Meet Meg, Bella and Celina—
three loving sisters, desperate to escape
the iron rule of their fanatical rector father…

One by one they flee the vicarage—
only to discover that the real world
holds its own surprises for the now
disgraced Shelley sisters! How will they
get themselves out of the scandalous
situations they find themselves in?

Can betrayed widow **Meg**
learn to love again?

Will pregnant and abandoned **Bella**
find the man to turn her blush of shame
to the flush of pleasure?

And how will virginal courtesan-in-training
Lina discover the meaning of true passion?

Find out in…

THE TRANSFORMATION
OF THE SHELLEY SISTERS

*Three sisters, three escapades,
three very different destinies!*

Louise Allen has been immersing herself in history, real and fictional, for as long as she can remember, and finds landscapes and places evoke powerful images of the past. Louise lives in Bedfordshire, and works as a property manager, but spends as much time as possible with her husband at the cottage they are renovating on the north Norfolk coast, or travelling abroad. Venice, Burgundy and the Greek islands are favourite atmospheric destinations. Please visit Louise's website— www.louiseallenregency.co.uk—for the latest news!

Novels by the same author:

VIRGIN SLAVE, BARBARIAN KING
THE DANGEROUS MR RYDER*
THE OUTRAGEOUS LADY FELSHAM*
THE SHOCKING LORD STANDON*
THE DISGRACEFUL MR RAVENHURST*
THE NOTORIOUS MR HURST*
THE PIRATICAL MISS RAVENHURST*
PRACTICAL WIDOW TO PASSIONATE MISTRESS†

Those Scandalous Ravenhursts
†*The Transformation of the Shelley Sisters*

**Look for Celina's story,
INNOCENT COURTESAN TO ADVENTURER'S BRIDE
coming soon in Louise Allen's
latest mini-series
*The Transformation of the Shelley Sisters***

VICAR'S DAUGHTER
TO
VISCOUNT'S LADY

Louise Allen

MILLS &
BOON

All the characters in this book have no existence outside the imagination of the author, and have no relation whatsoever to anyone bearing the same name or names. They are not even distantly inspired by any individual known or unknown to the author, and all the incidents are pure invention.

First published in Great Britain 2010
Harlequin Mills & Boon Limited,
Eton House, 18-24 Paradise Road, Richmond, Surrey TW9 1SR

© Melanie Hilton 2010

ISBN: 978 0 263 87602 4

Harlequin Mills & Boon policy is to use papers that are natural, renewable and recyclable products and made from wood grown in sustainable forests. The logging and manufacturing process conform to the legal environmental regulations of the country of origin.

Printed and bound in Spain
by Litografia Rosés, S.A., Barcelona

For the Romantic Novelists' Association
in their 50th Anniversary year

Prologue

12 February 1814

If James truly loves you, means to marry you—then I'll help, somehow. It was over five years since Arabella Shelley had said those words to her sister Meg and helped her to elope with her childhood sweetheart, James Halgate, the local squire's son.

It was nine months since she had hugged her weeping younger sister Celina and assured her that, if she could, she would help her run away from home too, away from the oppression and tyranny of their puritanical father who was convinced that all women were the vessels of sin and must be controlled and guarded against the slightest temptation.

Dreamy Meg and sensitive Lina had wilted miserably under this treatment, pining for laughter and music, flowers and books. And love. Oh, yes, they had all pined for love, Bella thought, grounding the watering can she had been using to fill up the pewter jugs of greenery set around the font. Flowers were permitted only grudgingly in the Reverend Shelley's Suffolk church, but ivy and sombre foliage would help remind the congregation of the graveyard that awaited them all, sinners that they were.

Bella sat down in the nearest pew, ignored the cold that soaked into her booted feet from the stone floor and wrestled with guilt once again over her failure to realise what Lina had intended. Without any help from Bella she had run away, leaving only a scrap of a letter from a sister of their dead mother, an aunt none of them had known existed until Lina had found her hidden letter.

The vicar blacked out Lina's name in the family Bible, as he had Meg's. If her sisters wrote, then their father intercepted the letters and destroyed them. Bella clung to the hope that if either of them had died, he would not have been able to conceal his knowledge of the bad end they had come to, but sometimes it was hard to hold on to the hope that they were still well and happy.

Bella rubbed her aching back and tried to push away the memory of Lina's sobs after she had been reprimanded for speaking to the curate. *He said I was a trollop, and wicked and leading Mr Perkins astray! How are we ever supposed to find husbands and get married if we may not even speak to Papa's curate?*

Goodness knows, had to be the answer to that question. But Bella knew that her own destiny was already ordained. At the age of twenty-five her fate was to be Papa's support in his old age. He had told her that often enough, with the certainty that an elder daughter should expect nothing more than to do her duty to her parent.

A lovable parent would be one thing, a sanctimonious, aggressively puritanical vicar, which was what the Reverend Shelley was, quite another. She had cherished hopes that dull Mr Perkins the curate would find one of them attractive enough to offer for, but after the confrontation following Lina's few words with him she did not deceive herself that he would risk alienating his vicar for the sake of either of them.

Her two younger sisters could not cope with the oppression, the carping, the sheer drabness of life at the vicarage. It was better that they had gone, for she, the sensible sister, was the one who could best cope with Papa who was becoming more suspicious and ill tempered as the years went by. Now she had no younger sisters to protect—only to worry about. It was time to accept finally that her life would be bound by the vicarage walls, and by her duty as the vicar's plain spinster daughter.

Something tickled her lip and she licked it, tasting salt. Sitting here weeping would not accomplish anything, except to put her behind with her duties, and besides, she *never* cried. What was the point?

Bella wiped her eyes and looked at the note tablets suspended from the old-fashioned chatelaine that hung from her waist. *Complain to butcher re: mutton; mend surplice; assemble sewing for Ladies' Circle; turn sheets side to middle. Church greenery*—that could be crossed off. Another tear trickled down and splashed on to the thin ivory. She dabbed it off, smudging the pencil marks, and bit down on her lower lip until she felt more under control.

Sometimes she did not think she could bear this any longer. She wanted her sisters—even a letter would do. She wanted a hug, a kiss, laughter, warmth. She wanted love.

Bella picked up the remains of the ivy fronds and then lugged the heavy watering can back to the vestry. Once upon a time she had dreamed of a lover coming for her. A knight in shining armour. A gallant nobleman who would sweep her away and cherish her.

Childishness, she told herself, buttoning her pelisse and pulling on her gloves. Fairy tales did not come true and it was not sensible to dream that they might, because waking up from the dream was always bitter disillusion. She locked the vestry and went out through the south door and down to the lych gate where she paused. Beyond it was the lane that led to the Ipswich road and freedom. The road she was never going to take.

She had forgotten her basket, Bella realised. Was it worth going back for it? She half-turned as a voice said, 'Is this Lower Leaming, ma'am?'

'No, this is Martinsdene,' she began, looking back. A stranger got up from the bench sheltered in the shadows of the roofed gate. 'Lower Leaming is that… way.' Her voice trailed off.

Blue eyes regarded her with interest and a sensuous mouth curved into a smile that was—surely not?—appreciative. The man was tall, relaxed, elegant. His riding coat was so plain it had to be expensive and a cabochon ruby ring glowed with sullen fire on his ring finger. He raised the hand that was holding gloves and whip and lifted his hat and she saw brown hair that shone, styled in a fashionable crop, the like of which had never been seen in this rural backwater.

'Thank you, Miss—?' he said in a voice that sent warm shivers through her chilled body.

'Shelley,' she managed. 'My father is vicar here.' Even as she said it, she cast a harried look down the lane to the vicarage as though her father's hawk eyes could see through the hedge from the study where he was engaged in writing next Sunday's sermon.

'Miss Shelley. I am Rafe Calne, Viscount Hadleigh.' And he bowed, as though she were a fine lady and this was Hyde Park. Bella managed to produce an answering bob of a curtsy. 'I am staying with my good friend Marcus Daunt at Long Fallow Hall and I must confess to being utterly lost.'

'Yes, well, in that case you do need the Lower Leaming road,' Bella said, thankful to be able to articulate something sensible. *A viscount, for goodness' sake!* 'It is past the Royal George inn and then you should take the left fork after the duck pond. If you come through the churchyard there is a bridleway that cuts off the corner—over there, by the holly bush.'

'Will you not walk that way and show me, Miss Shelley? I seem to have the knack of getting lost.'

'I—'

But he had already fetched a big bay horse from where it had been tethered out in the lane. He offered her his arm and Bella took it, lost for the words to refuse.

'You know, Miss Shelley, I have to confess to being somewhat blue devilled. Here I am, supposed to be resting—I've been feeling a trifle off colour lately—but I have been so bored I have not been able to relax. Poor Marcus can't work out what to do with me. So I came out for a ride, got lost and found this charming village and you. And I feel better already.'

Was she supposed to understand that *she* was making him feel better? No, of course not, Martinsdene was picturesque, artists had been known to stop to sketch it. Bella took a deep breath to steady her fluttering heart and tried not to notice how firm his arm felt under her hand and how warm he was, between her and the wind.

Oh dear, she thought. *Now when I daydream I will have a real-life aristocratic hero to visualise.* The bridleway was short and the pond soon reached. 'That way, my lord.' She pointed.

'Rafe, please. You are, after all, my rescuer.' He lifted her hand and kissed her fingertips. 'May I know your first name?'

'Arabella…Bella,' she stammered.

'Bella,' he murmured. '*Belle*. Beautiful lady.'

'Oh, no,' Bella retorted, common sense coming to her rescue. 'Now you are gammoning me, my lord.'

'Rafe,' he murmured.

'Rafe…this is…'

'I do not think you look in your mirror carefully enough, *bellissima*.' Rafe Calne swung up on to the big horse with enviable ease and smiled down at her. 'Until we meet again.'

Bella had walked to the butcher's in a dream, forgot what she had come for until she consulted her tablets and then walked home feeling as though she had been hit on the head. A real viscount, flirting with her. With *her*. Because he had been flirting—she was not so innocent that she did not recognise that.

'Arabella!'

'Yes, Papa?'

'Where have you been?' The vicar did not trouble to come to the door to ask, she had to go to the study to account for her actions over the past two hours. She did not mention the viscount. It would not be sensible, Bella told herself as she went to the kitchen to make sure that Cook was doing all she should with dinner. Not that it was easy to spoil hotpot with dumplings, boiled cabbage and stewed apple.

On Saturday she went to the church to make sure the prayer books had been gathered up after a wedding and checked the vestry to see that all was in order. Another surplice with a torn hem—doubtless discarded by the curate. She might as well take it and mend it along with her father's, she supposed, gathering it up and putting it in her basket.

Then, instead of going straight home, she wandered up the bridle path. There were the prints of Rafe's booted feet, big and masculine next to her small ones. Bella set her foot in one and then the next, wondering at the length of his stride. Those long legs and broad shoulders had troubled her dreams a little.

'Bella.' He was there, sitting on his big horse, Farmer Rudge's ducks wandering around its hooves.

'My lord!' He looked at her. 'Rafe.'

Bella glanced around as he swung down from the horse, but no one was in sight. 'Is something worrying you, Bella?' he asked, reaching for her hand.

'I—' She should pull away, but she could not. 'My

father would not permit me to speak to a strange man.
I should not be here with you.'

'I am sorry for that.' He looked sombre and the blue
eyes were shadowed. 'I felt the need to talk with
someone and you seemed... But if you must not, then
I will go away.'

'Talk? About what?' She left her hand in his.

'Here, in the country, I am beginning to see my life for
what it is. Futile, empty. Pleasure, money—I am a sinner,
you know, Bella,' he said earnestly, tucking her hand into
the crook of his elbow and walking slowly off down the
lane away from the village, the horse following.

'You are?'

'Oh, yes. And then I look at you—pure, innocent,
devoting yourself to your duties—and I see myself for
what I am. I wish some of that goodness would rub off
on me, Bella.'

'You just need to want to be good,' she protested.

'And you are satisfied with your life?' he asked her.
She could not answer, but she felt the guilty blush and
saw him see it too. 'Not entirely, I think?'

And so she had told him, all about how Papa had
changed slowly over the years, how Mama had died on
a visit to London, how Meg and Lina had run away, and
he had brushed a tear from the corner of her eye and
kissed her, just a fleeting, chaste kiss of comfort and her
world had shifted on its axis.

He had come to church on Sunday, serious and attentive, head bowed. After that she had seen him every
day. He was always careful, always discreet, but the long

walks, when she told him about living in the country and confided how difficult Papa was, and sympathised with his stories of London life and how it was turning to dust in his mouth, were like shining jewels in the dull ashes of her existence.

And on the eighth day he had kissed her, not giving comfort, not seeking it, but with a lover's passion, and she had clung to him, consumed with his heat and power and glamour.

'I love you, Bella,' he had murmured against her hair, their breath mingling in the crisp February air. 'Be mine.'

'You must talk to Papa,' she had stammered, dizzily aware that her dream had come true. Her knight had come for her.

'I must go back to London,' Rafe said. 'And speak to my lawyers. I will have them draw up a settlement so your father can see exactly what I will do for you. And I will bring back a housekeeper to look after him until he can choose one that best suits him.'

'But should we not talk to him first? I do not like to deceive him,' she protested.

'My darling, he sounds a most difficult man and I, I will admit, am the kind of rake of whom he will have the deepest suspicions.'

'But you are reformed now,' Bella protested.

'Yes, thanks to you.' Rafe caressed her. 'But he will believe it more when he sees the settlement, sees the ring I bring with me, knows his every interest—and yours—will be attended to. Then he might see the benefits of having the Viscount Hadleigh as his son-in-law. Would he like a better parish? I am sure I could influence something.'

'Oh, Rafe, would you? Perhaps he feels he has failed, never getting preferment, and if he did, he would be happier and less difficult.'

'For you, my love, I'll bow to every bishop in the kingdom,' he assured her. 'And find your sisters too.'

'Rafe.' And she had kissed him, deeply, clumsily.

'Lady Hadleigh.' He smiled down, suddenly serious. 'Will you really take me? I don't deserve you. Perhaps you will change your mind once I have gone.'

'No! Never. I love you.'

'Then be mine, Bella. Show me you love me. Show me you trust me.'

'But…before we are married?' she queried, anxious and confused.

'You don't trust me, I knew it. But what could I expect?' he said, turning away, his face stark. 'I will leave, now. It is better. We cannot marry if you do not trust me. I thought—'

He made a gesture of hurt rejection and she clung to his arm. 'Rafe. Of course I trust you. Of course I do.' He swept her up, his mouth hot and urgent on hers, his arms so strong and sure, and strode towards the great tithe barn.

Chapter One

~~~~~~~~~~~~~~~~~~~~~~

23 May 1814

It was a long carriage drive to trudge up in the drizzle, and the walk gave Bella far more time to think than she needed. *Rafe must listen to me*, she told herself fiercely. *He might ignore my letters, but he cannot refuse to help me, not face to face.* It was three months since she had lain with him in the barn on a bed of hay and felt his heart beating over hers.

Now she was apprehensive in her heart, queasy and weary in her body and bitterly angry, both with herself and with him. She had believed him. She had been so desperate to be loved, so sure of what she wanted, that when it appeared right in front of her, reached out for her, she had fallen, hook line and sinker for every lure of an experienced, conscienceless rake. And now she was with child. A fallen woman. Ruined.

No, please, she prayed as she walked. *Don't let him be without all conscience. Please let it be all right soon.*

Oh, Baby, forgive me. I am so ashamed. And unless he helps me, I don't know what to do, I don't know how I will look after you. But I will. Somehow.

And she was so tired with the pregnancy, with the travelling, with the fear. Rafe had not been in London; his fine house in Mayfair had been locked up and dark with the knocker off the door, but she was here now at the big estate he had described to her, dazzling her with images of her life with him as his wife. His viscountess. She had asked at the gate house and they said his lordship was in residence.

She pictured him as she walked. For a few blissful days he had made her glow with happiness. Rafe Calne, Viscount Hadleigh. Tall, handsome, brown haired and elegant with blue eyes that had smouldered their way into her heart and soul. Rafe Calne, her love and her seducer. She had tumbled into love and into his arms so easily, with every tenet of virtue and modesty forgotten in the whirl of emotion. She had dreamed of a fairy tale, was desperate for a fairy tale, and when she found herself in one she had believed in it implicitly. And now she was being punished for dreaming.

Ruined women like her were supposed to throw themselves into the river out of the depths of their shame. She had walked down to the Thames when she had found his London house deserted. She had looked at the swirling brown water. But she could not, would not, despair. She was the sensible sister, she reminded herself bitterly. She would come up with a plan.

And she was carrying a child and nothing, if she could help it, would hurt that baby. It did not matter what happened to her, it did not matter how much scorn he poured onto her head, the baby must be provided for.

Her feet were wet and cold. Rafe did not maintain his carriage drive in good order. Bella tugged her hood further over her face and shook the foot that had just trodden in a water-filled pothole. But he was a busy man, he had told her that. Doubtless his estate workers had not been supervised as they might. Rafe had been busy seducing another hapless innocent or flirting with some great lady, no doubt.

Bella's valise was banging uncomfortably against her knee and it was making her fingers numb. For the day after May Day, this was miserable weather: certainly it was not the day to set out on a three-mile walk through the countryside on an empty, unsettled stomach. It was probably a judgement for travelling on a Sunday, one more sin to add to the one she had so gladly, so recklessly, committed. The drive turned around an overgrown bed of shrubs and there was the house, Hadleigh Old Hall, sprawling low and golden brown and beautiful, even in the rain. It should have been her new home.

Bella straightened her shoulders as she reached the front door and banged the knocker. *Deep breath, keep calm.* He would be surprised to see her, shocked perhaps that she had travelled alone, angry when he heard what she wanted—of that last she had no doubt.

The butler's face as he opened the door spoke more than the words he was not uttering. Bella dripped in the shelter of the high porch and wondered if her nose was red or blue. She could imagine just what a sight she must present, soaking wet and travel stained after four days on the road, and she could see it in the way the butler looked at her. Eventually the man spoke. 'Miss?'

'Good afternoon.' His eyes narrowed at the sound of her cultivated accent and his face became expressionless. Bella took a deep breath and summoned up the tatters of her poise. She would pretend the butler was the butcher and she was having to complain about the meat again. 'I wish to see Lord Hadleigh.'

'His lordship is not at home.'

'Lord Hadleigh will wish to see me whether he is receiving or not. Kindly tell him that Miss Shelley is here.' She stepped forwards and the butler, caught off guard, stepped back. 'Thank you. I will wait in the salon, shall I?' She dumped her bag by the door.

The butler received her sodden cloak and then looked as though he might drop it, but in the face of her accent, her certainty and one lifted eyebrow, he ushered her into a reception room.

'I will inform his lordship of your arrival.'

It had been too much to hope the man would offer such an unconventional guest a cup of tea. Bella eyed the satin upholstery, decided not to sit on it in her damp skirts despite her shaking legs and tried to study the pictures on the wall.

She hardly had time to realise she could not focus on the first when the butler returned. 'His lordship will receive you in the study, Miss Shelley.'

The room tilted a little. *Rafe, at last. Please, God. Let me do this right. Let him have some shred of pity.* 'Thank you.'

The study was on the north side of the house, deep

in shadows. A fire flickered in the grate; the only light, a green-shaded reading lamp, was focused down on to papers on the desk. It illuminated the lines of Rafe's jaw, the edge of his cheekbones, the glint of his eyes as he stood, but not much more.

'Miss Shelley.'

So formal, so calm—he is concerned that the butler might come back. His voice seemed deeper; perhaps that was surprise at seeing her. He did not sound angry. That would come and she had tasted his anger, his fury at any attempt to thwart or contradict him.

'Rafe… My lord, I had to come.' She stepped towards him, but his left hand lifted, gestured towards a chair, and the firelight caught the flame of the familiar cabochon ruby on his ring. That hand, sliding slowly down over her breast, over the pale curve of her belly, down…

'Thank you, but, no.' It left him on his feet too, a shadowy figure behind the desk, but she was too agitated to sit. 'You will be surprised to see me.'

'Indeed.' Still no anger. Perhaps this cool distance was worse; he did not seem to even know her.

Bella felt a fresh pang of apprehension, a wave of hot shame that she was in this position.

'When you…left me you made it clear you never wanted to see me again.' *Silly little sentimental fool… Clumsy country wench—the only thing you can do on your knees is pray… So easy, so gullible and not worth the effort.* He had slapped her face when she began to weep.

Rafe shifted abruptly, then was still, remaining behind the desk. 'And yet you are here.'

She could not read the emotion in his voice. The

shadows seemed to shift and sway. It was necessary to breathe, to be silent for a moment or two while she fought the nausea and the shame. He was going to make her spell it out, he was not going to offer her the slightest help to stammer out her demands.

She felt her knees trembling, but somehow she dared not sit down. Something dreadful was happening, just as her worst fears had told her, and she needed to be on her feet to face it. He was so cold, so distant. *He is going to refuse.* 'I am with child. *Our child*, Rafe.'

'I see.' He sounded remarkably calm about it. She had expected anger, shouting. Only the flash of that ruby in the firelight showed any sign of movement.

'You promised me marriage or I would never have… never… I know what you said when we parted, but we must consider the baby now, Rafe.'

She could almost feel the emotion flowing from him in waves now, belying his calm tone. But she could not decipher it, except to feel the anger, rigidly suppressed. Perhaps it was her own fear and humiliation she could feel. Bella pulled air down into her lungs and took an unobtrusive grip on the back of the nearest chair.

'You are certain that you are with child?' That deep, dispassionate voice unnerved her as much as his words. Rafe had always been laughing, or whispering or murmuring soft, heated endearments. Or at the end hurling cutting, sneering gibes. He had not sounded like this.

'Of course! Rafe—' She took a step towards him but his hand came up again and she froze. There was a silence. She could tell in the light of the reading lamp that Rafe had bowed his head as though in thought. Then he looked up. 'And you came here thinking to marry Rafe Calne? That will not happen, child or no child.'

The room swam out of focus. Bella gripped the chair as though drowning. But she did not weep or protest. She had expected it and had planned for it and now, with the uncertainty gone, felt somehow stronger. A cold calm settled over her and from somewhere deep inside she summoned up her courage and her will; later she could weep—she had had enough practice at that when she first realised she was pregnant. But now she had to think about her baby. What was going to happen to them?

'You are responsible for this child,' she said, hating the way her voice shook, not wanting to show weakness. 'You must provide for it, even if you have no care for me. It is your moral obligation.' She would fight tooth and nail for her baby, she had realised as the days passed. Now her own emotions, her own happiness, no longer mattered. She would battle Rafe, however he wounded her, whatever foul words he hurled at her. What could he do to her that was worse than what had already happened?

'The situation, Miss Shelley, is rather more complex than you believe, although I cannot blame you for seeing it in somewhat black-and-white terms.' Rafe came out from behind the desk before she could speak.

She stared as he stepped into the light from the fire, the warm glow illuminating his face, sparking sapphire from eyes bluer than she had ever seen, gilding hair the colour of dark honey. 'You are not Rafe.' Bella sat down with a thump on the chair as her legs gave way.

'No,' he agreed. 'I am his brother Elliott. Rafe died

of a poisoned appendix ten days ago. You asked for Hadleigh—I now hold the title.'

Bella found herself without words. Rafe was dead. Her child's father was dead. The man she had sacrificed her principles and her honour for was dead. There were no tears, she realised hazily, nor satisfaction either. Only pain. Bella laid her hand over her cramping stomach protectively. She must be strong, for the baby's sake.

The stranger's face—Rafe's face in so many ways— was expressionless as he began to walk around the room, setting a spill from the fire to the candles. Bella fought for some composure. She had to say something or he would think her addled as well as wanton. She had given her virtue to his brother and now she was carrying his illegitimate child. This man would despise her. All right-thinking people would despise her, she knew that. Love was never an excuse, not for the woman.

'My sympathies on your loss,' she managed when he came and sat down opposite her, crossed long legs and settled back with the same casual elegance that Rafe had possessed. *Rafe is dead*, her churning thoughts clamoured. Rafe, the man she had thought she loved, was dead. He had betrayed her and Bella supposed another woman might rejoice that he was no more, but she could not. She just felt blank.

'Thank you,' Lord Hadleigh said and his face showed some emotion at last, a tightening, as if a migraine had stabbed at his nerves. 'We were not close, I regret to say. You were in love with my brother?'

That was abrupt enough. He certainly did not beat about the bush, this brother-ghost of her lover. 'Yes, of course I was.' His mouth twisted and this time it was clearly the hint of a smile. 'You think me immoral, wanton, I am sure,' Bella protested, goaded by his amusement. 'But I loved him. I thought he loved me. It was not easy; my father would not countenance me marrying, I knew that. We had to keep it secret.'

Was she making any sense? Her tongue and her brain seemed disconnected. It must be shock, she realised. How could she explain and make him understand the objections a country vicar might have to his daughter marrying a viscount?

He did not appear judgemental, just detached. 'I see. You were certain of my brother's affections?'

'Of course I was.' She blushed, surprising herself. Surely she was beyond that manifestation of maidenly modesty? 'He was so sweet, so passionate, so convincing.' She had to be frank, there was no point in trying to shield her privacy from this man. 'I never thought I would escape from Martinsdene,' she murmured. 'But I dreamed and my dream came true—a viscount fell in love with a vicar's plain daughter. Or so it seemed.'

'Are you plain?' Elliott Calne tilted his head to one side and studied her face. 'No lady would be looking her best just at this moment. I will reserve judgement.' His eyes laughed at her for a moment, and her heart turned over. Rafe's eyes, but deeper, more intent. Rafe's eyes alone could have seduced her without the need for a word spoken. These made her catch her breath and wonder at their secrets. 'I am sorry, this is no time for levity,' he said, serious again. 'You found you were mistaken in him?' He sounded regretful, but not surprised.

He must have known his brother was a rake, she realised. But he sounded as though he was fond of him anyway. The poor man was in mourning; she could not pour out her own fury and bitterness at Rafe to him, it was bad enough as it was. He did not need to hear the details of that brutal last day.

Bella wondered if she was going to be sick. She had heard that sickness only affected pregnant women in the mornings, and would go away eventually. But she was still feeling queasy most of the time. And tired and thirsty. And desperate to escape to the privy. And her breasts were tender and her legs and back ached. And there were about six more months of this still to be endured. *I am sorry, Baby*, she thought. *It isn't your fault.* Under her hand her rebellious stomach still felt as flat as usual.

'Are you feeling unwell? I should have thought to order refreshments, but your news was somewhat of a shock. Tea, perhaps. Plain biscuits? I understand from my cousin Georgy that they are a great help for nausea.'

That was perceptive of him. And kind. Was he truly kind or was he simply wary of a pregnant and distressed woman being ill in his study? Bella opened her eyes and studied the lean face watching her. He was not smiling now and he looked tired and rather grim. As well as losing his brother he had inherited a mountain of responsibility and now she had turned up, with this news.

'Thank you. That would be very welcome.' How calming civil politeness was—on the surface. Underneath she wanted to sob and shout. Rafe was dead, her baby was fatherless, she could not go home. Would this man help her or were tea and biscuits the extent of his kindness? 'Is there…are you married? If Lady Hadleigh—'

'No. I am not married.' The hope of some sympathetic female support vanished. Her question—or was it the concept of marriage itself?—seemed to amuse him. Perhaps he was another rake like his brother. But he could hardly damage her more than Rafe had already.

Elliott Calne tugged the bell pull and waited. Silence and stillness seemed to come naturally to him. Was he used to being solitary, or was his mind working frantically on the problem of how to deal with her with the least possible expense, fuss and scandal?

Then the butler came in and he smiled and she saw that, whatever else he was, he was not a man given to brooding bad humour. There were laughter lines at the corner of his eyes and that smile was more than a polite token for a servant.

'Henlow, please take Miss Shelley to Mrs Knight. She requires a bedchamber to refresh herself and rest. Have a tea tray with biscuits sent up. I will see you for dinner at seven, Miss Shelley; we keep country hours here just now.'

'Thank you. But, Lord Hadleigh, I cannot stay here, it is not at all—'

'The thing? No, indeed you cannot.' That smile again, as though she was still a lady, not a fallen woman, not his brother's discarded… No, she could not use the any of the words Rafe had hurled at her like sharp stones. 'We will discuss it over dinner.'

Elliott sat beside the fire in the small dining room, a book in his hands that he had not tried to read. He had felt the need to leave the study after that encounter—the atmosphere of distress and desperation could be cut with a knife. *God, Rafe. What have you done now?* For years, for all his adolescence, for all his adult life, he had been hoping that his elder brother would reform his ways, become the man Elliott was certain he must be, somewhere deep inside.

He wanted to love his brother as he had when he had been a child, but he had never been able to reach past the shield of disdain Rafe had erected against affection and contact. He knew there had been extravagance, dissipation, women. He had worried about Rafe's health and had tried to speak to him when they ran across each other in Town, but Rafe had always curled a lip and ignored him.

'You and your Corinthian set,' he had sneered. 'Sport and clean-limbed good fellowship while you batter each other's brains out in the boxing salon or waste good gaming time racing your damn horses. And when you aren't being smug about your muscles or your horses you are taking your bloody estate and its turnips so seriously that I think you must be a bastard of Farmer George's. Never thought our mother had had the King sniffing round her petticoats, but—'

Elliott had hit him, flush on the chin, and knocked him down. After that, they barely acknowledged each other. Occasionally one of his friends would have an embarrassed word when Rafe had offended yet another elderly lord, or ruined some young sprig at the card tables only to lose the same fortune the next day, but all of them knew that Elliott could not influence his brother.

Sometimes he felt like the elder and that oppressed him. He wanted to enjoy himself, to live life to the full, not to have to worry about anything out of his own control, and yet he found himself dragged back again and again to the waste and the anger.

And then there were the women. Rafe had kept a string of expensive ladybirds and actresses. Elliott doubted he had treated any of then well once the novelty wore off, but at least they had been professionals. But innocent young gentlewomen? Surely this had to be the first? Please God, Miss Shelley was the only one.

And not content with seducing and ruining her, Rafe had managed to impregnate her, the thoughtless, careless devil. He should have married her. Elliott stared at the flames. She might have been the making of his brother, the saving of him. He didn't want this damn title, he wanted his own life and his brother back, well and happy and settled, with the evil demon that had clawed its way into his soul cast out.

Chapter Two

'My lord.' The room was small and intimate, a cosy supper room, not the grand dining chamber she had been expecting. Lord Hadleigh rose to his feet from a chair beside the fire and put down the book that had been closed in his hands.

'Good evening, Miss Shelley.' That smile again. Despite everything there was a lightness there, a sense that he smiled easily. He watched her and she had the impression that he was looking at her as a woman and that, under different circumstances, he might have flirted with her. Yet she did not feel threatened.

'You are rested and feeling a little better, I trust.' He went to take the chair at the head of the small rectangular table and a footman pulled out the other chair set at right angles to his. Bella sat and had her napkin shaken out for her.

She had been fussed over by a pleasant housekeeper who had removed her wet clothes, found her a cosy wrapper and then tucked her up in bed with a cup of

tea and a dish of plain biscuits. Without in the least expecting to, she had slept deeply and dreamlessly for
almost two hours.

Neither the housekeeper, nor the maid who came to
wake her and help her dress, seemed at all surprised that
she had turned up out of the drizzle. It was curiously
hypnotic, this degree of comfort and luxury, the unobtrusive service, the lack of questions. It would not last,
but she would draw strength from it while she could. And
she so much needed strength. Strength to fight her own
guilt and despair, strength to fight the world's opinion.

She had woken, knowing what she must do for her
baby. Rafe might be dead, but the plan she had origi-
nally formed to deal with his almost inevitable refusal
to marry her must still be tried. She felt ashamed to have
to demand it now, but a steely determination had entered
her heart while she slept. She would do whatever it took
to protect her child, even at the expense of a man who
was innocent in all this.

'I feel much better, I thank you, my lord.' It was seven
o'clock on a dark, wet May evening, the seducer who had
rejected her was dead and she was virtually penniless
amongst strangers. Bella stamped on the rising panic; she
could say nothing with the footman in attendance.

'Serve the soup, Harris, and then leave us. I will ring.'

The savoury curls of steam made her almost dizzy
with desire. It was an effort to sip the soup and not to pick
up the dish and drain it. It must be forty-eight hours since
she had eaten a proper meal, but the rags of her pride made
it important to behave like a lady in this, if nothing else.

'Well, Miss Shelley.' Lord Hadleigh regarded her

with those deep blue eyes and she felt insensibly a little safer. 'Will you tell me your first name?'

'Arabella, my lord.'

'And when is the baby due?'

'Early December.' That was easy to calculate; she had lain with Rafe only the once, after all.

'You believed my brother would marry you? He offered marriage? Do have one of these bread rolls, they are excellent.'

'Yes, he promised. Perhaps you doubt my word?' she asked, the moment of reassurance vanishing. Elliott Calne shook his head. 'I am sure you think me wanton. I should be ashamed to even try to justify myself. But it was a fairy tale: my Prince Charming had hacked his way through the thorns to rescue me. You are doubtless wondering how a twenty-five-year-old woman could be such a romantic. It is not like me, I assure you. I have the reputation of being sensible and practical,' she added bitterly.

'Where did you meet? In London, I suppose.' He was too polite to comment on her morals and she was not sure how to explain it to him in any case. How could a man understand the impact his dazzling, treacherous brother had had on her? She was the lonely, dutiful, unhappy eldest daughter of the vicarage and Rafe had been the fulfilment of a fantasy.

'No, in Suffolk. I live—lived—in a village near Ipswich. I am a vicar's daughter. My two younger sisters, who could not bear life with Papa any longer, ran away some time ago. I remained. I am expected to support my father in his old age.'

'How old is he, for God's sake?' the viscount

demanded. He was certainly to the point, she observed, through her haze of misery.

'Fifty-three.' Bella took a wary sip of the red wine in her glass.

'A long wait for him to become decrepit, then. I gather he is not a joy to live with. More soup?'

'No. No more soup, thank you, and, no, he is not.' It was futile to lie. Lord Hadleigh needed to understand. 'He believes that females are natural sinners, the cause of wickedness, and it must be beaten out of them if necessary. "Woman is the daughter of Eve. She is born of sin and is the vessel of sin".' She quoted the sampler she had worked with her sisters. 'My middle sister eloped with a young officer, her childhood sweetheart, the youngest ran away and I was seduced by a viscount. Papa was quite correct, it seems. I do not know where either of them is,' she added with a pang. Bella put down her spoon with an unsteady hand and braced herself for this viscount to express his disapproval.

'So, with two sisters gone by the time Rafe happened along, you were ripe for escape?'

That was not the outright condemnation she had expected. Did Rafe's brother understand after all? It was hard to tell whether he was sarcastic or sympathetic. How to explain the magic of the week of February sunshine that had come with Rafe, like a harbinger of joy? How to convey the sheer wonder of having such a man—handsome, attentive, sophisticated—pay her attention?

'He had fallen in love at first sight, he said,' she began, haltingly explaining it to both him and herself.

'He was in the country, staying with his friend Marcus Daunt at Long Fallow Hall a few miles away. He admitted he was on a repairing lease because he was not feeling too well. The last thing he had expected was to fall in love, he told me.'

'That must have been the infection beginning,' Lord Hadleigh said. 'I wondered where he had been. He was in London when he died.'

It seemed odd that he did not know his own brother's movements. And how strange that she had not sensed that he was ill; somehow the baby made a connection between them that should have been tangible, however much she hated him. 'When was it? Did he…was there much pain?' The room blurred as she struggled to get her emotions under control. This was her baby's father; even after everything, she did not want him to have suffered agonies.

'He was in some pain at first, they tell me, but he slipped into unconsciousness very quickly. Miss Shelley—' He got to his feet and came round the table to crouch down beside her, his movements lithe. He was fit, she thought vaguely, and fast. 'I am sorry, that was too abrupt. Here, drink some wine.' He picked up the glass and wrapped her fingers around it, guiding hand and glass to her lips.

She drank a little. 'Thank you. I am all right. I wanted to know, it is better than imagining things.' She made herself go on with her story as he went back to his seat. It was hard to look at him: he was so like Rafe and yet, so different. He seemed kind, he seemed caring. So had Rafe—at first. *Beware*, the voice of experience whispered. *He's a man.* 'We loved each other—I thought—but I warned him about Papa, who became angry if I and my sisters so much as spoke to the curate.'

'Viscount Hadleigh is hardly the curate,' the current holder of the title observed drily. He got to his feet, removed her soup plate and began to carve a capon. 'Are the side dishes within your reach?' He handed her a plate with meat and served himself.

'Thank you, yes.'

'Go on, Miss Shelley. He loved you, you loved him, but your father would object because he wanted to keep you at home for his own comfort.'

'We spoke of marriage and made plans. Rafe would go back to London, organise the settlements and return to present Papa with a *fait accompli*—he was even going to employ a good housekeeper and bring her with him so Papa would not be abandoned. It all seemed perfect, that day. I was head over heels in love and... We became lovers. He asked and I... He said I could not love him, if I refused. So I did as he asked me.'

She could not go on. She was not going to describe the horror of it all disintegrating about her. The nightmare. She had loved Rafe, she knew she would have learned to please him in bed if she had had the chance, if he had cared for her in return and had wanted to teach her. But— 'That is all,' she concluded abruptly and looked up to find Elliott Calne's eyes studying her with something painfully like pity in them.

Elliott was silent, twisting his wine glass between long fingers.

Further intimate revelations seemed beyond Bella, but good manners insisted she try to make some kind of conversation. She could not just sit and sob, however bad she felt. 'Forgive me,' she ventured, 'but were you and your brother close?'

'You mean, I presume, how like him am I?' That question appeared to amuse him. The smile appeared, and goose bumps ran up and down her spine. It was some form of sorcery, that smile. In combination with those eyes it should be illegal. 'Not very, except in looks. I am the boringly well-behaved younger brother, after all.'

Boring hardly seemed the word. Bella made herself focus on him, not just on his resemblance to Rafe. Nor, she guessed, was *well behaved* an accurate description. There was an edge to Elliott Calne's observations that suggested a cheerfully cynical view of the world and a lack of shock at her story that made her suspect that he was quite familiar with the pleasures of life.

'You are?'

'For a long time I was the *poor* younger brother as well. That does put a slight crimp in one's descent into debauchery, unless one has no concern about debt or one's health. I enjoy sport, I enjoy working hard, being fit. I prefer to make money, not to squander it. Then when I had it I found that working for my wealth made me value it a little more than, perhaps, Rafe did his inheritance.'

He raised his eyes fleetingly to study the room and she glanced around too. Under the opulence there were small signs of decay, of money skimped on repairs and spent on show. Bella noticed a patch of damp on the wall by the window, a crack in the skirting, and recalled the potholes in the carriage drive. The fingers of Elliott's left hand tightened on the stem of his wine glass, the ring that had been Rafe's sparking in the candlelight. She realised that his eyes were on her and not the room. He glanced away again, went back to his silent thoughts.

Bella put down her knife and fork and studied the face that was so like, and yet unlike, his brother's. Rafe's face had been softer than this man's, though the searing attack of Rafe's anger had been sharp; she felt that Elliott's would be more ruthless and controlled under a façade that was more light-hearted than Rafe's. She shivered and he caught it at once; he was watching her more closely than she had realised.

'Are you cold?' She shook her head. 'Still hungry? Shall I ring for cheese, or a dessert?' The perfect host, yet this was very far from the perfect social situation and Bella suspected that much more was going on in that sharply barbered head than concerns over her appetite.

'No, thank you, my lord.' She was as warm and well fed and rested as she was going to be; now was the moment to say what she had resolved upstairs when she woke.

Goodness only knew how he would respond, but she was prepared to be utterly shameless. After a lifetime of doing what she was told, thinking of everyone else's welfare, needs and whims before her own, she was going to stand up and fight for her child. After all, the world would say she had put herself beyond shame. 'My lord.'

He looked at her, alerted by the change in her tone. 'Miss Shelley?'

'You are Rafe's heir, so I must ask you to do this—

insist upon it.' Her voice quavered and she bore down hard on the fear and the emotion. She had to get through this. 'I want you to provide me with a house—just a small, decent one—and enough money for me to raise my child respectably. I can pretend to be a widow, I need very little for myself. But I must ask you to pay for his education if it is a boy or for a dowry if it is a girl. I am very sorry to have to demand this of you, but I realise I must do whatever I can for my baby's safety and future.'

He studied her from under level brows and with no trace of emotion on his face. Was he shocked by her explicit demands? 'I am sure you will be a veritable tigress in defence of your cub,' he remarked at length, bringing the angry colour up into her cheeks. 'But, no, I will not set you up in some decent little house in some provincial town somewhere and provide for your child as you ask.'

Bella's fingers curled into claws. For a moment she felt just like the animal he had likened her to. 'You must—'

'I will not.' It was like walking into a wall. He did not move, he did not raise his voice, but Bella knew, with utter clarity, that this was not an unplanned reaction. He had guessed what she would ask and he had made up his mind.

He would have her driven back to the Peacock in Chipping Campden where she had left the stage coach, no doubt. Now that he had looked after her basic welfare and she had made her demands, he would want her out of the house. Well, she would go, she had no strength left tonight to fight him.

But she would be back tomorrow whether he liked it or not—Elliott Calne was her only hope and she would do whatever she had to until he gave in. Anything. She would come back, and back, until he either called in the constable or gave her what she needed. If she had to she would threaten a scandal, although she knew who was likely to come off worst if she did. Blackmail, shaming, threats— whatever weapon she could find, she would use it.

'I cannot argue with you now, but I will, I promise you. I should be leaving now. I will—'

'Indeed, yes,' he interrupted her, his tone as pleasant as if they had been discussing the weather. 'It is getting late and you have had a long and difficult day. I am afraid that the Dower House is draughty and my great-aunt querulous—although you will not see her tonight— but my cousin Dorothy is a pleasant enough female.'

'Your—' The Dower House and his female relatives? Was Lord Hadleigh insane? He could not deposit the woman who had been his brother's lover, who was carrying his brother's illegitimate child, on those respectable ladies. 'But I cannot stay with your relatives. I am ruined! They would be mortified if they realised.'

'They would be mortified if my wife-to-be stayed anywhere else.'

Bella's hand jerked and the stain spread like blood over the white tablecloth as her almost-full wine glass toppled. 'Your wife? You intend to *marry* me? *You?*'

'Why, yes. Have you any better suggestion, Arabella?'

'I came here with a perfectly reasonable proposition, and you refused me without even discussing it and now you suggest marriage!'

'It was not a suggestion. It is what is going to happen.' Elliott cut through her half-formed thoughts. From his tone he was both making a prediction and issuing an order. He looked as though he was negotiating a business deal, his eyes cold and steady. The charming smile had gone.

'It is ridiculous! I do not know you. Rafe is the father—'

'Rafe is cold in the ground.' She flinched, but he pressed on, ignoring her wordless gasp of shock at his frankness. 'And how well did you know *him*? I thought you wanted the best for your child.'

'I do! I would do anything for this baby…' Her voice trailed away as she saw where this was taking her. 'Anything.'

'Exactly. I assume you mean that. You did not come here really expecting to marry Viscount Hadleigh, did you? If Rafe had been alive, he would have refused and you know it, so you had, most sensibly, planned your demands.

'Now you will become a viscountess, move here, live in what—once I get this place into some sort of order—should be reasonable comfort. The difference is that you will be marrying me and not my brother. Is that such a sacrifice to make for your child or are you telling me you would prefer to live a lie in dowdy seclusion in some remote market town, bringing up a bastard?'

The sharp vertical line between his brows and the edge to his words told her quite clearly how little he wanted this.

'Of course I would not,' Bella snapped, nerves

getting the better of shock and distress and even the remnants of good manners. 'If I thought for a moment you meant it—'

'You doubt my word?'

Now she had impugned his honour and he was on his aristocratic high-horse. It would be nice to be able to complete a sentence. Bella hung on to her anger— it was more strengthening than any of the other emotions that were churning inside her. She tried again. 'I doubt you have thought this through. I have no desire to be married to a man who is going to bitterly resent it the moment the knot is tied. You would make an appalling husband.'

Judging by the way the corner of his mouth quirked, he appeared to find her completely unfair words mildly diverting, damn him. Bella had a momentary pang of conscience over thinking such a thing, but found she was beyond caring. This was a nightmare and somehow she had to wake up.

'Don't laugh at me!'

'Do you think I find this amusing? Then let me explain something, Arabella.' Elliott got to his feet, about six foot three of intense male at very close quarters. She did her best not to flinch away when he planted his hands on the table and leaned towards her, those deep blue eyes holding hers. 'I am Hadleigh. I am head of this family now. But if Rafe had done what he should have done and married you before he died, then I would be sitting here, a guest in *your* house, acting as *your* trustee until the birth of that child.

'And if it is a boy, *he* would be Viscount Hadleigh and I would be Mr Calne, his guardian, nothing more. Do you expect me, in all honour, to ignore that fact?'

Chapter Three

'**B**ut you are the legal heir. You hold the title now. You cannot want to marry me,' Bella protested.

'For God's sake, stop worrying about me or Rafe or anything else and worry about your child,' Elliott snapped. 'My brother should have left you alone or married you: one or the other. In fact, he should have married years ago. But he did not. Do you think I am grateful for his heedless behaviour because I now have the good fortune to inherit the title?'

He did not sound as though he considered himself very fortunate. 'All I can do, in honour, is to ensure that if it is a boy he will one day inherit, as my heir. It might not be legally imperative, but it most certainly is morally. No one will suspect—a child is presumed to be the offspring of its mother's husband. With any luck the birth will be full term or later—I believe that is not uncommon with a first child. We will have been assumed to have anticipated matters a trifle, however late it is.'

'Then people will believe you had—'

'I am Hadleigh,' he interrupted her again. 'After my brother, they expect that sort of behaviour from the viscount, I have no doubt. It will be a one-week wonder, the gossip.'

'But the staff here,' she protested, swept along by his vehemence, knowing she had capitulated but still protesting, 'they saw me arrive on the doorstep, on foot, sodden, having obviously travelled on the common stage. That is not how you would treat your betrothed, surely?'

Elliott sat down again and reached for the claret. 'Of course not, not if I knew you were coming. However, we simply use the truth about your difficult father, who does not approve of the immoral ways of the aristocracy and who has forbidden our marriage, despite the fact you are of age. His temper is such that you felt you had to run away to me before your condition became obvious and not wait for wedding preparations. You said nothing when you arrived to indicate that you were expecting to see Rafe and not me, did you?'

Bella shook her head. 'No. I behaved as confidently as I could and I only used your title. I feared the butler would show me the door before I could get to Rafe if I did not.'

There had to be something wrong with this, somehow. Her child would be legitimate? She was going to become the Viscountess of Hadleigh after all, despite her shame, despite her ruin? Yes, there had to be some catch, something she had not seen. Things that were too good to be true normally were just that. This seemed the perfect solution—but it would be like a diamond with a huge flaw in its heart. She felt too tired and dizzy and confused to think it through and find that flaw.

'You have had enough for one day, I suspect.' Elliott was at her elbow and she had not even noticed him move. 'You are in a delicate condition, you have travelled too far and you have had a shock.'

'Yes.' She was beyond arguing now; he was too strong to resist. And she should not resist in any case, but some voice kept nagging that she should not do this to him, that he did not deserve it. She had been prepared to make a sacrifice for her child; she had not expected the victim to be an innocent man.

'I cannot think straight any longer. We must talk again, but I would like to retire if I may. Your great-aunt and your cousin—what will you tell them, my lord?'

'Why, the truth, of course.' He eased back her chair and waited while she got to her feet. 'That ours has been a most secret and rapid courtship, and, given your father's irrational opposition, I intend marrying you by licence just as soon as I can lay my hands on one. Which is going to involve an early trip to Worcester tomorrow to see the bishop.'

She ought to say something, but it felt like trying to walk into a strong wind. 'You should stop calling me *my lord*,' he added just before they reached the door. 'We must appear to be on intimate terms.'

'Elliott,' she repeated obediently. It was a more solid name than *Rafe*, more real somehow. He *was* real, she realised. He was the only reality between her and utter ruin. Rafe was dead and she was safe from him, at least.

But he had been the devil she knew. This brother she did not know at all. 'This is… I don't feel—'

'And it would be as well if you were to come with me to Worcester, if you are up to travelling tomorrow. I expect you will need to do some shopping. Then back here by evening and we will be married the next day. Which reminds me, I must send a note down to Mr Fanshawe, the rector.'

'Married the day after tomorrow?'

'The sooner the better, don't you think? I have met the bishop before, which is fortunate. George Huntingford. Bit of a dry stick, but not inclined to be awkward. He won't have come across your father, will he?'

'I have no idea. But, Elliott, I cannot just confront a bishop and pretend—'

'Pretend what?' Elliott enquired with infuriating logic. 'You are of age, you are who you say you are and you are free to marry. There is no deception.'

'I do wish you would let me finish a sentence,' Bella said, her temper sparking through the fog of exhaustion. He was right, of course—why could she not simply accept it? She swallowed the tears of frustration, tried to think rationally. Was this really the right thing to do? It seemed so easy, far too easy. Perhaps she was dreaming.

'You are not very coherent tonight,' Elliott said in response to her protest. 'It is hardly surprising, but if I waited for you to finish we would be here until the small hours.' They looked at each other, his expression mildly exasperated, hers set into a frown that was probably making her even plainer than usual. He must surely be studying her and wondering what on earth he had done to deserve this.

It was irrational and ungrateful, but she was so angry with him, all of a sudden. He was utterly in control and she could do nothing because he was right: this was the best thing for her child. Her fists clenched; deep inside she knew that the man she wanted to strike was not him, but his brother. Striking the man who was going to save her and the baby from this nightmare was madness, but the temptation was strong. It did not help either that she had the conflicting desire to simply lean against his chest and sob.

'No, I am not very coherent.' Bella made herself speak moderately. 'I am usually calm, sensible, coherent and responsible. And before you say anything, losing my virtue to your brother before marriage was none of those things, I am well aware. But he…but I…'

'Your emotions overcame all else?' Elliott suggested, not unkindly.

'Exactly.' Bella clasped her hands tightly. 'I do not know if you have ever been in love, Elliott?' *Or are now. No, surely he would not have suggested this if he had any ties to another woman?*

'No,' he admitted to her intense relief. 'There is no one.'

'It sweeps away everything. It was the most powerful thing I have ever experienced.' Of course, it must have been only the illusion of love or she would have clung to Rafe, wanted him even when he hurt her and spurned her. It made it worse, somehow, that even her own emotions had deceived her. 'And just now I am bereft, tired, frightened, confused and adrift. And shocked. I presume you have never experienced any of those emotions either?' He did not look like a man who was easily discommoded.

'I have been shocked, certainly. Very recently.' The corner of his mouth moved in what was either a grimace of pain or a sardonic smile. 'You will agree that you have had a little longer to become used to your condition than I have.'

'I have had even less opportunity to become used to the notion that I am to marry a complete stranger and become a viscountess,' she began and then caught herself as her voice trembled. Elliott was being quite incredibly forbearing. And honourable. And she had put him in a most difficult position. 'You are being very kind.' That provoked a quizzical lift of one eyebrow. 'I do appreciate what you are doing for me, for the baby, but please, may we talk about this in the morning?'

'We can talk on the way to Worcester. I will collect you at eight, if you think you will be well enough for an early start.'

Bella swallowed. It was no effort to be up and breakfasted by then; at the vicarage everyone rose at six. But at that time in the morning her uncertain stomach was at its worst and just now she felt as if she could sleep for a week. 'Perfectly, thank you, I will be ready then.'

Her cloak was almost dry and the rain had stopped. Elliott insisted on carrying her valise to the carriage and then helped her out after the silent ten-minute drive. In the darkness Bella could make out a four-square house sitting in a hollow.

'The Dower House.' They waited for several minutes

until the door creaked open to reveal an ancient butler who peered out at them as they stood in the wavering light of the lantern he held.

'My lord? My lady has retired some time since. Miss Dorothy is in the small parlour, my lord.'

'Thank you, Dawson, we can announce ourselves. Miss Shelley will be staying for two nights if you could organise a room for her, and a maid.'

'My lord.' The old man shuffled off mumbling, 'Maid, room, fires', to himself.

'Dawson is about ninety,' Elliott explained, 'but he refuses to be pensioned off. Mind the lap dog, it will yap, but I doubt it will bite.' As he spoke he opened a door and stepped inside. 'Cousin Dorothy, forgive this late call.'

The dog did indeed yap. And Miss Dorothy exclaimed and dropped her tatting and it took several minutes to restore order. 'Your betrothed?' she enquired, peering myopically at Bella when Elliott began to explain. 'How wonderful. Had you told me, Elliott dear? I do not recall, and I am sure I would have done.'

'No, Cousin. Arabella has had to run away as her father does not approve of me.'

'Of *you*? Why ever not? If it had been that rascal Rafe, God rest his soul, one could understand. But *you*, Cousin?'

'Politics,' Bella explained, feeling as though she was in an opium-eater's nightmare now, things were so unreal. 'Papa is a—' She realised she had no idea where Elliott's allegiances might lie.

'Tory,' he finished for her, his interruption for once welcome.

Miss Dorothy, who was about fifty, plump and rather vague, nodded. 'Oh, politics. That would explain it.'

'We will be married the day after tomorrow,' Elliott pushed on. 'So if you could find Arabella a bedchamber for two nights, that would be very helpful. I did mention it to Dawson as we came in and I expect he's gone to speak to Mrs Dawson.'

'They will see to all that.' Miss Dorothy beamed at Bella. 'I do enjoy being a chaperon. One gets so little opportunity now Mama is frailer and we no longer go to many parties, but I used to look after all my nieces.'

'It is very kind of you, ma'am.' Bella dredged up her last reserves of will-power and did her best to behave politely. She felt as though she had been pushing against a locked door and it had suddenly opened, tipping her into space. She was still falling. 'I am sorry, I am afraid I do not know how I should address you.'

'Well, I am Miss Abbotsbury, but everyone calls me Miss Dorothy, my dear. Now, have you had your supper?'

'Yes, Miss Dorothy, thank you.'

'And have you brought a nightgown and a toothbrush? Elliott, where are you going?'

'Home, Cousin.' He paused at the door. 'I was just about to bid you both goodnight.'

'Without kissing Miss Shelley?' Miss Dorothy simpered. 'Such unromantic behaviour! I am not such a fierce chaperon as all that, Elliott.'

'Of course not. Arabella.' He came and took her hands in his and looked down at her face. It was an effort not to cling. She had known him a few hours and now this stranger was all she had. 'It will be better in the morning, you will see.' And then he bent and kissed her cheek, his lips and breath warm for the fleeting moment of contact. Bella had an impression of claret and spice before he straightened up and she made herself let go. 'I will collect Miss Shelley at eight, Cousin, if an early breakfast will not inconvenience you.'

'Not at all.' The chaste kiss appeared to have satisfied Miss Dorothy's romantic expectations. She beamed at him as he left, then turned to Bella. 'Well, my dear, I expect you would like to go to bed, would you not?'

'Yes, please, Miss Dorothy.' At last a question she could answer with perfect honesty and without having to think. The cosy, cluttered room was beginning to sway slightly. 'That would be delightful.'

Elliott sat in the closed carriage outside the Dower House at a quarter to eight the next morning and made mental lists. It was that or pull out the flask of brandy secreted in the door pocket and drown every one of the obligations Rafe had landed him with. Especially this one.

It would have been a perverse comfort to be able to mourn his brother and perhaps he was, even if what he was mourning for was the brother he never had: the close friend, the trusting companion. Rafe, jealous and suspicious, had never wanted to allow anyone close, even at the end.

But maudlin thoughts about brotherly love, or the lack of it, were no help in dealing with a neglected estate, over a hundred dependents, financial affairs that were tangled beyond belief and this latest obligation.

He was, it seemed, to be married to the plain daughter

of an obscure vicar. Why could he not have done what she asked and pensioned her off with enough money to support the fiction of a respectable widow? His damnable conscience, he supposed. Sometimes Elliott thought he had been given his brother's conscience as well as his own, for Rafe had certainly not appeared to possess one.

Yesterday evening it had been very clear what he must do, where his duty lay as a man of honour. If she had come to him after the child had been born, then he would not have offered marriage, for that would not have legitimised the baby. But she *had* come and he had been given the opportunity to do what was right.

All his adult life, it seemed, he had been attempting to make up for the damage Rafe had wrought to the estate, to his dependents, to those who crossed his path, and until now he had never been able to do more than stop one young sprig blowing his brains out after Rafe had ruined him at cards. Now all the wreckage had landed at his feet, as though a great storm had thrown it up on to a beach, and he must try to repair everything at once.

The little country lass had been so desperately bedazzled by his irresponsible rake of a brother that she had gone against everything she believed in—he had no doubt that she had been a chaste and virtuous young woman. But why should that surprise him? Rafe Calne had possessed the power to fascinate even the most intelligent women. It had always mystified Elliott how he had done it.

He rarely had trouble attracting female interest himself, but none of the women concerned ever appeared to have suspended every iota of common sense or judgement in the relationship as they did with Rafe.

He suspected that Arabella Shelley was not unintelligent, simply ashamed, frightened and confused. She was also angry with him, whether she acknowledged it or not. He was alive and standing in the place of the man she wanted to confront and force to acknowledge his responsibilities.

She had not known Rafe at all or she would never have fallen for him—she was not the sort of woman who wanted to flirt with danger. It hurt to acknowledge it, but Rafe had been a vicious, debauched, scheming rake who hid his true nature under a mask of charm when it suited him. And that charm had obviously deceived her all too well, for Elliott doubted that Arabella realised just how fortunate she had been. What if Rafe had lured her away to London and then abandoned her? It did not bear thinking about.

Best to put it behind them if they could. He was to be married and he had better accept it and move on from there as he hoped Arabella would.

He had never expected to find love in marriage, he thought as he stared unseeing out of the carriage window at the unweeded drive. He supposed he had that in common with most men of his class. But neither had he expected to take a wife who was not a virgin, one who was carrying someone else's child. They would have to become accustomed to that, somehow. It would be like wedding a widow virtually from her husband's open graveside.

He grimaced at the macabre image. He must think

positively. Surely Arabella would recover soon enough from the shattering of her infatuation with Rafe and the cruel realisation that she had been deceived. They could put it behind them and build a marriage based on reality.

It was, after all, time he settled down. He was thirty now. That had come as something of a shock. He had been teasing a small group of giggling young ladies at Almack's in March and had suddenly realised just how young they were. He could not go on flirting for ever, dodging the matchmaking mamas.

In the past few months he had begun to identify suitable young ladies who would make eligible brides and he had accepted an invitation to the Framlinghams' house party that would have given him time with a number of them, including Lady Frederica Framlingham.

Frederica was charming, assured and pretty. He suspected she would not be averse to an offer from him. Under the circumstances it was fortunate that the funeral, and then all the work he had found himself dealing with, had taken him from Town close to the end of the Season and before the house party convened and he could commit himself with Frederica.

The timing might work out well. Arabella would have until February to become used to her new role, to give birth and to prepare to make her dèbut next Season. Elliott pulled out his notebook and jotted a note to have the Town house refurbished. The front door opened. He pulled out his watch: on the stroke of eight. His betrothed was prompt.

Chapter Four

'Good morning, Elliott.' The footman helped Arabella in and he studied her face as she settled herself opposite him.

'Good morning. Did you sleep well?' She was pale and pinched and there were dark shadows under her eyes, which were bloodshot. He had never demanded beauty in his women, but he had expected a certain level of attractiveness. Miss Shelley was quite right, she was certainly plain. The image of Freddie Framlingham, pink cheeked, blue eyed, vivacious, flashed into his mind. Virginal, uncomplicated, good-natured Freddie.

'Thank you, yes.'

Elliott knew that was a polite lie. She must have spent most of the night worrying. 'Excellent.' There was no point in telling her just how ill she looked. 'There is Madeira wine and some dry biscuits in that basket.'

'How thoughtful.' The fleeting smile was a revelation. He stared at her; Miss Shelley, it seemed, was not quite so plain after all. Then the animation faded and once more she was wan and subdued. 'I have had a very careful breakfast. I hope this nausea will not last much longer.'

He did not refer to the fact that it was more than morning sickness that was distressing her so. They had no need to speak of the circumstances. 'You have a *confidante*, someone with experience of being with child?' It occurred to him that she would need one. Cousin Dorothy would be no help and Mrs Knight, his housekeeper, had her title from courtesy only. She too was a spinster.

'Our laundry maid has six children,' Arabella explained. 'I heard all about her health throughout several pregnancies so I have some idea what to expect. But other than her, no. Papa did not encourage close friendships.'

'Rest and a lack of anxiety should help.' Elliott hoped he sounded more confident than he felt. What Arabella needed was some experienced female companionship, not an unknown husband whose knowledge of childbirth was entirely derived from the stud farm and the kennels.

'A lack of anxiety?' That expressive smile suggested that she was far from agreeing with his choice of words.

'Now you know that your child will be secure,' he temporised.

'That is true.' She hesitated, then said, 'Elliott, are you quite sure about this? I lay awake thinking that you must be awake too. Awake and bitterly regretting what you had done.'

'I thought you want what is best for your child.'

'I do, but this is not your fault.'

'It is, however, my responsibility.' Damn it, he was beginning to sound like the prosy bore Rafe had accused him of becoming. 'A gentleman does not go back on his word.'

'No, Elliott. Of course not.' Arabella seemed to withdraw into herself.

So now he felt like a prosy bore who had kicked a kitten. He consulted his notebook. Might as well carry on behaving like a dull, domineering husband—at least that involved no messy, uncomfortable emotion.

'We will call on my lawyer, Lewisham, this afternoon and he will draw up the settlement so that you and the child are protected. I will also organise your allowance and arrange to have it paid to you quarterly, if that is convenient.'

'An allowance for housekeeping?' Arabella queried. He could see her making herself pay attention and wondered if dragooning her into coming to Worcester had been a good idea. But the alternative was to leave her with Dorothy and there she would have to pretend all the time.

'No, for your personal use. For gowns and whatever else you wish to spend it on. I thought fifty pounds, but you will let me know if it is not enough.'

'A year?' She was staring.

'No, a quarter.'

'Two *hundred* pounds? I can afford a maid.' She looked more stunned than pleased. She was way out of her depth, he realised. That was another thing that had not occurred to him—he was going to have to show her how to go on at this level in Society.

'I will pay for your maid, and later for the nurse and the nursery maid. And an allowance for the child. This is all for you, Arabella. We will discuss the housekeeping later, but you have Mrs Knight, who has been housekeeper for about ten years and she is very experienced. You will not have much to do in that department.'

'I know all about housekeeping,' she said with a touch of asperity. 'This will just be a matter of scale. But what am I to spend all that money on?' Then that unguarded smile reappeared. It was impossible not to smile back. 'Books! I can join a subscription library and have them sent. And journals. And embroidery silks— I would like to do fine work and not just darning and knitting. And then patterns for baby clothes.' Her hand came to rest, unconsciously, on her midriff and something twisted inside him that he could not identify. The baby was real, suddenly, not just an abstraction or a problem. Rafe's child. Elliott felt a strange pang, almost apprehension. He shook his head to clear it.

'And later you should have a dancing master. You will be called upon to dance very frequently, next Season. We will go up to London when you have recovered from the birth. Then you can have lessons, buy your ball gowns and court gown.'

'Court. Balls. Oh, my.' The smile faded. 'Elliott, I fear I am well out of my depth.'

'But I am not. I am used to the London Season, I have many friends in Town. You will soon find your feet and become an accomplished hostess.' And by then she would not rely so much on him. Life could get back to normal. He would attend sporting events, Jackson's Boxing Salon, his clubs. During the Season they would go to parties and to balls. And she would go shopping, make calls, look after the child. Out of

Season they would pay visits and live in the country. It was all very simple. No mistresses, of course. And no flirting.

'Thank you, you are very kind.' She fell silent and he let his notebook drop on to the seat and instead studied her face.

'You are quite easy to be kind to, Arabella.' He found that was true. But what would she be like when she had recovered her confidence and found her feet? 'Any husband would do as much.' *Husband. This time tomorrow, and we will be in church. Will I make a good husband? A good father?* There was that odd pang again. 'We are nearly there. Will you come with me to see the bishop?'

'I think I should.' She fiddled with her lank bonnet strings. 'He is going to think me a dowdy match for a viscount.'

'Would you like to buy a new bonnet first? And a new reticule? What you are wearing is perfectly acceptable, if plain.' Actually it was downright dull, but it would not boost her confidence to have him say so. 'But if it would make you more comfortable to have something new, we do have plenty of time. In fact, we could see to all your clothes shopping.' He rather enjoyed shopping with women, even spoiled and petulant mistresses. This country mouse would be amusing, exposed to the modest sophistication of the county town.

'Thank you.' Arabella bit her lip, obviously not thinking about bonnets. It would be entertaining to spoil her a little, make clothes a source of pleasure for her, rather than a necessity. 'I do not think we should mention who Papa is to the bishop, do you? I would rather he does not know where I have gone. Not yet.'

'As you wish.' She nodded and fell silent and there did not seem much more to say. He saw her wipe a tear surreptitiously from the corner of her eye. But there was a great deal to think about.

'Here we are—Worcester. See, there is Fort Royal, just ahead on the right as we go down the hill.'

Bella sat up straight and told herself to pay attention. Elliott appeared perfectly at his ease, businesslike even, with his notebook and his plans for her. The image she had begun to build of him last night, formed from the glimpses of rueful laughter, the decisive way he had dealt with her, the feeling that beneath the kindness was a man with a hint of danger about him, wavered. This was a rather solid, very responsible man. Just the sort one would wish for in a husband, she told herself.

This was all so strange, and so dangerously comfortable—an allowance beyond her wildest dreams, a new bonnet, a comfortable carriage, talk of ball gowns and dancing lessons.

Bella tried to look at Elliott objectively as he stared out of the window, his face a little turned from her. There was something about the way he held himself, something in the concentration with which he watched the passing scene that had her revising her opinion again. No, Elliott Calne was no stolid and indulgent benefactor, however kind and honourable he appeared.

Seeing the set of his jaw, she thought that she would not want to cross him. There was a feeling of power and force about him that his brother had not possessed, a suppressed energy as though he was confined within the clothing and trapping of an aristocrat, but wanted to shed them, do something explosively physical. He was a man who had an aim in life, not one aimlessly filling time.

Elliott sat back and took some papers from his pocket, bent over his notebook again and jotted what looked like calculations. Surely not her allowance still? He dropped a letter on the seat. Reading it upside down, she could see the words...*your instructions, have sold the stocks at a most advantageous price and have invested in the company you mentioned to the extent of one thousand pounds...*

No. Not her allowance, but business. Her husband must be a rich man. *You will be all right, Baby,* she promised. *You will grow up healthy and protected and you will never know your papa did not want you. I will love you and Elliott will be your papa instead and he will ensure your future.* It was easy to be glad of his money and his title for the baby's sake. But she felt uncomfortably mercenary to accept it for herself. She had sinned and now she was being rewarded. Yet without the marriage her child would not be legitimate, she reminded herself. Her own feelings and sensibilities must come second.

The carriage drew up and she looked out to find that they were in a busy street, lined with bow-fronted shops. 'I am sorry to be such an expense to you,' she said without thinking. 'And should we not be in mourning?'

'You are to be Lady Hadleigh and you must do the title credit. There is nothing to thank me for. And we have no family tradition of wearing mourning, certainly not in the country. Come.' And he held out a hand.

Bella stepped out of the carriage on to the flagstones. The sudden thought that this was the first step into her new life made her stumble. She was shopping to find a bonnet worthy of a bishop and the wardrobe of a countess. She would do it. And, somehow, she would learn to make this man a good wife.

Elliott caught her elbow and steadied her. She managed to smile at him and he smiled back, probably with relief that she was not being ill or difficult. A pair of young ladies passed them and she saw them glance at Elliott, their casual gaze sharpening as they looked. He really was a very attractive man, she realised, her lips tightening as she caught him returning the scrutiny.

He was taller and leaner—harder—than his brother. His smile was as ready, but no doubt far more genuine. Not as pattern-book good looking as Rafe, Bella thought critically, striving for detachment, but more overtly masculine. Dangerous in quite a different way to Rafe because it was less showy. This was a man who was utterly comfortable and confident in his masculinity. Elliott did not appear to feel the need to prove anything to anyone except himself. She felt a flutter of emotion that, for once, was neither apprehension nor nausea. Not, surely, attraction? No, not after what she had experienced with Rafe, she thought, hiding the shiver.

'Here we are.' Elliott had guided her along the pavement and into a milliner's shop without her realising. Bella pulled herself together and stared round at the hats on display. She probably looked like a child inside a confectioners, but she could not help herself studying the delicious concoctions with longing.

'*Monsieur*—but, no, I must say, *my lord*, is it not so?' A tall woman of a certain age swept down on them, obviously very familiar with Elliott. Which was interesting. Bella slid a sideways glance at him, distracted from her preoccupations. Did he bring his mistresses in here?

'Indeed, Madame Cynthie. And send all my accounts to Hadleigh Old Hall from now on, if you please. This lady, Miss Shelley, is to marry me tomorrow and she requires a bonnet for that occasion and one to meet the bishop this afternoon.'

'Ah!' Madame cast up her hands in delight before pouncing on Bella's bedraggled bonnet strings. 'And what colour is the wedding gown, Miss Shelley?'

'Er…' Elliott was no help, he merely lifted his brows at her in an infuriating manner. 'Green. Pale leaf green.' That was the gown she had dreamed about while she was waiting for Rafe: a dress the colour of spring.

Half an hour later the perfect wedding bonnet, wreathed in veiling and tied with bunches of utterly frivolous green ribbon, was in its box and Bella was staring blankly at two more perfect hats. She was not used to choice. The one with the cherry-red ribbons made her rather mousy brown hair seem darker and shinier and was very dignified. But the one with the bunch of primroses tucked under the brim made her eyes look greener and was so pretty she wanted to smile just looking at it.

'I cannot decide.'

'Both, in that case.' Elliott did not appear bored at

having to lounge around a milliner's shop while she dithered, nor annoyed that he was now buying three bonnets and not two. 'The red ribbons for Bishop Huntingford, I think. Put it on now. And throw the old one away,' he added to the milliner. 'Now for that reticule.' He waited until they were outside the shop before adding, 'And a green wedding gown.'

'I will never find anything to fit at such short notice.' She wanted to say that it did not matter, but, of course, it did. Elliott would be displeased if she did not look the part. The urge to demand that her old bonnet was packed up and returned to her died.

'Nonsense. Here we are.' Another little jewel box of a shop, this time a dressmaker's. And another shopkeeper delighted to see his lordship and obviously used to having him on her premises. Elliott met Bella's questioning glance with a look of bland innocence. Was he keeping a mistress? Of course he was, she must just learn not to mind about it. It would be easier with her emotions not involved; it was not as though she would be a real wife.

Mrs Sutton, could, of course, assist his lordship. She had just the gown and if Miss Shelley would only step into the fitting room to try it on, any alterations could be accomplished by mid-afternoon.

'And anything else you have to hand that would do,' Elliott called after them. 'Morning dress, afternoon dress, walking dress. Miss Shelley's luggage met with an accident.'

Bella was almost speechless by the time she emerged, but Elliott was ruthless and took her firmly off to find more shops. Reticule, shoes and gloves were easily dealt with, but the lingerie shop was another matter altogether. 'No.' She found her voice and dug her heels in after one glance at the froth of lace and gauze in the window. There were no actual garments on display, but she could imagine them only too vividly. 'I am not going in there with you.'

'Very well. Will you be all right out here for one moment?'

'Why, yes, but—' Elliott walked calmly into the shop leaving her, and the laden footman, outside.

'Right, in you go.' He emerged after a few minutes. 'Sanders, take the shopping back to the carriage and have it come round to collect Miss Shelley in half an hour. I will meet you at the Royal Oak.' He tipped his hat to Bella and strolled off.

It was impossible to vent one's feelings in front of the footman. Bella knew that she must preserve the illusion that she knew Elliott very well and not protest about having a stranger buy such intimate garments. She managed to keep a smile firmly on her lips, nodded to Sanders and went in.

It seemed Elliott had merely uttered a sentence containing the words *bride, wedding, tomorrow, everything* and left. After a few minutes Bella mentally added, *outrageous, extravagant and indecent.*

'This is transparent,' she protested, peering over the top of the garment being held up before her. 'And what is it, anyway?' She would look like the loose woman she now was.

'A nightgown, madam. Here is the négligé and the

slippers to match. I thought this set as well? And this. Oh, yes, and this would be enchanting with your colouring, if I might be so bold. Millie, only the best Indian muslin for Miss Shelley's underthings, mind. Oh, and that Swiss embroidery, as well. Now, stays...'

Whenever Bella tried to protest that there was enough the three assistants shook their heads and informed her that his lordship had been quite clear in his instructions and they would not dream of stopping until they had fulfilled them.

'And handkerchiefs,' the assistant said finally. 'There. Now we will just pack them up, Miss Shelley, if you would like a cup of tea?'

It was almost worth it to see Sanders's face as he was loaded up with dainty packages and bandboxes, striped and beribboned. Almost.

Elliott was lounging in a private parlour at the Royal Oak, the day's newssheets spread out on the table, a jug of coffee by his side, but he got to his feet as she entered. 'Coffee, Arabella?'

'Thank you, no.' Her stomach revolted at the smell. 'Tea, please.'

She could almost pretend this was normal, sipping tea in a strange city, alone with a man she had known for less than twenty-four hours, wearing a fashionable bonnet and expecting to visit a bishop. This was the sort of thing—without the bishop, of course—that she had once dreamed of doing with Rafe. The room blurred and she swallowed, disciplining her thoughts.

Chapter Five

⁂

'Is everything all right, Arabella?' Elliott enquired.
'Have you finished your shopping?'

'Thank you, yes.' Bella struggled between politeness
and honesty. 'I cannot help but feel that this has been
an entirely too-extravagant morning.'

'Did you not enjoy it?' Elliott watched her over the
rim of his cup and she could not decide whether he was
amused or displeased at her lack of enthusiasm.

'Of course not.' *I have a mind above such frivolity.*
But honesty won. 'No… Yes, I did. Most of it. It was
very pleasant to choose nice things.' She felt herself
colour up and his eyes crinkled at the corners in
response. Elliott appeared to like her blushes, which was
disconcerting. They had amused Rafe too, she reminded
herself, sobering instantly.

'It is the bare minimum, of course. But I thought
that you would wish to have the *modiste* call privately
at the Hall so you can discuss your requirements

when…' he waved a hand vaguely in front of himself '…your figure changes.'

'Oh, yes.' Something else to blush about. Perhaps it was better to abandon all pretence of modesty. 'I think that will happen soon, but the current mode is helpful in disguising things.'

There was a tap at the door and a waiter began to bring in food. Bread and butter, some cold meats and cheese, fruit cake. 'You have to eat properly,' Elliott observed, buttering bread for her when she sat and just looked at the table.

'I know. I was thinking about something else.' Bella added a little chicken to her plate and told herself that the baby needed the food and she needed her strength. So far, thank goodness, she had developed none of the cravings for strange foods that Polly the laundry maid had reported. Coal and honey had been one messy result.

But men were not interested in such feminine things, she knew. Elliott was being very forbearing, even discussing her morning sickness. Years of subduing her own feelings and desires came to her rescue as she searched for acceptable conversation. 'Who will be at the wedding?' she asked.

'Cousin Dorothy, my great-aunt Lady Abbotsbury, if she feels up to it, and my friend and neighbour John Baynton, who will be my groomsman.' He frowned. 'Who can give you away?'

'Miss Dorothy?'

Elliott laughed, the first time she had heard him do so out loud. The sound made her smile, it was so infectious. 'She would love that, I am sure, but it would cause even more talk if we do something so unconventional.' His amusement vanished as he studied her face. 'What is it?'

'You sound just like Rafe when you laugh. It was the only time his voice was as deep as yours.' Rafe had laughed a lot. All the time, except when he was suddenly intense, gazing deep into her eyes, his own so blue. She had thought they must be the bluest eyes in the world until she saw Elliott's, darker, more vivid, like deep ocean water with cold, dangerous currents beneath the warm surface.

'I am sorry. I must be a constant, painful reminder.' His lips thinned as he helped himself to a slice of beef and added mustard lavishly from the pewter pot. She must stop this, he did not need her throwing her memories of his brother in his face at every turn.

'No, not at all. I will become accustomed. It is simply a matter of self-discipline and I will learn to forget my experience with Rafe,' she added bleakly. Soon, surely, she would be able to look at him and not see Rafe's face like a translucent mask overlaying Elliott's? She had to remember that this was another man altogether, one she could trust, one who would not abuse her. She had to believe that.

'In the meantime I will endeavour not to laugh.'

Was that said sarcastically or was he in earnest? She would have to learn to read him if she was to be a good wife.

'Thank you, but that will not be necessary,' Bella murmured, fighting down the panic at the thought of everything she must learn. A good wife, a good mother and a good viscountess: three new roles to learn and so many things that she could do wrong. She ate another slice of bread. She was a competent, experienced housekeeper, so the domestic side of things held no terrors. She would love the baby, so she could trust her instincts there. Elliott would tell her what she needed to do to be a proper viscountess. But how was she to learn to be a good wife to a man she did not know and did not love without blundering, hurting them both—assuming he ever cared enough to be hurt by her clumsiness?

'Have you finished, Arabella?'

'Thank you, yes.' How long had she been sitting there brooding? 'Is it time to go and see the bishop now?'

'It is.' He stood up and held out his hand to her. 'Just curtsy, call him *My lord* and leave the talking to me. If he asks something difficult, simply look to me adoringly and I'll deal with it. Can you do that?'

'Yes,' she said. It was becoming quite easy to think that Elliott was someone she could look to for help. Whether or not she could manage a look of adoration, she was less sure. She must remember that for him, this was strictly a matter of honour and duty, she must not come to rely upon him emotionally.

'Thank you, my lord.' Bella managed a creditable curtsy and took Elliott's arm. In his other hand he held a wedding licence. *Soon*, she thought, *soon you will be safe, Baby.* Resisting the urge to back away, as though in the presence of royalty, she preceded Elliott out through the door, keeping silent because of the liveried footmen and a passing cleric with an armful of papers.

'That went very well,' Elliott observed as they walked across College Green behind the cathedral.

'Yes,' Bella agreed. To her relief the bishop had shown no surprise at Lord Hadleigh arriving with a red-eyed, drab female on his arm and requesting a special licence. Elliott sounded quite pleased, not at all as though he was merely resigned to this wedding. Her heart lifted a little. 'Elliott, do you mind so very much?'

He caught her meaning and his lips firmed, making him look rather formidable. 'I mind a lot less than I would having you and the child on my conscience. I told you, Arabella, this is my duty; you need have no fear that I will not perform it to the best of my ability.'

It was not his duty she was worried about, it was his feelings, but the wretched man seemed ready to discuss anything rather than those. 'No, I was not—' she began.

'Elliott!' The man crossing the greensward was as tall as Elliott, but darker, slimmer and, as a ready smile creased his face, apparently more light-hearted at the moment.

'Daniel.' Elliott held out his hand and as the other man shook it enthusiastically she saw he bore a resemblance to both Elliott and Rafe.

'Good to see you out and about after the funeral. Who would have thought it? In his prime, poor Rafe. I am having trouble believing it. Difficult for you.'

'You could say that. Arabella, allow me to introduce you to my cousin, Mr Calne. Daniel, Miss Shelley.'

Bella smiled and shook hands. They were friends, she could tell at once. Elliott and his cousin had exchanged looks that said more than they had put into words. Why had he not told Mr Calne at once that they were to be wed? Surely the more relatives present, the more normal the whole thing would appear, not that she wanted to face them. Perhaps he thought she would be embarrassed. She nudged Elliott's booted foot with her toe and he looked down at her. 'I wonder if Mr Calne might not be free tomorrow?'

'Of course. Our interview with the bishop has sent my wits wandering, obviously.' He smiled. 'Daniel, you must congratulate me. Miss Shelley and I are to be wed.'

There was a moment while his cousin stared at Elliott blankly. Bella had the fleeting impression that he was very surprised indeed. Then he seemed to pull himself together. 'My dear fellow!' Mr Calne slapped Elliott on the back and beamed at Bella. 'My felicitations. And am I to guess from your reference to Bishop Huntingford that the ceremony is to be soon?'

'Yes, tomorrow. Miss Shelley's father does not approve the match, although she is of age, and things were becoming a trifle uncomfortable for her at home, so we have expedited matters.'

Bella took a firmer grip on Elliott's arm and smiled warmly, trying to look like a loving fiancée. 'Perhaps Mr Calne could solve our problem, dearest.'

Elliott's eyebrows rose a trifle at the endearment. 'Which one, my love?' he countered, the corner of his mouth twitching.

There are so many, Bella thought, fighting the impulse to smile back. 'Why, someone to give me away, of course.'

'Of course.' He smiled at her; obviously she had said the right thing. 'Daniel? Will you do that duty?'

'I would be honoured!' Mr Calne beamed at both of them and Bella found herself smiling back. Elliott was pleased, at least one of his family was pleased and she liked the enthusiastic cousin.

'Come for luncheon,' Elliott said. 'The ceremony will take place at three. You'll stay the night?'

'That would be delightful, if the new Lady Hadleigh has no objections. I have concluded my business in Worcester and I will be returning to my home, which is some way beyond Hadleigh Old Hall,' he explained to Bella. 'It would be most pleasant to break my journey. Now, I will bid you farewell—I am sure you would much prefer your own company just at the moment. I will see you this evening, Elliott. Until tomorrow, Miss Shelley.' He resumed his hat and strode off.

'He seems very pleasant,' Bella commented. Elliott was silent and her heart sank. She had erred, been too forward, and they were not even married yet. 'I am sorry,' she ventured. 'I'm afraid I—'

'There is no need to apologise,' Elliott said brusquely. 'You are about to become the Countess Hadleigh, you are not the vicar's daughter any longer.'

She *was* afraid, that was the problem—there were so many things she could get wrong—and now perhaps she had irritated Elliott and, whether he liked it or not, just now he was the only stable point in her universe. She bit her lip; it seemed at the moment that she had the strength for only one thing at a time, and a dissatisfied fiancé was one too many. *Courage*, she told herself.

'I'm sorry.' Elliott stopped and looked down at her. 'Of course you are anxious. Daniel's a good fellow, and an optimist. I sometimes think he will be making a merry quip in the middle of the Day of Judgement. He's a lawyer, a hard worker. He got on Rafe's nerves—too solid, not enough fun.'

Bella heard the edge to his voice when he mentioned Rafe, but at least he was not cross with her. She let him tuck her hand under his elbow as they began to walk again.

'His father, my Uncle Clarence, who died some time ago, was my father's only brother. His widow lived in London with my father's two sisters until she died last year. You will meet them when we go up to town next year.'

'Will you not invite them to the Hall?' Surely that would be usual, with a new wife to introduce to the family. 'Or should we not visit them?' She dreaded the thought, but there would be no avoiding that duty. All families with any pretensions to gentility kept up the tradition of bride visits. She glanced round as they passed under the great medieval gate arch, momentarily distracted by the pinkish stone, so very different from Suffolk plaster and brick.

'They rarely travel and I imagine you would prefer to find your feet before entertaining a houseful of demanding ladies.' Elliott put out a hand to stop her as a man went past with a basket full of salmon on his head, still dripping from the river. 'As for going up to London before the end of the year, I do not think the Town house is in a fit state.'

That must be an excuse. Rafe had mentioned his London home; he could hardly have been living in squalor. Presumably Elliott did not want her exposed to his relatives until she had acquired some of the polish a viscountess required, or he was embarrassed because her pregnancy would show by then.

It was lowering that he was ashamed of her, but, under the circumstances, hardly unexpected. And perhaps he had his mistress in London, another lowering thought. Fashionable marriages accommodated such unsavoury realities, she knew. She must learn to accept it and not embarrass Elliott with her provincial attitudes.

'Very well, Elliott.' Out of the corner of her eye she saw him give her a quizzical look, but he did not challenge this meekness. 'Then your relatives at the Dower House are on your mother's side?'

'Yes. Great-Aunt Alice is my mother's older sister, Lady Abbotsbury, and Dorothy her unmarried daughter. There are three other daughters, all married and living some distance away. I expect you will soon make acquaintances in the area.'

'Is local society congenial?' The thought of new friends, probing and becoming intimate, was unsettling. They would be more people to hide the truth from.

They were back at the Royal Oak and the carriage was waiting. 'Congenial? I hardly know. They came to the funeral, of course, and made duty condolence calls, but I cannot say I know any of them.'

'But surely you know the neighbourhood very well?' Bella settled back against the squabs, thankful for the physical comfort after the aching misery of the stage the day before.

'I have not lived at the Hall since I went to university.'

'But you must have visited frequently?'

'No.' It seemed he had not intended to expand on that

monosyllable, but the surprise must have shown on her face. 'My mother died just before I went up and then my father had a hunting accident while I was at Oxford. I assumed Rafe would want me to manage the estate— he had no taste for that kind of thing and had made it plain often enough that it bored him. But it appeared he felt more…territorial about it than I had foreseen.'

'He rejected your offer of help?'

'He accused me of wanting to take over, usurp his position in local society. For some reason he appeared to find me a threat. I was young enough to be hurt, and for that to appear as temper. We had a blazing row, I punched him on his very beautiful nose—you may have noticed the slight bump—and that was that. We hardly exchanged a civil word for eight years and I was *persona non grata* at the Hall.'

'How awful. I cannot imagine being at odds with Lina and Meg. And you were both very young—if only you had been reconciled later.' How strange of Rafe. Surely he would have welcomed a brother's help with the country estate he seemed not to have cared for? Without thinking, Bella put her hand over Elliott's. It was stiff and unresponsive and she lifted her own away, feeling she had erred.

'It was doubtless good for me, as things turned out. I was forced back on my own small inherited estate. I learned to run that and how to invest wisely. Then I turned to speculation—mines, canals, housing—and found I had the knack for it. Rafe felt I dabbled perilously close to trade for one of our class and made that clear whenever our paths crossed in Town.'

'Rafe seemed unused to rural life,' Bella murmured. 'He was out of place in the country, I thought.' Elliott made no response, so she blundered on, 'I expect he was much happier in Town. He was so sophisticated in our little village. He seemed to be polished, somehow, like a gemstone, all hard glitter.' *Stop talking about him. I don't want to remember, Elliott does not want to hear this.*

She had been nervous at the thought of London society. Then Rafe had told her that she made rustication in the sticks bearable, that she would convert him to country living, to the fresh purity of the simple life, and she had believed him and been comforted. Now she saw his lies like layer after layer of deceit.

'Oh, yes, Rafe was polished. You will find that I am less so. Less polished, more direct. I belong to the Corinthian set—sportsmen. I box, I drive, I race. I attend prize fights.' That explained the lean, hard look of him. 'Do you find the thought of those kind of activities distasteful?' Bella shook her head. If truth be told, she found the idea rather exciting. The picture of Elliott, stripped to the waist, fists raised, made her pulse race.

'And perhaps I am even more demanding than he was.' She was unsure how to respond to that—was it a threat or a warning? 'Here we are at Mr Lewisham's offices.'

Bella leaned back against the squabs and stared rather blankly at the passing countryside. Her heart still felt hollow, as though Rafe, wrenching himself from it with his harsh words, had left it wounded. But now his face was becoming mercifully blurred with Elliott's; his voice was lost in the other man's. She wished she could tell Elliott everything, bring herself to talk about that dreadful afternoon in the tithe barn, tell him what Rafe had said and done and how she had felt. But she must hide her deepest feelings from his brother, who had his loss to contend with. Elliott clearly knew how badly Rafe had let her down, but however much Elliott might have been estranged from Rafe, he had wanted to make peace, she was sure. How could she tell him how foul his brother had really been to her?

And, besides, he did not need the fact that she was plain and naïve and unsophisticated reinforcing. Rafe had made that clear; Elliott had eyes, too.

She sat up straighter and tried to take an intelligent interest in the scene outside. It appeared they grew a great deal of fruit, hereabouts. She saved that observation up to make conversation later. A lady discussed neutral subjects of interest and she very much doubted that she had as many of those as a viscountess ought to be able to muster.

It would help if she did not keep thinking about those piles of clothes. Elliott was right, of course, she had to look the part, but even so, he could hardly have been expecting to outfit a wife who did not even bring her own trousseau with her.

'What is worrying you now?' Elliott asked, making her jump.

'How do you know I was worrying?' she asked to put off answering.

'Your teeth were caught in your lower lip, and you were frowning. Is there something you want to ask me?'

'I wanted to thank you for all the lovely clothes.'

'I told you, it is necessary that you look the part.' He sounded a little impatient.

'I know. The gowns and bonnets and so on, I understand about that. But the other things.' She could feel her cheeks warming. 'The…undergarments and the nightgowns. I have never had pretty things like that before; it was kind of you to buy those for me.'

Elliott's mouth twitched, she could see out of the corner of her eye. Bella turned on the seat so she could look at him directly. 'Why are you smiling? Have I said something amusing?'

'No, forgive me. It is just that a man really needs no praise for buying things that contribute to his own pleasure.'

The amusement had been replaced by a curve of his lips that reminded her acutely of Rafe, just before he kissed her, and it took a sick moment for his meaning to sink in. The carriage went through a deep cutting in the road and shadow fell into the small space, almost hiding Elliott's face. It gave her courage to utter the question. 'You mean you expect a…a real marriage?' she said all of a rush as they emerged into sunlight again.

Chapter Six

'A real marriage as opposed to what, exactly?' Both Elliott's dark brows winged upwards.

'What we will be doing. Or not doing. I mean, we are marrying in the expectation that the baby is a boy, your heir. So we would not need to…to share a bed afterwards. If it was. A boy, I mean. If it is a girl, I can see you would want an heir, so…' But that was a long time away, she did not need to think about that now.

'Arabella, are you suggesting that I do not come to your bed until after this baby is born and that if it is a boy that I never do?' Elliott demanded.

'Well, yes. I mean, you do not want to marry me because you love me, or anything like that, so…'

Elliott twisted on the seat to face her, but she turned away abruptly and stared out of the window, presenting him with the rim of her new bonnet and what she knew was a pink-flushed cheek. *How did I ever get into this conversation? I am ready to sink…*

She heard him draw breath in through his gritted

teeth. 'Arabella, we are getting married. I am prepared to do my duty by Rafe's child and by you, but I am not prepared to become a monk in the process!'

His voice deepened to a growl and she turned back, even more flustered by this sign of the temper she had suspected lurked beneath that calm and controlled exterior. 'Oh! But I thought—but I do not know you!' And, surely he did not *desire* her? Elliott showed no sign of finishing her sentences now. He sat and watched her flounder, his expression unyielding.

Eventually he said, 'How long did you know Rafe?'

'Eight days,' she confessed.

'You were constantly in his company? You became intimate in every way, understood him, mind and soul?'

'Why, no. We could only meet in a clandestine way, snatch an hour here and there. How many couples know each other mind and soul before they marry? I *loved* him. I mean, I thought I loved him. I did not know him at all, of course,' she added with wrenching honesty.

'You fell in love with a man you had known for a handful of days, if you add up those snatched hours,' Elliott said remorselessly. 'Rafe was complex and complicated, just like any other human being. You could not possibly have thought you knew him any better than you know me.'

'But I do not love you!' she threw at him.

'True.' Elliott nodded. 'What was it that so destroyed your judgement, your instinct for danger? Were you were dazzled, desperate, beguiled or seduced?'

'No! Yes, I mean I was all of those things. But haven't you a mistress?' Bella asked rather desperately. She had to know, she realised.

'No, not just at the moment.'

'But you could get one,' she suggested. 'I wouldn't mind.' *Please take one. Then I will not have the humiliation of my ignorance, my clumsiness. My fear.*

It was obviously entirely the wrong thing to say. Elliott looked thunderous. 'Then you should mind,' he growled. 'Why should I in any case, when I will have a wife? As it happens, I believe in marital fidelity.'

'Then you would want to come to my room.' Best to be quite clear. 'Next year, I mean, after the baby is born?'

'I was rather expecting to do so tomorrow night,' Elliott said. His voice was dry, but she could hear his temper tightly reined beneath it.

'*Tomorrow* night?' Her insides seemed to have become entirely hollow.

'It is usual on a wedding night to consummate the union.'

'But you do not love me,' she protested. *How naïve, this is not some green boy, this is an experienced man who expects to gratify his physical desires. He thinks I have been Rafe's mistress so I will know what to do. And what if he is just as angry as Rafe was when he realises how inept I am?* And Elliott did not think her pretty. How could he, looking as ill and drawn as she was? So this was duty, as he saw it. No mistress, faithfulness to his inconvenient, unsuitable wife. A nightmare and twenty-four hours to anticipate it in.

'Love is not a necessity, you know,' Elliott said, confirming her thoughts. 'You are not repelled by me?'

She shook her head. No, of course she was not repelled by him. Part of her looked at him and ached with a very shocking and basic desire to touch him. To be touched by him. He was big and strong and very masculine and she needed to be held and comforted. But that was nothing to do with what a man and woman did in bed. Marital intimacy was quite another thing.

'Or frightened of me?' Another shake, a little slower that time. Bella kept her eyes fixed on the reticule she was holding in a death grip. She was terrified, but how could she tell him? The humiliation would be even worse than keeping silent. 'We will consummate this marriage.'

'Must we?' It came out as a whisper.

'Yes. There is no way I am going to contemplate a sham marriage. This is for the rest of our lives. I am doing my duty, Arabella—I am asking you to do yours.'

He was quite right, of course he was. She understood duty and she understood obligation and she must pay the price. This man was saving her from poverty and shame and her innocent child from all the stigma of its conception. 'Yes, you are right, of course. You will require an heir if this is not a boy and you are entitled to a proper marriage whatever happens.' Could she counterfeit whatever was necessary for him to be satisfied with her?

'I would not force you. Physically, I mean. I would never do that. But I will come to you tomorrow night and we will see what happens.'

'I will not refuse you,' she murmured, her fingers still crushing the worn reticule.

'And you must always tell me if you are indisposed, naturally.' How calm and unembarrassed he sounded, as though they were discussing whether she could hold a dinner party or accompany him to the races.

'I do not make excuses,' Arabella said, trying not to sound reluctant and hearing her own voice, colourless and flat.

'No, you do not, do you?' Elliott shifted across into the corner so he could look at her more directly and she made herself meet his gaze, her chin coming up a little. 'You have little experience of men, I assume.'

'Very little indeed,' she agreed. 'It has not been very successful so far,' she added with an attempt at a dry little joke.

'I will have to see what I can do to improve that,' Elliott said. Mercifully he did not begin to explain just how he would set about it.

He was going to be her husband and he expected to be so, fully. Her brain did not seem to be working very well. Why had she not realised that he would require… *that*? She had known instinctively that there was a flaw with this perfect solution and here it was.

Somehow she must learn to please Elliott as she had not pleased Rafe, she *must*. She kept trying not to think of that, of what it had been like. Afterwards she had thought it had been her fault for being so ignorant, for crying out at the pain, otherwise he would not have risen from their makeshift bed so soon, without holding her, without so much as a caress. Now she tried to tell herself that he had behaved like that because of who he was and it was no fault of hers. But a voice inside hacked away at her confidence. *Repressed, ignorant vicarage girl*, it whispered in Rafe's voice. *You are frigid… You will never please a man. Stupid, clumsy, plain.*

The next day she had hardly seen him, his kisses had been brief, almost brutal. And then, when she had clung to him, he had turned on her, his words full of angry, acid spite. At first she had not understood, then as the truth had sunk in she had clamped her hands over her ears, trying not to hear. She was a bore in bed, a bore for wanting to cling, a bore for not realising this was all a game to entertain him while he was stuck in this God-forsaken backwater. There had not been one word about her feelings, about her, at all.

Now, her resolution not to think about the act itself could not entirely suppress the thought of those quite shocking nightgowns. Elliott was expecting her to wear one tomorrow. Everything she would be wearing, every day, right down to her skin, was ordered and paid for by him. He owned her and she must do what he said.

A shiver ran down her spine. And he would own her baby, too. Yes, the diamond had a huge flaw in it, she could see it now so clearly. But that was the price she was going to have to pay for the security she and the child needed.

'Would you like to rest?' Elliott asked. Thank goodness, he showed no inclination to restart this discussion. He must have decided the matter was closed. Her husband-to-be had spoken. 'It has been a long day. Stretch out on the seat. There is a rug you can use as a pillow.'

'Thank you.' Bella took off her bonnet and lay down. She was tired, now she let herself think about it, but more than that, if she pretended to sleep there would be no danger of any more conversation. Elliott folded the rug for her and she rested her head on it and closed her eyes. *He is kind*, she reminded herself. And honourable. And he will not be satisfied until he bends me absolutely to his will.

* * *

But you do not love me. That whispered protest seemed to echo in his brain. Of course he did not. Gentlemen did not expect love in marriage. *And neither had Rafe.* The words had been on the tip of his tongue, but he had not said them. He could not be so cruel as to remind her of that, not when Arabella looked at him and fixed those wide hazel eyes on his. Why had he not noticed before how clear her eyes were and how lavish the dark lashes?

If it had not been so serious he could have laughed at her innocent assumption that he would marry her in name only. It was not often that he was at a loss for words, Elliott reflected. But this time Arabella had succeeded in silencing him for several seconds.

Women were emotional creatures, he told himself. Yesterday she had been exhausted, she had received a huge shock and she was with child. Just one of those circumstances was enough to make any woman hesitate when faced with a man insisting he share her bed, although, without vanity, he knew himself to be an experienced and skilful lover. Arabella would not be dissatisfied, he vowed. He would be gentle and considerate and not ask too much of her, not for some time yet. But he would go to her bed, put down the marker that he belonged there.

She would do her best to be a good wife, he believed that, although she had so much to learn, not just about him or the household but the entire world of the *ton* and her role as viscountess. But *duty* was obviously a word with meaning to her and she would try and he must help her.

Elliott made himself more comfortable in the corner and watched Arabella's sleeping face. When she had blushed, putting colour into her wan cheeks, the effect had been rather charming. Perhaps he should make her blush more often. The thought of how he might achieve that brought a smile to his lips and a pleasant tightening in his groin. Yes, he was looking forward to tomorrow night.

He had felt a brute when he had won that argument, though. And when he had become angry he had the clear impression that she was used to being shouted at. She needed confidence to fulfil her new role and she was not going to get it if he was impatient—in bed or out of it.

At least he had been able to tell her the truth about his lack of a mistress. Keeping a *chère amie* and planning to court Frederica at the same time had seemed inappropriate to him, so he had paid Lucille off two months past. The lack of female companionship had been the least of his problems recently, but now it occurred to him that the dubious charms of celibacy were fast wearing thin.

Elliott crossed his legs, the heat of desire fading to be replaced by a mental image of Arabella regarding him reproachfully over the edge of the bed sheets. Patience was going to be needed, but she would soon become accustomed. It was fortunate that he did not suffer any lack of self-esteem in the bedchamber.

He made himself think of other things. He was beginning to admire Arabella's courage. He tried to imagine what it would be like to be young, female, pregnant, to find your lover had rejected you and left you all alone. It was not easy for a self-confident, wealthy, privileged male to put himself in those shoes. Then he recalled the days after his father's death, the shock of bereavement, the hurt of Rafe's rejection, the loss of the comfortably familiar future he had naïvely imagined would be his, the insecurity of a small income with no open-handed father to bale him out.

That had been bad, but he'd had his freedom, a small estate, the status of his family name, a man's lack of constraints, his friends and pastimes. The shock had spurred him to take risks and forge his own, successful, path. But Arabella was a woman with no power and no freedom.

Together they could build a marriage, he felt confident, just so long as he could remain patient and she was open with him.

Arabella stirred in her sleep and he smiled. Yes, *charming* was the word, with those long lashes and her hand tucked under her cheek like a slumbering child. Her lips moved and Elliott leaned closer.

'No,' she murmured. *'No!'*

'Arabella.'

She woke, confused, on a bed that rocked, woken by Rafe, who was dead and who she must fight. She had been dreaming about him, that blissful moment when he had lain his long, hot body over hers, had parted her softness with demanding fingers—and then the nightmare had begun.

'Arabella, we are home.' Not Rafe, but Elliott. Safety. Bella rubbed her eyes, remembering and wondering at the relief that filled her when she saw who she was with.

Home. She swung her feet off the seat and sat up, pushing back her hair. Elliott looked tense. He must be impatient, chasing about the county because of her, dealing with her fears and her emotions, when he had so much to do here.

Bella reached for her new bonnet and tied the ribbons, managing a smile for him. He stared back, serious, looking as though he was trying to read her mind. 'This is a lovely house,' she said, snatching at conversation. 'I think I will enjoy discovering it and learning about my new home.'

'You must make what changes you wish,' Elliott said. 'I have no sentimental attachments to anything here.'

'Oh.' That was rather chilling. She had hoped to explore with him, find treasures from his childhood that he would tell her about, learn the history of the old house and get to know him in the process. 'What is your smaller estate like? Is it close?' The carriage swept past the front of the hall and turned towards the Dower House.

'About ten miles south of here, towards Moreton in Marsh. The house is more a yeoman farmer's than anything more grand, but the land is good.' Despite his measured description Arabella could hear affection and pride in his voice.

'What will you do with it, now you have this?' Bella allowed him to help her down from the carriage, wishing the dusk was not falling. It would be good to see her new home in sunlight. 'What is it called?'

'Fosse Warren. It is close to the Fosse Way, a Roman road. I have no choice but to leave it in the hands of my steward, he's a good man.' There was something in his eyes that told Bella that it was a wrench to leave the estate in other hands, however trusted.

'And the house will be standing empty,' she said,

thinking about damp and keeping rooms aired. She must find out about housekeeping there.

'I will let it out, I expect,' Elliott said, steering her round a hole in the drive. 'I will not dispose of it; it can become the second son's portion.'

'But it is your home,' she protested, managing not to blush at the reference to another child. But Elliott would do his duty to this land, this house and its people, just as he was doing his duty to her. Of course he was thinking ahead, making plans for the future of the family.

'Hadleigh Old Hall is my home now. And yours,' he added as he knocked. 'Ironic, is it not? I never expected to live here, while you thought you were to be its mistress although you had never seen it. And now we must both call it home.'

The door opened before Bella could respond. 'My lord, Miss Shelley.' Dawson seemed less frail today, or perhaps he had been expecting them and had not been alarmed by the knocker. 'Her ladyship and Miss Dorothy are in the drawing room, my lord.'

Bella took a deep breath. Miss Dorothy had been charming, but Lady Abbotsbury would be an entirely different kettle of fish, she suspected. How had Elliott described her? Querulous, that was it. She had managed with the bishop, now she must manage with the dowager; she could not let Elliott down.

'Elliott? What is this Dorothy tells me?' The sharp voice began the moment Elliott stepped through the drawing room door. 'Marriage to some country girl no one has ever heard of? What are you about? Eh?'

Chapter Seven

A country girl no one has heard of. That is exactly what I am, Bella thought. *His family are going to hate me, I am not good enough, he will realise…*

'Great-Aunt Alice, Miss Shelley is here,' Elliott said reprovingly, with a squeeze of Bella's hand. The panic subsided a little.

'I can see that! Come here, girl.'

Bella dropped her best curtsy and stood in front of Lady Abbotsbury, summoning up all the calm she used in the face of Papa's worst moods. 'Lady Abbotsbury. Thank you for allowing me to stay here.'

'Not much choice! Harum-scarum way of doing things, I must say.' The old lady's cheeks were plump and brushed with rouge, her hair was piled high, augmented with false curls and padding and her gown was of the last century: brocade and panniers and lace. But her eyes were sharp and dark and interested entirely in the present moment as they studied Bella. 'You're very pale, child. What have you got to say for yourself, Miss Shelley?'

'I will do my best to make Lord Hadleigh a good wife, Lady Abbotsbury.'

'Glad to hear it. What do you say to that, eh, Elliott? You've done better than that rakehell brother of yours, bringing home a nicely behaved young lady who thinks as she ought.' The black eyes showed no softening as she pronounced her approval.

'I will do my best to make Arabella a good husband,' he replied, bending to kiss his great-aunt on the cheek. She responded by fetching him a smart blow on the arm with her fan, but Bella guessed she was pleased with the gesture. 'Thank you for looking after her for me. She is pale because she is tired; she has had a trying few days.'

'Hmm.' The knowing eyes studied Bella, but Lady Abbotsbury made no comment. *She knows*, Bella thought. *She knows about the baby.*

She waved them to the sofa. 'What is happening tomorrow? No one ever tells me anything.'

'We will be married in the parish church by licence at three. Daniel Calne will give Arabella away. There will be a dinner afterwards, which I hope you will feel able to attend.'

'Doesn't matter if I feel up to it or not,' the old lady snapped. 'You need it to be seen that I approve. I'll write to all my acquaintances, never you fear. Arabella will be accepted despite this hugger-mugger affair. You'll be making the round of visits to all the family at once, I dare say.'

'I thought not,' Elliott said smoothly. 'Arabella has a lot to learn here and I expect to be much occupied with estate matters.'

'Will you, indeed?' The chuckle was wicked. 'That's one way of describing it! So we can be expecting a happy event in the new year?'

Bella could feel herself turning scarlet. She had heard about the outspoken language of some of Lady Abbotsbury's generation, but she had never encountered it before. Obviously the old harridan had second sight. She made a conscious effort not to lay her hand protectively over her belly.

'So, you've found yourself a good girl who knows how to blush, Elliott. Excellent. Most of these modern misses are too brassy to remember how.'

'As you say, Great-Aunt.' Elliott got to his feet. There was no sign of a blush on *his* cheeks, Bella noted with resentment. 'I will leave you now, Arabella. Daniel Calne and the carriage will be here for you at a quarter to three.'

'Thank you, Elliott.' She remembered to smile affectionately at him.

'Well, take her out on the terrace and kiss her goodnight, Elliott!' Bella regarded her hostess with fascinated alarm. They were true after all, the stories of shockingly lax behaviour in Grandmama's day. 'I don't know what modern young men are coming to. No imagination, no passion. Shoo, the pair of you, do your canoodling, then I can stop being a chaperon and go to my bed.'

'Arabella?' Elliott offered his hand. 'I am reminded that I am shockingly remiss as an eager bridegroom.'

The fascination turned completely to alarm as she strove for something light to say. She could hardly bolt from the room like a scared rabbit. 'No doubt it was the interview with the bishop this morning,' she suggested, getting to her feet and allowing him to guide her towards the doors leading out to the garden.

'Of course, that must have had a sobering effect.' His eyes were amused, even though his expression remained perfectly serious.

So, he has a sense of humour. Perhaps the strains of his brother's death and her arrival had buried it deep, for that was the first sally she had heard him make, although his smiles were warm. It was a relief to find her mild joke had been appreciated. The pleasure of that lasted just long enough to take her out on to the terrace amidst shadowed urns and tubs of clipped evergreens.

She turned, her hand still in his, and found herself close, almost toe to toe with him. In the dim light he looked so very like Rafe that she shivered and took half a step back in alarm.

'Arabella?' The deep voice was Elliott's. This was not Rafe, she told herself, this man was kind and honourable and she must not show any reluctance. Tentatively she lifted her free hand to his lapel. Elliott did not need any further encouragement. He drew her to him, keeping her right hand, still clasped in his, trapped between their bodies as his left hand came round her shoulders. Bella felt the heat of his body down the length of hers and tipped back her head so she could look into his face, so disturbing and familiar in the shadows, yet so subtly different.

'What is it?' she asked, when he made no further move. *What is he going to do?*

'I am learning your face.' Again, that thread of amusement under the serious tone.

'In the dark?' Perhaps he thought her too plain to look at for long in daylight.

'I can see the shape of your face and the gleam of your eyes and the way you tip your head to one side when you are puzzled. I can smell the rosemary you use to rinse your hair.' The hand that was flat against her back slid up and rested lightly at her nape. One finger moved, stroking. It felt as intimate as a touch on her bare breast and, despite herself, her body responded, heating, shivering as the tension coiled low in her belly and the breath caught in her throat.

As she gave a little gasp of shock that she could respond so, he bent his head and took her parted lips, sliding his tongue between them with a directness that had her starting in alarm. The hand at her nape held her still as his mouth explored hers and the intimate invasion was sensual, not forceful. But there was a demand there, behind the gentleness, that reminded her of his insistence on a true marriage.

Bella made herself kiss back, let her own tongue touch his in a tentative exploration that she knew was untutored, gauche. *He will become exasperated in a minute*, she thought. *This cannot be right.* But Elliott did not seem to find it displeasing, for he held her closer, angling his mouth over hers to caress the delicate moistness until she was lost in the feel and the scent and the disturbing heat of him. It seemed, strangely, that he was concerned for her pleasure as well as his.

When he lifted his head and freed her mouth she found her fingers had curled tight on his lapel and she was standing on tiptoe, the better to give him access to her lips. Blushing, Bella released the crushed coat and stepped back. 'I think perhaps…' *How could I have done that, taken pleasure from kissing a man I do not love?* she thought, shaken. Was her father right after all, and this was wantonness? Yet she did not want anything more than Elliott's kiss; everything else terrified her.

'I think perhaps I had stopped thinking,' Elliott said. He sounded somewhere between breathless and amused. 'I had better take you back inside or even my great-aunt's eccentric views on chaperonage may be outraged.' They stepped into the light cast from the room across the flags and he looked down at her. 'I have made you blush again; that will please the old reprobate.'

'Is she? A reprobate, I mean?' Bella snatched at the chance to let her pink cheeks cool a little before going back. She felt disorientated, as though she hardly knew herself.

'Outrageous in her day, I assure you,' Elliott said with a chuckle. 'A string of lovers as long as your arm, if my mama was to be believed. She is the product of a more robust age than ours. And she still has an eye for a well-made footman.'

Bella was smiling as they stepped back into the drawing room. The amusement, and resisting the temptation to stare at the formidable old lady, tided her over the awkwardness of their return and Elliott's respectful kiss on her cheek as he left. Then she was alone with the two women and the knowledge that by this time tomorrow she would be married to a man she scarcely knew who was wedding her only because his rigorous code of honour dictated it.

Chapter Eight

'**Y**ou must eat!' Lady Abbotsbury sat enthroned in a vast brocade chair that had been dragged into Bella's bedchamber. She had been supervising the bride's preparations all morning and Bella suspected she was having the time of her life. She only wished she felt the same.

'I cannot.' Bella stared at the cold meats and fruit that had been laid out on a side table, her stomach revolting. She hoped the old lady did not realise that this was morning sickness as much as nerves and comment as much.

But even without that, her emotions were in such a turmoil that she had hardly slept. And now it was hard to work out which was uppermost in her mind—guilt for placing Elliott in the position where he had to marry her, fear at the thought of the wedding night or the residual confusion over the way his kiss last night had made her feel.

Her response to Rafe had been almost entirely emotional, she could see that now. She had been dazzled,

flattered, swept off her feet by the handsome, sophisticated, wonderful man who was powerful enough to take
her away, whatever her father said to the matter. She had
tumbled headlong into love with Rafe. She had loved
with her heart and not her head and she had given herself
to him because of that, but somehow she had never been
as physically aware of him as she was with Elliott,
when they had lain together.

In Elliott's masterful kiss she had discerned respect
and the desire to please her even as he had demanded
and taken. And he had ignited feelings in her that were
entirely novel. It was alarming and humiliating and left
her in a confusion of guilty sensation. What would he
think of her if he realised how one kiss had made her
feel? He would think her even more abandoned than he
must do now, she decided. Or perhaps he would be
pleased—and then very, very disappointed.

'Have a cup of tea and some bread and butter,' Miss
Dorothy coaxed. 'We must start getting you dressed by
one at the latest and it is twenty to the hour now.'

'Mr Calne will not come until a quarter to three,'
Bella protested. She had bathed—fortunately without
an audience—and then the maid rubbed her all over
with some deliciously lavish cream that smelled of
roses and came, apparently, from Lady Abbotsbury's
private hoard. Then her hair had been washed and
rinsed in rosemary infusion, at which point Elliott's
great-aunt and cousin had arrived to direct the drying
and brushing.

The maid had trimmed her nails and buffed them
with a kidskin polisher, then her gown and undergar-

ments and shoes had been laid out and inspected minutely while she was ordered to rest with her feet up, attired in one of the extravagant négligés she had bought the day before. Lady Abbotsbury expressed complete, and embarrassing, approval of it.

Now Bella could not imagine what else there was to do except get dressed and that would take half an hour at most. She did not relish the thought of sitting around in all her finery for an age with nothing to do but think.

'We barely have time,' the dowager said. 'Eat! There's your hair to dress, that will take almost an hour. No macquillage these days, more's the pity, all you whey-faced modern misses—powder and patch and rouge, that's what you need. Then your corsets—good and tight, that takes time. A man likes a small waist and a good bosom on display.'

Bella picked up a slice of bread and butter and made herself chew. Her real fear was that this alarming old dame would start lecturing her on the marriage bed. She knew she needed some frank advice, but she also knew she would never dare ask, however much some reassurance would help calm her nerves.

By the time Mr Calne arrived a glance in the mirror told Bella that she was white as a sheet. She stood in the drawing room when he was ushered in, too afraid of crumpling her gown to sit.

'Well, now!' Mr Calne stopped on the threshold, eyebrows raised, his hands full of yellow-and-white roses. 'Elliott has caught himself a beauty, and no mistake.'

Bella blinked at him, then risked a second, longer glance at the overmantel mirror. She stared back at herself, eyes huge, lips deep pink against her pale skin. She was, if not a beauty, prettier than she had ever looked.

'Mr Calne, thank you.' She recalled her manners and went forwards to shake his hand, only to have the roses placed in hers. 'You've brought me my bouquet, how kind!'

'Elliott arranged that,' he protested, waving away her thanks. 'I am just doing my duty as the surrogate brother who will give you away. Which reminds me, I have something else from the bridegroom.' He delved in an inner pocket of his elegant tail coat and produced a flat blue morocco-leather case.

'For me?'

'But of course for you. Here, give me those flowers back and open it.' They managed the transfer and Bella stood staring at the case. 'Go on, it won't bite.'

His teasing tone broke her paralysis and she clicked the catch. Inside, on a bed of satin, was a double rope of pearls and a pair of pearl drop earrings. 'Oh, but they are lovely.' *Elliott has given me these?* Her immediate reaction was surprise and delight and then she realised: she was about to marry him, to become a viscountess. She would be required to wear appropriate jewellery at all times. The gift was merely protocol.

'The Hadleigh pearls,' Daniel said, reminding her that he was Elliott's cousin and might be expected to know these things. 'Brought into the family by a seventeenth-century bride.'

'Good.' Lady Abbotsbury approved. 'The rest of the Hadleigh gems are in the bank in London, I expect, unless Rafe pawned the lot of them, which would not surprise me in the slightest. The diamond parure will suit you, but this is more suitable for the occasion.'

But wealth and glitter did not concern her. Diamonds, indeed! She would look ridiculous, the church mouse in the borrowed finery, but she must try to live up to Elliott's expectations. *Society's expectations.* It was her duty. The thought of living up to his expectations in the bedchamber was another matter altogether. You could not learn to satisfy a man in bed by careful study of etiquette, only by practice and intimacy.

'My ears are not pierced,' she realised in dismay, dragging her thoughts back to the present.

'Pink silk,' Miss Dorothy suggested, producing a handful of skeins from her bulging embroidery bag.

Mr Calne insisted on fastening the necklace for her while Miss Dorothy, after carefully matching skin tone to silk, managed to secure the pearl drops.

He offered his arm. 'Now are we ready? I fancy we will be the desirable ten minutes late at the church.'

'Mr Calne—'

'Daniel—we are to be cousins, are we not? And I stand in the place of a brother today.'

His smile was charming, his good spirits infectious. Bella smiled back. Somehow she would make this work. She must, for the child's sake. 'Daniel. And I am Bella. Thank you for helping us today. It means a great deal to me that Elliott's family are not offended by the suddenness of this match.'

'Come then, Bella.' He checked over his shoulder that Miss Dorothy and Lady Abbotsbury were attired in their bonnets, the dowager leaning heavily on the arm of the tallest, and best-looking, footman. 'Off to church we go.'

The church was full of the fragrance of roses and lilies from the estate hothouse. Elliott felt his head swim as he stood at the altar steps, taking deep breaths. Unexpected butterflies were making free with his stomach and he needed to calm them. Just what was he getting himself into? Whatever it was, it was too late now to step back from it.

Beside him stood John Baynton, stolid and reliable as ever, reading through the form of service. He had already checked that the ring, a band of plaited gold that had belonged to Elliott's grandmother, was safe; now he looked up and ran a critical eye over Elliott.

'You are as white as a sheet,' Baynton whispered. 'Very correct behaviour in a bridegroom. I am impressed.'

'I always endeavour to do the correct thing,' Elliott whispered back, making a joke of it. What was there to be nervous about? He was doing what he must for the family honour. And he was marrying a young lady who appeared pleasant, well mannered and dutiful.

True, there was the small matter of the baby on its way, his own brother's child. And the fact that he now had a vastly increased estate to manage—and drag back from neglect. And his new viscountess had never experienced life beyond a Suffolk village. And he suspected that the Earl and Countess of Framlingham were not going to be best pleased to discover that, far from courting their daughter Frederica, he had spent his period in mourning getting married to a nobody.

Ah, well, a challenge is always welcome. Elliott smiled grimly, saw the Reverend Fanshawe's startled expression and modified his own into what he hoped was reverent anticipation. There was the tap of a cane, the small flurry as his great-aunt and cousin took their places. Then the organ struck up. He kept his eyes forward until he heard the rustle of silk and the sound of Daniel Calne's shoes on the stone slabs, then he turned.

Arabella was veiled, of course. There was no clue to her emotions behind the cream lace that fell from the bonnet, although the bouquet of roses trembled slightly. She came to a halt by his side and then glanced round as if confused. Elliott braced himself, almost expecting her to bolt, but Dorothy, more familiar with the details of weddings than he, was already coming forwards to take the flowers.

Mr Fanshawe gave them a moment to collect themselves, then began. 'Dearly beloved...'

'...you may kiss the bride.'

Arabella was holding on to his hand as though she was drowning. He lifted her veil, trying to communicate reassurance, and saw her face. *She is lovely*, he thought with a jolt. Her skin was flushed with delicate pink, her eyes were wide and bright, her lips full, tempting. Where had the drab, miserable little vicarage miss gone? But there was apprehension in those hazel eyes and the full lower lip was not quite steady. No need to alarm her, he thought, dropping a light kiss on her mouth.

* * *

Bella curled her fingers hard into Elliott's grip to steady herself. *The bride. I am now Lady Hadleigh.* His face came into focus as he lifted the veil, pale and serious, those startling eyes almost ink blue as he studied her face. *He is realising that he has committed himself irrevocably*, she thought as he bent to kiss her. Her lips wanted to cling to his for reassurance, but already he was straightening; the firm pressure had lingered for just the right amount of time for the place and occasion.

How competent he is, how assured, how certain of how things must be done. And I am none of those things. But she had been, until Rafe had come into her life and turned it on its head. She had been a dutiful daughter, a competent housewife, an efficient support to the parish. Would any of those talents be of use at all now? It was time to learn to be a viscountess.

Bella lifted her chin and straightened her back as she placed her hand on Elliott's arm. Deportment and dignity were important. She took her bouquet from Miss Dorothy and matched her steps to Elliott's slow stride as he began to walk back down the aisle. Following his example, she looked from side to side, smiling and nodding to the strangers who were watching her. There was an unexpected number of people filling the pews. On her way to the altar she had been too nervous to look.

Many must be the staff, inside and outside, from the Hall and the Dower House. But there was a neat little woman who was perhaps the vicar's wife and a young lady with a little girl on her best behaviour at her side, both of them smiling at someone behind Bella and Elliott—Mrs Baynton, she guessed.

For all the short notice, this was not a hole-in-corner affair, which was a relief. She had worried for Elliott's reputation if there was gossip now. That would come when her pregnancy became obvious, but perhaps by then people would have got over the shock of the sudden marriage, provided she comported herself suitably.

Elliott had arranged matters so that it seemed just what he had said—a hurried marriage because of the bride's unreasonable father. *I must write to Papa*, she realised, then pushed away the unpleasant thought until tomorrow at least. There was too much else to deal with today.

They emerged into a sunny May afternoon, the guests flocking out behind them, to find the churchyard full of curious and smiling villagers. 'I am glad this is a country wedding,' she whispered to Elliott and he smiled down at her.

Something tugged at her skirt and she looked down to find a small boy holding out a fistful of wild flowers. He was solemn, chubby and with a front tooth missing. 'Just one moment,' she said to him and tossed her own bouquet up in the air.

There was a laughing scramble as girls ran for it and she stooped again to the child. 'Those are very pretty. Thank you so much.' He thrust them into her hand, solemn with nerves. Bella looked at them, an unkempt tangle plucked from the hedgerow instead of the elegant and sophisticated bouquet. *Just like me*, she thought. 'And what is your name?'

'Charlie Mullin, mum.'

'Where do you live, Charlie? May I come and visit you one day?'

'Pa's the baker, mum.'

'Then I expect he makes excellent bread, I must buy some.' She straightened up laughing, and he ran off to grab the skirts of a plump woman who was pink with embarrassment at her son's bravado.

'That was well done,' Elliott said as they began to walk again.

'I must get to know the villagers as well as your tenants,' Bella said, waving to a group of little girls. 'I have a responsibility to them now and I am used to this kind of work from my parish duties. I expect Mrs Fanshawe will be able to advise me who is in need.'

'It will come as a shock to them if someone from the Hall calls,' Elliott said, his voice dry. 'I doubt they have had any attention from Rafe.'

Rafe would not have understood the need to be sure if frail elderly villagers had warm bedding and someone to cook for them or whether the village children learned their letters and he had probably not cared in any case. Elliott *would* care, but these things were not something the lord of an estate was expected to deal with. This was something she, the viscountess, could do, she realised. 'Well, I will call,' she said. 'And I will tell you what needs doing and we can discuss it.'

The look he gave her held amusement and a degree of surprise at her decisive tone. 'And I expect you will be asking me for money for your good works?'

'Naturally,' Bella said, delighted to find something she was equipped for.

Whereas for this, now, she was not. Elliott was turning to speak to the stocky man who had stood by him on the altar steps. 'Arabella, may I introduce John Baynton, my groomsman and a very old friend, and Mrs Baynton. And this is Miss Baynton.'

'Prunella,' the little girl said, producing a curtsy. 'I am five.'

The first of Elliott's friends. Daniel did not count, he was family. 'Good afternoon, Prunella,' Bella said. It gave her time to compose herself, to manage the sort of amiable yet dignified smile that she supposed a viscountess should favour. 'Good afternoon, Mrs Baynton, Mr Baynton. Thank you for coming. I am glad Lord Hadleigh had friends at his side today.'

Mrs Baynton did not seem too concerned about composure and dignity as she shook hands. 'And I am delighted to meet you, Lady Hadleigh, and to discover that Elliott has such a romantic streak in him! I will call in a week or so, once your honeymoon is over: I am sure we will be firm friends.'

Honeymoon? Of course, with a runaway bride and a precipitous marriage, the presumption must be that this was a passionate love match and that she and Elliott would be spending their days and nights in intimate seclusion. It was the last thing she wanted, whereas becoming close to this friendly young woman with her warm brown eyes was exactly what she needed.

It seemed Elliott thought so too. 'Honeymoon? I only wish we could, but under the circumstances, with so much business following Rafe's death, I am afraid I will be sadly neglecting Arabella.'

'Yes, do call soon,' she urged as the Bayntons gave way for the vicar to introduce his wife.

'Are they coming to dinner?' she asked as Elliott turned finally to the waiting carriage.

'Yes. The Bayntons, the Fanshawes, Daniel, my great-aunt, Dorothy.' He waited until they set off and the noise of the wheels masked their voices from the footmen up behind, then bent and murmured, 'And I believe Anne Baynton is increasing again, which is convenient, should you two become friends.'

'Oh, yes.' It would be a huge relief to have a female friend who had already carried a child to talk to. But she would have to deduce what to tell Mrs Baynton, who would surely work out that her new friend had not conceived on her wedding night but was already three months gone. If she confided that a baby was on its way, then Anne Baynton would conclude that Elliott was the father, and that they had had a liaison. Could she let the wife of one of his friends think he had behaved in such a way?

'May I tell her?' she whispered. 'She will guess, I am sure. Bu—'

'But not the full truth?' he murmured back. 'Yes, let her think I am impulsively passionate. It will amuse John.'

'I do not want anyone amused at your expense!' she retorted in an agitated whisper, surprising herself at how defensive she felt on his behalf.

'What man would object to being thought capable of seducing such a virtuous beauty?'

That was hardly reassuring. Bella slanted a wary look at his face and then faced forwards hastily. He was smiling, but there was a gleam in his eyes that sent a warning shiver down her spine. She had seen that expression on Rafe's face. Elliott was thinking about seduction in rather more than the abstract.

And she was not a beauty, or virtuous, so he was being sarcastic, she supposed, which was disappointing—she had thought him kinder than that. She tried to ignore the hurtful sting of his words and focus on the good news—she would have a female friend who could support her through this pregnancy.

They drove the short distance to Hadleigh Old Hall in silence. By the time they arrived Bella had a composed smile on her face and two firm resolutions— not to expect anything from Elliott and to think only of the here and now.

Elliott helped her down. 'Well, Lady Hadleigh?'

'Very well, my lord.' Her dignified composure was shattered as Elliott swung her up in his arms. 'Elliott!' The other carriages were drawing up around them. There was a burst of applause and a cheer as she buried her face in his shoulder and was carried through the front door.

Chapter Nine

The hall was full of staff, laughing and smiling. For one appalled moment Bella thought Elliott was not going to stop and she would be swept up the stairs and into his bedchamber. Her heart thudded with fear and excitement, then he set her on her feet, his long fingers laced into hers.

'Three cheers for our new ladyship.' Henlow stepped forwards. 'Hip, hip, hoorah!' The staff needed no urging from the butler and the hall rang with their enthusiasm.

Bella felt her eyes beginning to swim with emotion—they genuinely sounded happy that she was there. Everyone was being so kind to her. She untied the wide satin ribbons on her bonnet and one of the maids came forwards to take it and her gloves.

'Bella! I insist on being the first to kiss the bride in her new home.' Daniel took her by the shoulders and dropped a smacking kiss on her lips. 'You're a lucky fellow, Elliott.'

'I am indeed,' Elliott turned, bringing Bella with him,

and walked towards the dining room. *'Bella?'* he enquired, low-voiced.

'I thought…as he is your cousin, family, that it was unexceptional. He asked me to call him Daniel. Was I wrong?' Had she erred already, committed some breach of etiquette?

'Why does he not call you Arabella?' The guests were behind them, but not crowding too close. There were a few steps still to the table.

'Bella is my pet name. Rafe…I mean, everyone uses it. My family…' she started to explain.

'I see. One you do not expect me to use.' Elliott brought her to the foot of the table where a footman was holding her chair. 'Your place, *Arabella*, my dear.'

'Thank you.' Somehow she kept the smile on her lips as Elliott went to the head of the board and their guests found their places. She must never have told him that to everyone who mattered to her she was simply *Bella*. And now he was hurt that she had given his brother and his cousin the right to use her pet name, but not him, her husband.

Part of her, the part that was still smarting from his sarcasm in the carriage, was glad. But that was petty; she must make this marriage work as well as possible.

John Baynton took the seat on her right hand, the rector on her left. Elliott was flanked by Lady Abbotsbury and Anne Baynton. In the middle of the table Daniel was already teasing Dorothy about something while Mrs Fanshawe shook her head indulgently at him.

Bella swallowed. She had never been to a formal dinner party before. She knew that as a guest she should make conversation to her right for the first course, then to her left. But now she was the hostess with a duty to promote conversation generally.

'Are you both from this part of the world?' she asked. 'It is very beautiful. So many fruit trees,' she added a little wildly, recalling yesterday's drive.

'Yes, I was born not six miles away,' John Baynton began when the sound of a knife blade against crystal had them all looking towards Elliott.

He was on his feet, a champagne flute in his hand as the footmen finished filling the glasses down the length of the table. 'Great-Aunt, Cousins, friends. I give you Arabella, Viscountess Hadleigh.'

The men rose and everyone lifted their glasses. 'Arabella!'

She sat, blushing and charmed, while the diners settled themselves again. Elliott was watching her, his eyes steady on her face. And then he lifted his glass again. She saw his lips move. *Arabella*. And then they curved into a smile that reached his eyes and made her feel hot, flustered, special, and she felt, all at once, that she could manage a dinner party for the king himself.

It was half past nine. Elliott shook hands with the departing guests and decided that timing such a departure was a delicate matter—if guests rushed off too early then it pointed up the fact that this was the wedding night. If they lingered too long the unfortunate bridegroom would be champing at the bit.

He glanced across at Arabella, who was smiling at Anne Baynton. She had done well, he decided. With experience would come confidence, but she had natural grace and a real interest in her guests that could not be counterfeited.

But now she was tired. Her skin was pale under the slight flush that heat and excitement had brought to her cheeks and she was resting one hand on a chair back for extra support. For a while he had forgotten her condition, forgotten that this was a match neither of them had wanted.

'Goodnight, John.' He gripped Baynton's hand. 'Thank you for standing with me today.'

'My pleasure. She is charming, your Arabella.'

'Yes, I believe so,' he agreed thoughtfully. His friend shot him a look of surprise at his measured tone. 'I had no idea how easily she would take to company,' he added to excuse his unlover-like lack of ardour.

Then, at last they were alone. 'That went very well, I thought.' Strange to have to make conversation on one's wedding night, if he had thought of such a thing before then he had imagined his bride falling into his arms the moment the guests had gone and... He was being as romantic as a girl, Elliott thought, smiling at himself.

Arabella sat down on the nearest couch, but she kept her back straight, her head up. 'I am glad you think so. I like the Bayntons very much. Mrs Baynton *is* increasing, you were correct. That is such a relief.'

Elliott wondered if he should sleep alone tonight and let her rest. But there was a point to be made, and one night apart might well slip into two and then three and there would always be an excuse not to take that step and make her his in body as well as in law.

'Elliott,' Arabella said, her hesitant tone pulling him

out of his thoughts. 'I am sorry I did not think to ask you to call me Bella.'

'I prefer Arabella.' It was a pretty, gracious name that reflected her inner dignity.

'Yes,' she agreed, getting to her feet. 'I can quite see it is more suitable for a viscountess.'

It was not what he had meant, but he did not labour the point; she did not appear to be in the mood. 'Would you like to go up? I will linger over my brandy for half an hour before I join you.'

She looked at him, her hazel eyes widening. 'Yes, of course, but I do not know where my room is yet.'

Next to mine. Anticipation ran through him and he saw her recognition of it reflected in those big eyes. The tip of her tongue emerged, touched the curve of her upper lip. It was nerves, but it was also an innocent provocation that had his groin tightening in almost painful response.

'No, of course, you have not seen around upstairs yet.' He opened the door. 'Henlow, please show her ladyship to the viscountess's suite and ring for her maid.'

Arabella's lips parted in surprise. She was going to be even more surprised when she saw the suite in question, Elliott thought as he closed the door behind her and went to the sideboard to pour a glass of cognac. He had scoured the rooms himself, removing such souvenirs of Rafe's female guests as stockings, garters, a collection of illustrated books that he had pitched on to the fire after a quick glance, several lengths of silken cord and a set of black satin bedclothes. Even so, there was no hiding the fact that the rooms had been decorated

with a very different woman in mind than a decorous
wife and viscountess.

There had not been time to do anything about the mirror
set into the underside of his own bed canopy. It would definitely be better to go to her bedchamber, although the
thought of that sweetly curved body reflected in the glass
as she lay on the dark green silk coverlet was powerfully
arousing. But that was for the future.

Elliott knew it would be no hardship to make love to
his new wife once he had her confidence. In the garden
she had responded with an innocent ardour that had
seemed to surprise her as much as it had him.

The clock struck the hour. The brandy glass in his
hand was still full. Elliott set it down, stood up and
looked at his own reflection in the mirror. The face that
stared back was harder than Rafe's, less charming. But
he was not going to put on a false face for Arabella—
this was not a one-night *affaire*, this was for life. From
today they had to learn to live with each other.

He went out to the hall. 'Thank you, Henlow, that
will be all for tonight.'

Should she get into the bed? Arabella regarded it
warily, wondering what Elliott would expect. It was
large and tented in pale pink silk from a corona fixed to
the ceiling. Not a colour she would have chosen herself.
Nor would she have lavished all these frills around the
room, nor had quite so many mirrors. The paintings and
ornaments appeared to be very…sensuous and made her
uncomfortable without quite knowing why. The sitting
room next door was *soft*. That was the only word for a

room with so much fabric and so many cushions. No bookshelves, no writing table, no sewing basket in sight. And as for the dressing room, it was positively sybaritic.

There was the marble tub big enough for two with a cistern that could be filled with hot water that showered down at the pull of a chain. There were gilded swan-necked taps. There were heaps of soft pink towels and a *chaise longue* and more mirrors and endless wardrobes and drawers where her new clothes looked lonely in all the space.

Instinct told her that the entire suite had been created with pleasure in mind. Rafe had used this for his lovers, not a wife, and it made her uncomfortable to think of what had happened in these rooms, where every step was muffled in sensual luxury.

She came back to the bed, distracting herself by observing how its shell-pink drapes contrasted unpleasantly with the green of her négligé. Elliott had said she might change what she pleased; well, she would start with this suite.

On the other hand he might like it as much as Rafe had done. What had he said about the lingerie she had thanked him for—that it was as much for his pleasure as hers? Just how much like his brother was he? Probably all men were alike when it came to the sexual act. And if that was the case then he would feel all those things that Rafe had told her he felt. Only Elliott would not be so cruel as to berate her with her clumsiness and ignorance, her plainness and lack of sophistication. He would be too well mannered to refer to the fact that she was pregnant. He would just think all those things.

She sighed, leaning her forehead against one of the elegant bedposts that reached almost to the ceiling. There was so much to worry about, so much to learn.

'Arabella?' She turned and found Elliott standing just inside a jib door that she had not noticed before, its fabric covering matching the wall it was set into. It must open on to his own rooms. He was wearing a long blue robe, the shirt under it open at the neck to give a glimpse of dark hair. A jolt of desire lanced through her and she grabbed the bedpost behind her with both hands, shocked by the intensity and unexpectedness of the reaction.

'Are the rooms to your liking?' He came right in, closing the door behind him with a click that made her jump.

'Yes, delightful.' His eyebrows rose and a hint of that wicked smile touched the corner of his mouth. 'They are very luxurious. Very…pink,' she said, not adding that she imagined this was what a bordello looked like.

'Certainly pink,' he agreed. 'It is not your colour. Change what you wish.'

It seemed so wasteful to change a suite of rooms simply because pale pink made her look washed-out—as of course he had just noticed. But, Bella reminded herself, this is the setting for his lordship's pleasure, intended to display the woman who lived in this padded casket of luxury. She must look her best here. Perhaps she could make the sitting room more comfortable, more of a retreat of her own.

'Thank you.' Her hands tightened on the bedpost as he came closer, his soft morocco slippers soundless on the deep pile of the carpet. It was all silent, like a dream, except for her heart thudding so hard that she thought he must hear it and the rush of blood that buzzed in her ears.

Elliott stopped, close enough for her to see that he had shaved, close enough to pick up a subtle woody tang of cologne. 'You look like a maiden tied to a stake waiting to be rescued from the dragon,' he remarked. 'An amusing game, perhaps, but not, I think, for tonight.' His eyes were heavy-lidded, dark with anticipation, and she shivered, caught between fear and something else she did not quite understand. Elliott raised an eyebrow. 'And perhaps I am the dragon?'

'No. No, not at all.' She released her grip on the post and then did not know what to do with her hands. Elliott solved her dilemma by catching them in his and drawing her close. She thought he was going to kiss her lips, but his mouth found the angle of neck and shoulder instead, nuzzling under the soft frills of veiling gauze, his breath hot and his tongue hotter, until her whole body seemed to glow, just from that one contact.

Elliott. She thought she had spoken, but no sound escaped her parted lips except a whimper that became a sob. He released her hands and her arms went around his neck, to keep herself on her feet or hold him to her, she was not certain which.

'It is all right,' he said softly, and she realised she had him in a stranglehold. 'It is all right, Arabella. There is nothing to be afraid of, we are just going to bed together.' He might have been murmuring reassurance to a nervous filly, his hands gentling over her. He set her back against the post and untied the ribbons of her négligé, pushing it over her shoulders, then he stepped aside to where the covers had already been turned down and pulled them back further.

'Is this side all right for you?'

The prosaic question was so unexpected, so far from her lurid imaginings of what was going to happen next that she gaped at him. 'Oh. Yes, I don't mind, really.' The bed was huge compared to what she was used to; she would be adrift in it wherever she slept. Elliott was waiting patiently so she let the négligé drop and climbed into bed. He flipped the covers over her legs and went round to the other side, discarding his robe as he went.

Bella looked fixedly at the opposite side of the room, but out of the corner of her eye she could still see him. And he was wearing a nightshirt, thank goodness. She did not think she could cope with him naked, not yet.

The bed dipped, there was the tug of bedclothes being adjusted, then he remarked, 'You could lie down, you know.'

Could she? Bella felt as though she was made out of wood. If her back went down, her legs would shoot into the air, like a peg doll whose joints had seized up. She tried, legs tight together, and stared up at the underside of the canopy.

Elliott moved closer, leaned over her, one hand on the pillow beside her head. 'Just kisses for the moment, Arabella,' he murmured and leaned in. 'You know you like kisses. Only kisses until you are ready.'

It was gentle, like last night and, like that kiss on the terrace, she did not mistake the gentleness for a lack of confidence, or experience. He knew what he was doing, he knew what he wanted and how to take it but, mysteriously, he seemed interested in *her* too, not just her breasts or that part between her legs.

Elliott stroked softly into her mouth with his tongue, teasing and tasting; he nibbled along her lips, sucked her top lip into his mouth, bit it gently and released it, only to do the same to her lower lip.

It was as if he found the taste and the texture of her pleasurable—which was very strange. Surely the entire point of what they were doing was for him to penetrate her, which would give him his release?

Every now and again he paused, as if he was waiting for something. Surely not for her to reciprocate? Did he want her to nibble and suck? To slide her tongue into his mouth too? She had done it last night, she remembered, embarrassed. Just the very tip. His mouth had been hot and moist and his tongue almost indecent in the muscular way it had moved against her lips. As if it were another part of him altogether.

She was feeling very strange now. Warm and restless and aching. And she did want to kiss him back, to taste and feel the textures of his skin. As her tongue slid into his mouth he shifted his position with a grunt that sounded like satisfaction, moving down the bed to hold her more closely, the hand that had propped him up coming round to cup her cheek and hold her steady.

Emboldened, Bella pulled back a little, then kissed the corner of Elliott's mouth. She felt him smile, so she ran her tongue along the join of his lips and kissed the other corner. Definitely a smile now. It was very strange, almost as though he found this *fun*, as though he wanted to play.

He tipped her head and his mouth found her ear, his tongue tracing the whorls, his breath hot. Bella shivered. It should tickle. It was her *ear*, for goodness' sake. But her breasts were aching and she wanted to rub against him and molten heat was gathering, low in her belly.

Then his lips closed over her ear lobe and he began to suckle it. Bella gasped. It was utterly…indecent. But it was only her ear lobe. He might as well be sucking her elbow! Yet it seemed to swell in his mouth, the insistent tug stimulating the morsel of flesh almost to the point of a discomfort that was perversely pleasant. Now her breasts really were too tight. She moved, restless, and felt her nipples, as hard as if she had splashed them with ice water, fretting against her nightgown.

He tugged and the nightgown came off. Somehow his nightshirt had gone already.

Elliott growled deep in his throat and shifted closer and then she felt it, the hard brutal length against her hip. He had promised only kisses, but then, for men, it was impossible to stop once they started, she understood that. So, it was going to happen now. She tried not to stiffen, to move away from him, but she could not help her body tightening as he moved his weight over her.

'Arabella?' She made herself look at him. His eyes were deep, fathomless blue in the candlelight, his lips slightly parted. He was controlling his breathing, she realised. His hand moved over her belly and she felt the chill of the familiar ring, the ring that had been on Rafe's hand. His fingers probed between her legs where she knew she was shamefully hot and moist.

'Oh, yes, you are ready.' He seemed pleased. But

Rafe had seemed pleased until… He entered her, firmly and strongly, and her entire body seemed to tighten with the fear. *Too tight, too big. It hurts…I must move. I am supposed to move and to hold him and…* But all she could do was lie there like the wooden doll she had imagined earlier. Lie there under him while the big, hard body surrounded her, crushed her, filled her. Used her.

Don't think like that. It is your duty, his right. Bella opened her eyes on to Elliott's intense blue gaze. He was rapt, lost in sensation, but somewhere, deep, she knew that all was not well, that something was missing.

'Arabella—' Then he closed his eyes, his face tensed and he gave a stifled shout as his body convulsed into hers until she thought he would break her apart. After a moment he went limp, his body crushing down on hers. There was heat and the slide of sweaty skin and the roughness of the hair on his chest and legs.

Between her own legs a strange pulse quivered and ached, unsatisfied as her body began to protest at the treatment.

'Arabella?' He was looking at her, hair in his eyes, his expression bleak and unguarded. 'That was not good, was it?'

'I'm sorry,' Bella began, with no more words assembled in her brain to continue.

'There is nothing to be sorry for,' Elliott said. But a dry undertone to his voice contradicted his words. She had been right, he was too kind to tell her how disappointed he was in her. He rolled off and tugged until she came against his side, her cheek on his shoulder. 'Go to sleep now.'

'But—'

'We have consummated the marriage, Arabella. That is enough to be going on with.'

Bella looked up so she could see his face. 'Was…was that how it is supposed to be?'

'Do you think so?' He lay watching her, expressionless, not giving her any help at all.

Of course it was not. How disappointed he must be to have been forced into marriage with her. Her shake of the head was so vehement that he laughed. 'There you are, then. We can work on it. Come back here and sleep, Arabella.'

I amuse him? Is that better than scorn and insults and violence? It has to be. She lay down, her cheek against man-warmed linen and closed her eyes. Perhaps if he would do it again in the morning, before she was properly awake, that would be better. She would be relaxed, it would be over before she had time to be afraid and for it to hurt and he might find it more enjoyable.

Chapter Ten

~~~❦~~~

Elliott woke in the early morning light, every muscle tense with arousal. It took a moment to realise where he was and who was lying, relaxed in slumber, against him. His wife. Arabella was about the only relaxed thing in the bed, he thought grimly. She was just where she had fallen asleep last night, her cheek pressed to his shoulder. In the night she must have moved her arm for it now lay across his body, her hand lightly clasping the erect length that ached for her to tighten the lax grip.

Last night had been…frustrating. He had thought her ready for him, willing, but something had gone wrong. Was she associating lovemaking with Rafe's betrayal afterwards? Or had he simply misread her, failed to see that nerves were overcoming her sensual responses? The temptation was to simply roll over, rip off his nightshirt and take her again before she had the chance to wake up and remember her nerves. *No.* Elliott tried breathing lightly, controlling the need to move under her palm. No, she had to know what she was doing, be fully involved with it. With him.

It had taken him a long time to get to sleep last night, puzzling over Arabella's responses to his lovemaking. She reacted as he would expect a virgin to react, not like a woman who had had an *affaire* with an experienced rake. Perhaps it was the pregnancy. But he was hardly on such terms with any mothers that he could ask them how child-bearing had affected their love lives.

Elliott inched out from under her arm. As he slid out of the bed he saw her face clearly, the track of one dried tear down her cheek. His wife had wept on her wedding night. He had no idea how to comfort her or what to say. *You are safe now? I am not like my brother, even if you probably see him every time you look at me? I won't abandon you and your baby?* 'I promise I will look after you,' he murmured. But she knew that by now, surely? It seemed she needed something he did not know how to give her.

Elliott closed the door into his dressing room with care, walked through into his own bedchamber and closed that door too. Only, it was not his bedchamber, it was Rafe's, just as that was not his woman in the pink boudoir that had been decorated for a whore. She was Rafe's cast-off mistress and, somehow, they had to forget that.

He was not used to sleeping in a nightshirt. Elliott dragged it over his head, hurled the balled-up linen at a wing chair, missed, swore and threw himself on the bed. From the mirror above his reflection, naked, still half-erect, glared back at him.

He looked like a working man compared with his elegant, sleek brother. Rafe would not have dreamed of joining his farm hands in the fields to help in the last push to bring the crops before rain fell. He would not have sat up with the shepherds in the lambing fields in the small hours or found pleasure heaving roof timbers with the carpenters when there was a building to repair.

Rafe would not have enjoyed getting sweaty and battered in the boxing ring, then laughing in some comfortable inn afterwards with the friends who had just been trying to land him a facer. He would certainly not have relished a long hard road race in all weathers, pitting skill and the horseflesh he had chosen and trained against the best the Corinthian set could muster.

Rafe had been going soft, Elliott had thought when their paths had crossed in London. Those meetings had always been in gambling hells or society ballrooms, never in the fencing schools or the boxing salons where Elliott drove himself hard for the strength and stamina he prized.

He got off the bed, shrugged into his robe and yanked the bell pull for coffee. He had never felt himself in competition with his brother and he was not going to start now in the bedchamber. What he was fighting here was nothing as rational as physical appearance or intelligence or charm, but a broken heart and betrayed dreams.

She had shed one tear. He did not want Arabella to cry, he wanted her to smile for him, blush a little. He wanted her to laugh and sigh and moan in his arms. *Damn this.* He had thought to be rational and clear in his requirements as though he was appointing a new member of staff, not forging a relationship with a wife. He had spelled out what he expected from her in the bedroom and she had forced herself to do her *duty*, he was sure of that. And he was in here with a severe case of frustration because he did not want to distress her this morning and she was fast asleep in there.

What was the matter with him? He could surely feel compassion for the poor girl without getting himself this wound up about her feelings. He was over-analysing, Elliott decided after another length of the room. She had allowed Rafe to seduce her, she was old enough and intelligent enough to know what she was doing. She had got herself into a mess, he had rescued her from it and now they were stuck with each other. He was not used to women finding anything but satisfaction in his arms, that was the trouble, he thought with a rueful smile.

'One day at a time,' he said aloud. 'One night at a time.'

'My lord?' Franklin, his valet, was standing in the dressing-room door looking a trifle bemused.

'Coffee, Franklin. And then my riding clothes. I want to look at the Hundred Acre Wood first thing.'

'At what time does his lordship normally take breakfast?'

'Lord love us! Begging your pardon, your ladyship, but you did give me a start.' Cook put down the basket of eggs she was holding. 'At eight, normally, my lady. He comes back in then.'

Arabella walked into the kitchen and surveyed the preparations. 'Back in? I am sorry, please can you remind me of your name?'

'Mrs Tarrant, my lady. And that's Bethan with the coffee grinder and Annie in the scullery.'

My lady. Goodness. I'm my lady *now.* 'Good morning, everyone.' There was a flurry of bobbed curtsies.

'His lordship goes out to the estate every morning at six, my lady. He sends down for a cup of coffee, then he's out until eight. Not like his late lordship—he would take his breakfast in bed at about ten.' Her pursed lips looked incongruous in her cheerful face.

'And what does his lordship take for breakfast?' Arabella was determined to be a perfect, attentive wife in every possible way. She might be a disappointment to Elliott in bed, but everything else would be faultless.

She had slept last night, worn out by emotion, she supposed. But she had dreamed of Rafe again. At least, she thought it was Rafe, and she had wanted to run away, but every now and again the man in her dream had turned with a sharp, alert grace that was different from Rafe's languid elegance. His face had been blurred, as though she could not quite recall the difference between the two brothers. And her body had ached and tingled with the disturbing aftermath of Elliott's possession of her body.

Rafe had been right: she was hopeless in bed. Elliott had been kind, but he had been disappointed in her. He thought her plain, no doubt, and soon she would be very obviously pregnant, and none of that helped the fact that she had no idea how to respond to him, how to arouse him. How to satisfy him. Her husband had done nothing to deserve such a…*useless* wife.

Elliott had been gone when she woke and the hollow in the bed was cool when she touched it. No morning kisses, no attempt to make love again. Would his patience snap and would she hear the same jibes, the same reproaches from him as she had from Rafe? *Useless, wooden, plain, frigid...* It was agony to imagine that she would hear words like that from him, see in his eyes that he despised her for being a failure as a woman.

As she had dressed, trying to get used to the hovering presence of Gwen, her new maid, sent up from the Dower House with Lady Abbotsford's compliments, Bella had resolved that at least she could be the perfect mistress of the house. She would not fail at that, and she would not mope; Elliott would not want a miserable wife.

It was easier decided upon than carried out. Arabella made herself focus. The preparations in the kitchen seemed somewhat meagre for a gentleman's breakfast, she thought.

'Toast and coffee, my lady. I did ask when he first came here, but he said that was all he'd take.' Cook folded her reddened hands on her apron front. 'I can't pretend I was not disappointed, my lady. I like to put on a good spread, and one thing I will say about his late lordship, he knew how to entertain.' Again that enigmatic tightening of the lips.

Bella was not going to think about Rafe. The practicalities of feeding her husband were much more important. 'And where does he eat his toast?' If Elliott retreated into his study it was going to be a problem.

'In the breakfast room, my lady.' Cook seemed not to find it odd that she did not know her new husband's tastes, or that he had gone out early as usual the morning after the wedding. Arabella suspected that Mrs Tarrant was a perfectly capable cook if she was given firm orders, but she lacked initiative or curiosity.

'Very well. Today please serve toast and coffee as usual. I will take tea. But I think we should have something more as well, just in case his lordship has an appetite. Shall we have a look in the larder?'

'Heel!' The pair of pointers stopped dead in the middle of the hall and looked back guiltily. Toby, the terrier, who always treated orders as suggestions to be considered and then disregarded, trotted on and sat in front of the breakfast-room door, head on one side, stubby tail rasping on the flags.

Elliott dropped his hat, whip and gloves on the hall chest and sniffed. *Bacon?* 'Henlow!'

'My lord?'

'I can smell bacon.'

'Yes, my lord. Her ladyship is in the breakfast parlour.'

Avoiding Arabella was out of the question, it would be discourteous. But bacon? Surely not the choice of a woman suffering from morning sickness who might be expected to take a light breakfast in bed.

Elliott pushed open the door and went in, the dogs at his heels. Arabella was standing by the sideboard, the silver dome of a serving platter in her hand. A heap of bacon, crisp and tempting, was piled on one side opposite a small mountain of scrambled eggs.

'Good morning, Elliott.'

'Good morning.' A footman appeared through the serving door, placed his coffee pot on the table next to a tea pot. The dogs, impatient, pushed past Elliott's legs and went to lay on the hearth rug as usual.

'Dogs, out!'

'Do they usually come to breakfast? I do not mind them.' She was smiling and immaculate in a cream-muslin morning gown, her hair twisted up into a simple knot. 'Those two are very handsome.' She clicked her fingers at the pointers and they turned their long intelligent heads towards her.

This was the woman he had left tear-stained in her nest of pink satin frills and now here she was, cool and outwardly composed. Elliott fought back a strong sense of unreality. He had expected shyness and reserve. Yes, the reserve was there behind the smile. 'If you are sure? Lie down.' The pair obeyed, still watching Arabella. *The woman with the bacon*, Elliott thought. *Cupboard love.* 'I did not expect to see you for breakfast.'

'No?' She put down the cover and picked up a plate. 'Some bacon and eggs? There is sausage as well.'

And preserves and fruit on the table, and a double rack of toast and a platter of butter. 'I do not normally eat much for breakfast, I do not have the time.' Toast was easy to eat with all his attention on the papers and his post. They lay neatly folded and stacked beside his place, as always, but next to them was a small vase with a posy of flowers. *Flowers?*

'Will you not join me, just this once?' She was already filling a plate, carrying it across.

'You do not have to wait on me,' he said as she placed the plate on the table before him. He sat. To do anything else would be impolite. Just this once, though.

'But you must not waste time.' Arabella's voice was earnest as she went back to the sideboard and filled her own plate. She came and sat at right angles to him, as he had placed her at dinner the night she had come to the house, and reached to pour his coffee. 'Do you take cream? Sugar?'

'Neither, thank you.' Elliott had a strong sense of being outflanked and out-manoeuvred, but the scent of the bacon was making his mouth water and the room seemed somehow warmer and more welcoming than usual.

'Oh! Another dog.' Arabella was looking down beside her. 'What a very *interesting*-looking animal.'

'That is Toby. Doubtless he is begging. Ignore him.'

'I would not dream of feeding your dogs titbits. No, Toby. Good dog, go and lie down.' She waited a moment. 'Of course, he will not obey me.'

'Nor me,' Elliott admitted. 'He adopted me when he was a puppy, but he has not grasped the concept that I am the master. You can try reasoning with him, that sometimes works. Provided you understand that this is *his* house now and we are here for *his* convenience, he will be happy.'

'Ah.' She smiled and he found himself smiling back. 'A dog who thinks he is a cat.'

'Arabella.'

She caught the change in his tone and put down her knife and fork. 'Yes, Elliott.' All the laughter had gone out of her eyes, and colour touched her cheekbones, but her expression remained pleasant and attentive.

'About...' He had been going to talk about last night, but he realised he had no idea what to say or even what he wanted to convey. He had made her his wife, that ought to be enough. He could hardly ask her over breakfast why she had so obviously found the entire experience so unsatisfactory.

The candid hazel eyes gazed back, as she waited for him to speak. He wished, suddenly, that she was not so obedient and compliant. It would be easier to deal with temper and a tantrum. He saw the colour ebb and flow under her pale skin.

He said the first innocuous thing that came into his head. 'How do you intend to spend the morning?'

'I want to explore the house. I will ask Mrs Knight to show me around. Then I will discuss the week's menus with Cook. I have a letter to write,' she added, the animation ebbing away to leave her voice colourless.

'Your father?'

'Yes. I really cannot delay it any longer.'

'I have already written, setting out the provision I am making for you,' he said. 'Even though you are of age, I felt I should put his mind at rest. You could enclose your letter in mine.'

'You have not told him—'

'That he is to be a grandfather? No. I have also been rather vague on how we met. If he makes enquiries he will find that Viscount Hadleigh was staying in the neighbourhood in February and he can draw his own conclusions.'

'Thank you.' Arabella returned to taking small forkfuls of food. 'I will write this afternoon.'

'You are feeling more like eating today?' The bacon was delicious. Elliott cleared his plate and got up to explore the other dishes. Fat sausages, mushrooms—he dug in.

'A little. I know I must make the effort to eat properly.'

'Would you like me to show you around the house?' It had not been his intention, but he had a sudden interest in how Arabella would deal with this rambling mansion. It must seem daunting after a country vicarage.

'You will be busy,' she demurred. But he saw her eyes. It would please her if he did this. 'Cook said that you did not normally eat much breakfast because you have so much to do and I have already delayed you.'

'You are more important.' Elliott found he meant it.

'Where are we going?' The stairs seemed endless. Elliott had ignored the ground-floor reception rooms, the main bedroom floor, and just kept climbing as the shallow treads of the old staircase got narrower and narrower.

Bella glanced to either side as they passed landings and glimpsed more steps, doors, changes in floor level. The house rambled, she realized; it would take time to learn it.

'Do you want to rest?' Elliott paused at last. There were no more steps, only a dusty landing with corridors to either side. Toby, who had been trotting behind them all the way up, took off down one, nose to the floor, stumpy tail wagging.

'No, the exercise is good.' It was invigorating to stretch her legs again. She worried fleetingly if it was all right for the baby, then decided it must be better than sitting around.

'Just one more flight, then.' Elliott opened a door to reveal steep stairs. 'I'll go first.'

Bella followed, telling herself that it was only natural to admire the long legs climbing in front of her. Elliott had muscles she did not recall Rafe possessing, but then, she had spent most of her time with him looking into his eyes, not staring immodestly at his nether limbs.

'Do you mind heights?' Elliott called back as he reached up and threw back a trap door. Light flooded down the stairs.

'No, not at all. I always enjoyed raising the flag on the church tower.'

He climbed out and stretched down his hands to help her out through the low door into the sunshine. Bella found herself, still handfast with Elliott, on the flat leads between the slope of the stone-tiled roof and the edge of the waist-high parapet.

'How lovely!' The view stretched for miles across the Vale of Evesham, off into the distance to the misty bulk of hills that must almost be in the Welsh Marches.

Elliott moved to be between her and the edge. 'Keep hold of me.'

It seemed very right to do so, somehow. He was strong and solid and steady, Bella thought, freeing one hand, but leaving the other one in his warm grip. He would make a reliable father, she was certain.

As she looked out over what had been Rafe's land until so recently she realised that she could never tell the child who its real father had been. To do that would be to betray Elliott, and Rafe certainly did not deserve any posthumous devotion from the child he had so carelessly created. But should a child not know its own parentage?

'What is wrong?' How alert Elliott was to her mood, to her physical reactions.

'I feel a little melancholy. I am sorry, that is the last thing I should be saying the day after we were married.'

'It is hardly surprising. Did you expect to feel better once you had a husband?' When she stared at him, startled, Elliott was looking out over the view. The thumb of the hand that held hers brushed gently against her wrist. He must have felt her pulse jump at his frankness.

'I wish…I should wish I had not lain with Rafe, but I do not regret the child,' she said. 'But I am ashamed at what I did, what I felt. I should have known better, I should not have allowed passion and my desire for escape to overcome everything I had been brought up to believe was right.' *But surely needing to love cannot be wrong?* It was all so muddling. 'I am ashamed at putting you in this position. I thought it would be better when I did not have to agonise about providing for the baby, but there is so much else to worry about that I know I am not behaving as I ought. I will do my best to be a good viscountess, Elliott.' *And a good wife. Somehow.*

'So you feel a sense of duty?' The thumb stilled its soft caress.

'To you? Of course. And gratitude. And liking,' she added, looking up, shy at what she would see on Elliott's face.

'That is something, then.' He turned so his back was against the parapet and she was standing in front of him, toe to toe, his body shielding her from the breeze.

'Last night…' she managed, her eyes fixed on the simple knot of his neckcloth.

'Yes?'

'You… I did not satisfy you.' *Lord, but this was difficult.*

'I did not say that.' But he did not smile. 'Rather, you were the one who was unsatisfied, I think.'

'That is my fault,' she confessed. He shook his head,

opened his mouth, but she stumbled on. 'I will try my best, truly I will. Tonight will be different.'

'Tonight will be no different unless you can convince us both that you *want* me to make love to you.'

Bella jerked up her head and stared at him. 'Convince you? But how do I do that? I submit—is that not what you want?'

'No, it is not.'

Her heart sank. She even had that wrong. Now he would tell her just how unsatisfactory she was. Kindly, no doubt, for this was Elliott, not his brother. 'When you want to make love, then you will know how,' Elliott said.

Chapter Eleven

He is smiling, but he is not amused, Bella thought, looking into the blue eyes that held no trace of laughter in them. *Is he angry?* But he did not *feel* angry, not with her. 'I like it when you kiss me,' she admitted, offering the thought as if to mitigate her failings. *How can I ask him to show me what to do?* A proper *woman knows it instinctively.*

'So I should hope.' Now his eyes were smiling and she smiled back. This was a different Elliott, the one she had seen glimpses of before. This one was light-hearted and flirtatious and ready to laugh at himself. 'Without wishing to brag, I am considered an accomplished kisser.'

'Do you practise much?' she asked, greatly daring.

'I have been known to,' Elliott admitted. 'But now I must perfect my technique with only you to help me.'

That was encouraging. Did he mean he would not go back to his mistress? She thought about his words and saw the amusement in his eyes at her all-too-obvious thought processes. But the laughter was not unkind.

'But I do not have any technique at all,' she said at last. This all sounded very complicated. Arabella had assumed that a kiss was a simple placing of lips together. Rafe had felt almost...brutal. He had apologised so charmingly, she remembered, when she had pulled back, shaking, her fingertips pressed to her bruised lips. It was the uncontrollable passion she aroused in him, he had explained, leaving her feeling guiltily that it had been her own fault.

And now it was her duty to learn to kiss her new husband properly. Only, it did not feel much like a duty, more like a pleasure. This was so confusing and the fact that she was standing between Elliott's braced legs—how had she moved that close?—made it oddly difficult to think through the tangle of shame and need and fear.

'I can assure you, Arabella, that when you stand there, so close, with the tip of your tongue just touching your upper lip like that,' he said, his voice husky, 'you need no technique whatsoever.'

My tongue? She whipped it back in and closed her mouth, but too late. Elliott leaned forwards and kissed her. Arabella let herself go, gave herself up to the sensation, stopped thinking. Things seemed to happen quite without any conscious thought. Her lips knew how to part, her tongue knew how to touch his, to explore the heat of his mouth, slide over teeth, caress the delicate inner flesh. *Oh, I can do this!* Her hands knew how to move up his chest until she could feel his heart beat under her palm...

Elliott shifted, pulling her in closer between his thighs. Bella felt the heat of him pressing against her belly and her breath hitched. That was what it was all about, not this drugging, sensual kissing. It was all about *that*.

Kissing she could learn, it seemed. But *that* was different. How did she learn to do something that hurt so much? She flinched like a child expecting a cuff around the head.

'What is it?' He freed her mouth and his hands slid down to cup her buttocks as he leaned back a little to see her face. The movement brought her tight against his erection and unexpected sensation, a hot, molten, desperate urge to rub herself against him, flared through her. Desire hit like a big wave on the beach, knocking her off balance with the shocking force of the need. She struggled against it, knowing she would be clumsy and inept, and jerked back just as Toby erupted on to the roof, sending the pigeons into the air in a panic of flapping wings.

'Bad dog!' Bella turned, twisting out of Elliott's arms. 'The silly creature—as though he could catch one. My goodness, he did make me jump. Toby, come back here!'

'Was that what was wrong?' Elliott asked, straightening up.

'Of course. I think I would like to go down now.' Quite deliberately Bella let her hand rest on her stomach for a moment and saw Elliott's eyes follow the gesture. There was absolutely nothing wrong with her other than the shameful effects of Elliott's kiss and her own fears and she felt a pang of guilt. She was deceiving him for the first time. Lying, in effect, to extract herself from a situation she had no idea how to handle.

The guilt tightened its grip as she saw the concern on his face. 'I should not have dragged you up all those stairs.'

'I enjoyed it,' she said, managing a smile. 'I am much better today.'

'Then let us go down,' Elliott said, getting through the door first to help her. 'And you must go and rest.'

But that was not what she wanted. She wanted to continue exploring the house with Elliott, not resting with nothing to think about but that kiss and her body's reaction to it. Bella negotiated the steep steps with care, wrestling with her feelings.

She had lain with Rafe because she thought she loved him and—she could see now—he had blackmailed her into it, not because she had felt uncontrollable carnal desire. Now here she was with his brother, whom she hardly knew, and every time he touched her, her whole body ached for his caresses. That was wrong, surely? What was happening to her? She had no idea, except that the fear was still there, the knowledge that she could not willingly do more than surrender her body to Elliott.

But if she let him keep kissing her—would that help? Only it was not fair to him to arouse him and then be such a disappointment in bed; she understood enough now about the male body and its needs to know that.

Elliott was standing at the bottom of the stairs, his hand held out to her. 'I am fine,' she said. 'Thank you.' It was easier when they did not touch.

'If we go this way…' he gestured down the right hand passage '…we come to the stairs that lead directly to your suite. You can rest; I will have tea sent up.'

'I do not want to rest.' Bella made her way down the uncarpeted passage in front of him.

'But you will, won't you?' His tone did not encourage discussion.

Bella firmed her lips. It was almost more comfortable to bicker than to kiss. Only, she was the one doing the bickering, Elliott was simply laying down the law. An alarming hint of rebellion stirred inside her. After years of obeying one man's every order, she found herself prepared to argue with this one, which was disconcerting. A woman was supposed to obey first her father, then her husband, in all things. But one did not choose one's father, whilst a marriage was a partnership, was it not?

A door stood slightly ajar, a distraction from her troubling thoughts. 'What is in here?' Without waiting for Elliott's reply she pushed it open and went in. The room was large and would be airy and light if the windows were cleaned and opened wide, Bella thought as she turned slowly to look at it. There were two little beds on either side, a wooden horse, a drum, a shelf with a line of red-coated soldiers marching to do battle with dust and spiders, and something shrouded in a dust cloth.

'A nursery! But so far away from the main floors.'

'It was ours until we reached six,' Elliott said from the doorway as she went to peek into the room leading off. It was obviously the nurse's room, with adult-sized furniture. 'There's a scullery on the other side where the nursery maid would make our meals and do the washing. It is quite self-contained.'

'But—did your mother not want you with her?'

'We would be taken down for an hour before bath time to see Mama in her room.'

'Oh.' *How cold.* 'And you and Rafe both lived up here?'

'He went down to a suite on the floor below when he was six, so I was by myself after that. He had his own room and there was a chamber for his tutor, and a school-room. When I joined him I had my room there as well.'

'Poor little boy,' she exclaimed. 'How lonely you must have been up here.'

Elliott still had not moved from the doorway. He shrugged. 'It is what I was used to. It is normal in big houses.'

'Well, it is not going to be normal here any longer,' Bella said. Tradition was all very well, but this isolated room made her uneasy—it was as if children were banished for the crime of being young. 'I must have the baby close. What is this?' She flicked back the dust-sheet. 'Oh, a cradle—how lovely. Is it very old?' Under her hand the dark oak was tactile, almost a living thing. Her touch sent it rocking gently. She peeped under the high gabled hood and smiled, imagining her baby lying safe inside smiling up at her.

'That is the heir's cradle,' Elliott said. 'It is Tudor, I think. You'll see it in several of the portraits in the Long Gallery. See the coat of arms on the back of the hood?'

Bella shifted round to see. The carving was strong and bold and she could read it easily. A falcon held an arrow in its grip, its head turned arrogantly to face the watcher. *'I hold what is mine,'* she read. 'I will have it taken downstairs and polished.'

'If the child is a boy, that will be his. If it is a girl, she will have another cradle.' It seemed Elliott held fast to tradition.

'Of course.' A cradle was not worth fighting over, but the location of the nursery was. 'I will have a look at the rooms close to mine and decide on a nursery.'

'This is suitable. It will be cleaned and repainted and you can choose new furnishings,' Elliott said.

'No, you do not understand.' Bella straightened up and faced him. 'It is too far away.'

'We will employ a competent nurse. You will need your rest, not a crying child.' His face showed no sign of any sympathy.

'Elliott,' Bella said, keeping her voice even with an effort, 'either the nursery is downstairs or I will move up here.'

'An ultimatum?' One eyebrow rose. Bella fought the urge to edge away. It was not that she was frightened of him, but there was something else going on here, something more than a disagreement over the position of a nursery and she did not understand it. What she did understand was that she was feeling extremely emotional all of a sudden. It was not grief, it seemed to come from nowhere, filling her with an overwhelming desire to weep.

'If you like,' she said. 'I am sorry, Elliott, but I feel very strongly about this and I am afraid that if we have to stand here arguing about this any longer I am going to cry. I don't know why. I just feel very…very…' She gulped.

'Oh, for goodness' sake,' he said, striding into the room and scooping her up in his arms. Toby, who had followed them into the room, let out a volley of barks.

'Put me down!'

'No.' He smiled at her ruefully. 'I expect it is your condition making you feel weepy. I tell you, Arabella, pointer bitches in pup are a lot less trouble than women.'

'Really, Elliott!' She tried to struggle, then gave it up

as futile as he walked along the corridor and down the winding flight of stairs at the end, the terrier skirmishing around his feet and making him swear under his breath. It was rather pleasant to be held in his arms as though she weighed next to nothing and the shift of muscles as he moved was intriguing. There was something about being carried that made her feel extremely feminine and her head rested against his shoulder in a most satisfactory way.

It was weakening to the will and the constitution of course, being carried about like a child. She must assert herself. 'About the nursery,' she began as Elliott reached her bedchamber door.

'Yes?' He set her on her feet and regarded her with what looked like resignation.

'It will be down here.' They watched each other in silence. He looked unyielding, but he did not actually refuse. 'Please.'

'I wondered how long it would take,' he said enigmatically. 'Very well—but out of my earshot, mind.'

'Yes, Elliott.' Bella felt smug, then saw the shadows in his eyes as he turned away. No, this wasn't a game, this learning the boundaries of a marriage.

'And rest,' he tossed back over his shoulder. 'Can you do as you are told in that respect at least?'

'I am going in now,' Bella said. She opened the door and stepped into the room. Toby shot in before she could prevent him.

'Good.'

She shut the door and leaned on it. She had said she was entering her room, not that she would rest there. Elliott would be riding out soon, she was sure, and then she was going to explore on her own and find her perfect nursery.

Elliott had wished that Arabella was less compliant; it seemed he was getting his desire. Whether this would prove to be a good thing remained to be seen. One could not dismiss an argumentative wife as one could a demanding mistress.

Elliott swung up into the saddle of his bay cover hack and turned its head towards the Home Farm. Turner was going to wonder what had happened to him today. He had been spending virtually every morning with the estate manager since he had come here, trying to get the land and the tenants' cottages back into the state they had been in when Rafe had inherited. His brother had shown not the slightest interest in the property that earned him the bulk of his revenues, but neither would he delegate sufficient power and resources to his steward to allow him to do what was necessary in his stead. It seemed he was as unwilling to yield any authority to an employee as he had been to his brother.

Even when Elliott had dealt with the lack of investment and neglect it would still be a long way behind Fosse Warren where he was experimenting with the latest techniques and had been spending heavily for several years. At least Turner was happy now, with authority to lay out money and an employer who was taking an intelligent interest.

Elliott held the bay back to a walk despite its fidgeting. He was in no hurry to discuss the value of turnips in crop rotation or whether they should buy some orchards down in the Vale as Turner was suggesting. Thinking about Arabella was more absorbing and thinking about Arabella and sex kept the other, darker, more difficult thoughts at bay.

She was naturally sensuous, he was certain of that, although after last night, it was hard to see why he was so certain. Elliott shifted in the saddle as he thought. She enjoyed kissing, he could feel her body's response to him, her innocently provocative exploration. *His* body was in no doubt what it wanted, uncomfortably so, and whenever he touched her it seemed that this time he was going to have her yielding, completely. But as soon as things became more intense, she either recoiled, or, as she had last night, passively submitted.

It could be that she was responding instinctively to him and then being brought up short when her natural modesty and her duty to him as her husband were in conflict, or it could be something else. Her pregnancy? Something about him? Rafe?

Arabella was proving an infuriating enigma. She was apparently dutiful and meek—and yet she dug her heels in over the location of the nursery and he was sure that, however many sleepless nights they had when the baby was born, she was not going to be convinced that it should be on the upper floor. She knew he did not take more than toast for breakfast, yet she had somehow cajoled him into eating a veritable feast. She was pregnant with his brother's child, and yet she seemed as nervous as a virgin. She was deliciously, provokingly sensual and yet she recoiled the moment things moved beyond kisses.

And now, just when he'd wanted—no, *needed* —to have a frank, firm discussion with her she had become weepy. That at least was down to the pregnancy, he was certain; Arabella had seemed as surprised to find herself so emotional as he had been. But even so, it was enough to make him feel like a bully.

Elliott was not given to bullying anyone. Firmness, fairness and an authority he had learned young worked much better and earned loyalty as well as good work.

He was not given to deceiving himself either. There was more to his unsettled mood this morning than an over-emotional wife—it was time to face it. His reaction to seeing that nursery had been visceral, a jolt in the guts that had surprised him. He had not been unhappy up there as a small child. He could recall Nanny White's smiling face and playing soldiers with Rafe and the taste of porridge with honey in it and the longed-for delight of that hour with Mama before bedtime.

Even when Rafe had moved downstairs he had not been sad, content to play by himself with his toys and in his head. He had missed Rafe, though—he hardly saw him once he had graduated to the world of the school-room—and he had looked forward to the day when he joined him downstairs.

But Rafe at almost eight was different from the playmate upstairs and a small brother was, apparently, an inconvenient nuisance. Elliott learned to keep his hands off Rafe's toys and Rafe's books, not to sit at Rafe's desk, not to ask for their tutor's attention until Rafe had received all the assistance he demanded.

When he was twelve he had begun following their old

steward around, asking questions, taking an interest in the estate. Everything about it was fascinating and soon he was having ideas of his own that Peters encouraged. One day their father had praised him for his knowledge about the herds within Rafe's hearing.

'I am the heir,' Rafe had hissed at him as soon as he got him alone, twisting his arm painfully. 'You're just the spare. This is going to be mine—the title, the house, the land. You're nothing, *Mr* Calne, and don't you forget it.'

And for the first time Elliott had lost his temper, hit his brother, fought him with all the fury and desperation of baffled hurt. And he had won, had routed Rafe, who had taken his split lip and black eye off to their mother so Elliott got a whipping. But Rafe never attacked him directly again and Elliot discovered that he could stand up for himself.

No, it had not been unhappy memories of life in that nursery that had hit him, but the realisation it was Rafe's child who would lie in that cradle now and not his own. That was why he had wanted the nursery so far away, he acknowledged. It was as petty and shameful as that. So much for his impassioned declaration to Arabella that in all honour he must be certain that if the baby was a boy it would inherit one day. He had meant it then, he knew that. He had not even had to think it through, he had known it was the right thing to do. It was still right.

So why was he resenting it now? If he and Arabella had a son together, he would leave Fosse Warren to him. Until a few days ago that had been his only ambition for the land, to leave it to his son, a boy who would grow up to be plain Mr Calne, just as he had. So what had changed?

Elliott shook his head, frustrated and annoyed with himself. And ashamed. Damn it, he had felt good about himself for doing the right thing, for marrying Arabella, and now he realised he wasn't the rational, emotionless man he had thought. 'You smug devil,' he said to himself. The bay sidled, confused by the voice and the tightening rein. 'Come on, let's do some work,' Elliott told it, using his heels to urge it into a canter. 'I've wasted enough time on the roof and looking at cradles.'

Chapter Twelve

'Mrs Knight, are you free to go through some of the rooms with me?' Bella found the older woman in the stillroom, frowning at a list in her hand.

'Of course, my lady.' She put down the list and smiled at Bella. 'I was just wondering where all the beeswax polish has got to. I could have sworn we'd got enough made up to last another month, but I can see we'll be raiding the hives before long at this rate. Now, where would you like to be starting, my lady?'

'The main bedchamber floor, if you please, Mrs Knight.' Bella picked up her skirts and walked upstairs side by side with the housekeeper. 'I would like to see what we have available for guests.' Elliott would have many friends and she was determined that she would be an excellent hostess for him. Surely warm hospitality and goodwill would make up for her lack of sophistication and knowledge of the *ton*?

The master suites were in the central block of the house with two wings on either side. Mrs Knight led the way along to the far end of the West Wing and began to open doors for Bella to see the rooms. 'There are six rooms along here, my lady. Best for bachelors, I always think, for they've no dressing rooms.'

'This little chamber at the end would make a good location for a water closet,' Bella suggested. She had read about such luxurious indoor plumbing and was determined to persuade Elliott to invest in some.

'Running water, my lady? In the house?'

'Yes, indeed, Mrs Knight. And more than one of them, if possible. So much more pleasant than the old earth closets, don't you think?'

'I wouldn't know, my lady, I'm sure.' It was obviously a radical thought, but Bella, although grateful for the indoor earth closets after a lifetime of the vicarage's privy in the garden, was inspired by the idea of modern plumbing. 'It will be an awful lot of disturbance, won't it? All those pipes?'

'And I think we will need a tank, so that the closets can be flushed.'

'It's a good thing his lordship's a progressive man,' Mrs Knight said, still dubious. 'His last lordship wouldn't have stood for it and that's a fact.'

'No?' Bella was surprised. Rafe had struck her as a man who would have wanted the latest comforts. 'I hope we will be having house parties here before long,' she added, changing the subject. She did not want to talk about Rafe any more than it seemed Mrs Knight did.

'That will be nice,' the housekeeper said, and sounded genuinely pleased at the thought of all that extra work.

There did not seem to be much wrong with these rooms, they could certainly wait until she had dealt with the pink draperies in her own suite. They were almost back to it now. 'What is this?' The door opened onto a sitting room with furniture under dust cloths.

'A sitting room for guests in this wing, my lady. It was a suite at one time, I think; there's a dressing room off it that is used for storing things now.'

Which would be perfect for the nurse's room. And it was next to Bella's own sitting room. All it would take would be a door knocked through. She had found her nursery. But she could hardly tell Mrs Knight that. Although she itched to have it converted immediately, it must wait until her pregnancy was acknowledged fact.

'Shall we look at the other wing, Mrs Knight?'

'There are the rooms we use for married couples and single ladies, my lady. They've all got dressing rooms.'

'There are a lot of rooms,' Bella commented. 'But not so many large ones for couples.' Perhaps some rearrangement could be carried out to create better dressing rooms and make small suites?

'Oh, yes, my lady. The rooms are rather old fashioned. But his late lordship did not give that much mind—his house parties were mostly single gentlemen and females.'

'Females?'

'Yes, my lady.' The housekeeper fiddled with her keys. 'Not ladies, if you get my drift.'

'Indeed.' *My goodness, Elliott might have had a mistress, but at least he does not bring loose women home.* Then it struck her that he could have been holding veritable orgies at Fosse Warren and Mrs Knight would not have known. She doubted it somehow, even though Elliott obviously had a healthy interest in sensual matters. 'Thank you, Mrs Knight. I will go back to my room and rest now. Could you ask someone to bring me up a tea tray?'

'My lady.' The housekeeper bustled off, her bunch of keys swinging at her side, and Bella went to her sitting room, making a conscious effort not to drag her feet. Elliott had told her to rest, and she should obey him, she knew. And now she *was* tired, so there was no virtue in her obedience, she acknowledged wryly. Marriage was not easy, especially if one had a conscience.

The next morning, as soon as Elliott had gone out, Bella went straight back to the room she was already thinking of as the nursery. They had enjoyed a very civilised breakfast together with no reference made to the fact that he had not come to her room last night, saying that she seemed tired and should get a good night's sleep. How long such forbearance would last she was not sure, but thinking of something else was decidedly more comfortable than speculating on when Elliott might return to her room and demand that she work harder at satisfying him. The very thought filled her with alarm for she knew that nothing had happened to make her any more likely to please him.

Bella stood in the middle of the space and half-closed her eyes, imagining the chairs and tables replaced with a cot and a nursing chair. There would be light curtains at the window and soft rugs on the floor. Toys would be scattered about… 'Perfect.'

'Perfect?' said Elliott's voice behind her.

'This room, for a nursery,' Bella said as she turned. But it was not Elliott, it was Daniel Calne standing there in breeches and riding coat, looking windswept. And *almost* handsome, she thought, making the comparison with Elliott and finding that Daniel did not quite match up to his cousin in looks.

'You sound so like Elliott.'

'People often remark that we sound alike—he and Rafe and myself.' Daniel came into the room, big and amiable and smiling. He was restful to have around, she thought. She felt quite safe with Daniel, a friendly man who wanted nothing from her she could not give. 'A nursery, two days after the wedding? You are obviously a planner, Bella.'

She knew she was blushing, knew her hand had gone betrayingly, to her stomach. 'I…'

Daniel Calne's face changed from cheerful greeting to what, under other circumstances, would have been amusing astonishment. Then he had his expression under control again. 'You are with child?'

'Yes, I am. And I would be obliged if you would keep that in confidence, Daniel.' All she had to do was be calm, he could not possibly guess it was Rafe's child, Bella told herself. 'You may imagine I am a trifle embarrassed about it, as well as delighted, of course. I will not be able to conceal it for much longer.'

'I will be discreet.' He had gone positively pink. 'I was momentarily taken aback. I was convinced Elliott was cour—convinced he had no notion of marriage in mind… I am delighted, of course.'

What had he almost said? Not *courting*, surely? Elliott had told her he was not in love with anyone. She felt uneasily that it had not been the entire truth.

'I have been clumsy, I am so sorry. I should have kept my mouth shut. I felicitate you on the forthcoming happy event and I will be suitably surprised when I hear about if officially, so to speak.' Bella turned her head away, still worrying about that unfinished word. 'Bella, forgive me. I will not speak of this to anyone, I swear.'

'Thank you. I would not have Elliott embarrassed for the world. And there is nothing to forgive.' She should ring for tea. It still had not quite sunk in that she was mistress of this house and could order the staff as she wished.

'And what is Daniel to be forgiven for?' *How could I have ever mistaken someone else's voice for Elliott's?* Bella wondered. His was deeper than Rafe's, more flexible and expressive than Daniel's.

'For making Bella jump out of her skin just now,' Daniel answered before she could think of anything to say. 'She was lost in thoughts of wallpaper and curtains and I walked in and startled her.'

'I was just going to ring for tea,' Bella interjected. Now she was committed to a lie, Daniel was taking her request for discretion to include mentioning it to Elliott. It seemed she had done nothing but deceive him recently and it made her miserable. Or perhaps she was refining too much upon it and it was simply her unsettled emotions that were to blame.

'Daniel has just got here—I did not realise that you

two had a meeting.' Elliott stood back punctiliously as she went through the door, then they both followed her along to her own sitting room and waited while she rang the bell and sat down.

'We do not have a meeting,' Elliott said. 'I came back because I had forgotten some paperwork. You're a fair ride from home,' he remarked to his cousin. 'But it is good to see you.'

'I have a new hunter I wanted to try and I dropped by on the off chance. But there is a matter of business, if you have the time. Perhaps I can ride with you a little when you go out again.'

'Discuss it now,' Elliott said as the maid came in and was sent away for the tea.

'Yes, of course,' Bella said, remembering that a dutiful wife would not want her husband to be drinking tea with her when he could be attending to business. 'The girl can bring your tea down to the study.'

'I meant here. I would not miss your first tea party, my dear.' He smiled at her and Bella felt a rush of pleasure.

Daniel looked doubtful. 'I do not wish to bore Bella with such things, but if you insist… I was wondering if you are going to lease Fosse Warren. Or sell it, perhaps.'

'One of your clients interested?' Elliott enquired and Bella recalled that Daniel was a lawyer.

'No. I am.' Elliott stared at him and Daniel shifted, colouring up. 'I thought I would try farming myself. A sideline, you understand. I don't intend giving up the law.'

'I had no idea the practical rural life held any appeal for you. Well, I am sorry, but I only intend to lease the house and pleasure grounds. I have hopes of a returning nabob or some cit wanting a country retreat. I shall retain the estate and the farms. But feel free to come and talk farming any time you want.'

'Thank you, I will take you up on that. You'll be putting a manager in?'

'My steward is very competent, but I will be keeping a hand on it. I don't want it neglected while I bring this estate around.'

'Rafe was never one for rusticating, he always said the country was a dead bore,' Daniel remarked as the maid brought in the tray.

'A pity he did not delegate sufficient authority to Jim Turner for him to keep things running, in that case,' Elliott said. 'He's a good man. If Rafe had trusted him, the land and the buildings wouldn't be in the state they are now. Thank you, Arabella.' He took the cup she passed him and smiled, a sudden flicker of warmth breaking through the intensity. He was still unhappy about leaving his own home, she thought with a sudden flash of insight. 'The tenants' cottages are a disgrace from what I've seen so far,' he added, serious again.

'I must start visiting the tenants,' Bella said. Perhaps she could be helpful to Elliott in pointing out which were the priority cases if repairs were needed.

The two men moved on to speak of a local political scandal and Bella studied the two faces, so obviously related and yet so different. She was becoming used to seeing the likeness to Rafe in both men, although she was finding it harder and harder to recall his exact appearance, to remember his voice when Elliott's deeper tones were in her ears all the time. Perhaps all her memories of those few days would blur mercifully, in time.

'Where is Rafe buried?' she asked and both men turned to face her, their faces as alike as brothers in their shared surprise. She should not have blurted it out, she realised, but she needed to know. She did not want to come across the grave unexpectedly and betray any emotion that might betray her.

Elliott recovered first. 'In the family vault in the church where we were married,' he said. 'You will see it on Sunday, although the memorial is not finished yet, of course.'

'Just a plain plaque?' Bella enquired, trying to sound as though she was taking an interest in a total stranger's grave. Rafe had lain so close to her when she had married Elliott. The thought made her feel cold. Perhaps it was best that she had not known.

'I thought a plaque, yes. Name, dates, title and the family crest. White marble,' Elliott added. She saw the way he was studying her face and wondered if she had said something that might betray her feelings to Daniel.

'What, no statue of Rafe in heroic pose showing his best profile and with scantily clad maidens mourning at his feet?' Daniel joked. 'He'd have appreciated those.'

'Calne.' Elliott frowned.

'My apologies, Bella.' Daniel's smile was rueful. 'And I must be going. I keep forgetting that you are on your honeymoon, such a practical pair of lovebirds that you are—curtains and agriculture are most unconventional entertainments two days after the ceremony.'

He took himself off, leaving Elliott audibly grinding

his teeth. 'He is not usually tactless.' He sat down next to Bella on the sofa. 'I am sorry, did that disturb you?'

'Talking about Rafe's tomb? No, and I raised the subject after all, which was foolish of me. I did not want to come across it unexpectedly, that is all. I should have waited and spoken to you when we were alone. My thoughts and emotions are all over the place—is it my condition again, do you think?'

'I imagine so.' Elliott smiled and her heart warmed. He was so kind to her. 'Not that I would know. I have considerable expertise with brood mares and pointer bitches, none at all with wives. Perhaps if you were to develop a wet nose, a glossy coat and a tail I might be better able to advise.'

'Oh, Elliott.' Bella dissolved into laughter. 'Would you tell me *sit* if I did?'

He caught her in his arms and pulled her on to his lap. 'Certainly—*sit*! I have never seen you laugh before. It suits you.'

Her giggles died away as she found herself held very close. There were laughter lines at the corners of those blue, blue eyes and Elliott's lashes were dark and indecently long for a man. His arm was firm around her and she balanced securely, one hand pressed to his waistcoat, conscious of the strength of his thighs beneath her, the occasional flex of the muscles and the alarming realisation that Elliott was finding this arousing.

'Elliott?' She licked her lips and saw him watching her. His heavy-lidded regard stirred disturbing sensations deep inside. 'Elliott…' She leaned towards him and pressed her lips to his.

Everything about Elliott became tense, from his arms around her to the hard evidence of his sexual interest beneath her. Bella could almost hear him thinking before his lips moved under hers and he leaned back against the support of the sofa, bringing her to lie against his chest. It meant she was on top of him, in control of the kiss. It felt exciting and dangerous and wicked, even though he had not even opened his mouth beneath hers, even though his hands remained light on her back, quite still.

He is leaving it to me, she thought and the sense of power eclipsed all the other sensations. Elliott wanted her and she was in command and she knew her kisses did not displease or disappoint him. It seemed to her, in a flash of insight, that this was a brave thing for a man to do, to abdicate sexual power to a woman. She could not imagine Rafe doing so for a moment and yet Elliott was not doing this out of weakness, but out of confidence.

Bella ran her fingers into the hair at Elliott's nape, rubbing over the taut tendons, the muscle. She had the illusion that she could hold him like this, powerless in her grip, so she could pillage his mouth at her leisure. Part of her mind laughed at her—he could have her on her back in a moment—but the fantasy was delicious. As she probed at his closed lips with her tongue-tip and he resisted her she realised he was playing too.

Her fingers closed in his hair, commanding obedience as she slid her tongue inside his mouth. The tightness was exciting and his surrender, as he opened to her, delicious. Bella shifted so she cupped his face with her other hand, holding him while she explored, tasted, teased. His mouth was hot and slick and he tasted of tea and, under that safe, domestic taste, something male and dangerous and wild.

Panting a little, she drew back so they were nose to nose. 'Take me?' he suggested, his voice husky, his hands sliding down to the curve of her hips. 'Here, now…'

Chapter Thirteen

*T*ake me. Could she? Dare she? Of course not, she would be utterly inept, laughable. All the magic drained away, leaving her mortified and awkward. 'No,' Bella muttered, wriggling free. 'Not here, in broad daylight.' She was blushing, she could feel it. How she must disappoint him after his mistresses, chosen, of course, for their sensual expertise.

'Later?' Elliott sat upright as she landed inelegantly on the other end of the sofa. He did nothing to disguise the bulge in his breeches.

Bella looked away. She had to try to respond sooner or later, even though it would be a disaster. 'Tonight?'

'Tonight,' Elliott agreed. He sounded as though they were discussing whether or not to have fish for dinner. Was that simply good manners or was he hiding anger and frustration under the civil tone? Of course he was.

There was a silence while Bella regarded her toes and wondered what to say next. Her mind appeared to have gone numb and her body was a confused riot of sensations, most of them urging her back into Elliott's arms.

'What were you doing in that sitting room?' Elliott asked. He crossed his legs, so she felt it was safe to look at him again. 'I thought you would want to start any decoration with your own rooms.'

'It will be ideal for the nursery,' Bella explained. It would have been better if she could have given this more thought before springing it on him, she thought as his brows drew together. 'A door could be knocked through to my sitting room and there's a small room for the nurse to use.'

'You will never get any peace.'

'I will. The nurse will be there and my own sitting room is between my bedroom and the nursery.'

'Very well.' He agreed so suddenly that she was taken aback. 'But we had better wait until your pregnancy is official before we start knocking holes in walls.'

'Of course. Thank you, Elliott.'

He made a dismissive gesture and, just for a moment, Bella thought she saw something almost like shame in his eyes. Then it was gone. He was good at hiding his emotions, but she thought it was because he valued self-control, not because he had set out to deceive her.

Elliott had a certain dangerous edge of physicality to him that made her wonder if he was exactly comfortable in the high *ton*. She imagined him stripped to the waist boxing, or fencing, driving home an attack with a flashing blade, and swallowed hard.

'I must go,' Elliott said. He stood and looked down at

her and his voice deepened, sent a shiver down her spine. 'Until dinner, my dear. I look forward to it—and to later.'

Bella got through dinner somehow. Elliott must have spoken to Henlow, for the meal was formally served, even though there was only the two of them. Elliott was teaching her, she realised, demonstrating the etiquette she must learn in the safety of their own dining room without guests.

All the leaves had been taken out of the table so they could converse, he at the head, she at the foot. An array of cutlery hedged her plate, glasses were ranked across the top of it. There was a vast starched napkin to control on the slippery silk of her evening gown and a succession of dishes to identify the correct flatware for.

And Elliott kept up a constant stream of conversation, mostly on subjects she knew nothing about, so she had to deal with a quivering aspic mould while finding something sensible to say about the fact that there would be a by-election next month for the Evesham constituency.

Then, just as she was trying to decide what to do with the saddle of lamb and the tiny, highly mobile white onions she was being offered, he asked her opinion about Napoleon's abdication. 'I am afraid I have no idea whether Elba is a sensible place to put him or not, my lord. This lamb is excellent. Is it from your...our own flock?'

'Oh, yes, Lady Hadleigh, it is ours.' She decided he was pleased with her reference to the farm. 'I feel Napoleon would be safer further away—Elba is too close to France for my liking.'

'You think he might escape and we would have war again?' That was an alarming thought after only a few weeks of peace. 'Perhaps wiser counsel will prevail and he will not be sent there.'

'Perhaps.' Elliott went on to talk about the government's views on the subject; the names of ministers and opposition politicians made her head spin. She strongly suspected him of trying to distract her from what would take place later in her bedchamber, but she tried to keep up with him. It was obvious that she would have to start reading the newspapers if she was not to appear a complete dunce when they had dinner parties.

Somehow she managed five courses and remembered to leave Elliott to his port without needing to be reminded. She sat and pretended to read until he joined her and then braced herself for at least another hour of scrupulously polite and highly educational conversation until the tea tray was brought in.

'Lady Hadleigh.'

'My lord.' He was going to say something about her reluctance this afternoon, or what he expected when they went to bed, she knew it. Bella sat up straight, put on her best, brightly interested, face. She could do this. She must do this, and the longer she put it off, the worse it would be. Elliott was her husband now, she owed him a duty. And another, more cynical, sense nagged her that she must attach him for the sake of the child. That the happier he was with her as his wife, the better he would accept the little cuckoo in his nest.

'You preside over the dinner table with great grace.'

'Thank you.' Oh, thank goodness, he did not want to

talk about bed yet. Then what he had said sank in and she bit her lip to control the smile that was in danger of becoming an unladylike grin of delight. 'It is such a relief to hear you say so—I was well aware that you are doing your best to make me familiar with the etiquette.'

Elliott sat down, crossed his legs, steepled his fingers and regarded her over the top of them. He should have looked formidable, instead he seemed reassuring. 'I hope I can help; it cannot be pleasant to be pitchforked into this.'

'I never thought of the practical implications of being married to a viscount,' she admitted ruefully.

'I imagine not,' Elliott said wryly, then, to her great relief, changed the subject instead of observing that she had not appeared to have given much thought to *anything* but her infatuation or she would not be in this position now. 'Shall I invite the Bayntons to spend the day soon? If the weather is fine John and I will ride out—I want his advice on some woodland—and you and Anne can have a comfortable time together.'

'Oh, yes, please.' The prospect of having a female friend who could explain the mysteries of childbearing was almost overwhelming. 'Thank you, Elliott. I am conscious of how much trouble I must be to you.'

'Not at all. I am beginning to see the advantages of having a wife,' he said. What those were for him she could not imagine; just now she seemed to be causing him nothing but problems. Perhaps he thought that after tonight... His smile with its wicked edge sent little flutters of alarm through her. 'You must let me know whenever you want to go into Worcester for more shopping—clothes, refurnishing your suite. Perhaps you and Mrs Baynton would like to have an expedition one day?'

'I am not sure the bills I might run up will count as advantages.'

'We need to make this our home,' Elliott said. 'That will cost money—I am quite resigned. I have put repairs in hand to deal with the damp and the cracked windows.'

'Well, in that case…what are your views on water closets?'

Elliott gave a gasp of laughter. 'I hardly dare enquire why you ask. Where were you considering locating such an object? And how the devil do we get the water to it?'

Bella launched into a description of her reading on the subject and they were well into considerations of water tanks, lead pipe and ventilation by the time the tea arrived.

'I can just imagine what Daniel would say if he could hear us,' Elliott observed as Bella poured, nervously aware of the age and beauty of the Worcester tea service she was expected to deal with. 'If he thought us unromantic before, can you imagine his comments on sanitary engineering as a honeymoon topic?'

'I would not dream of discussing such things with anyone else present,' she hastened to assure him. 'I know it is not something ladies should speak about, but I do feel I can talk about anything with you.'

'Thank you.' Elliott's expression of satirical amusement softened. 'Now that *is* a romantic observation, Lady Hadleigh.'

Bella wondered just how romantic Elliott was feeling an hour later as she sat at her dressing table while Gwen brushed out her hair. Such dull hair, she thought. Straight and brown and ordinary despite rosemary rinses. Did men notice such things, or did the fact that she was not a beauty mean that details such as the colour of her hair or the shape of her nose were ignored? Perhaps it was best not to brood on what men found attractive, not with her husband expecting her to… In fact, best not to think at all, about anything, if that could be managed.

'Which nightgown tonight, my lady?'

'The fawn one with the copper ribbons,' Bella decided at random. At least it did not clash as unpleasantly with the pink draperies as the green had done.

It was, if anything, more revealing than the green. There seemed to be an inadequate amount of fabric in the bodice and very little substance in the skirts unless she stood stock still. 'And the négligé, please, Gwen.'

The maid brought the robe, which did little for decency other than add another filmy layer, and placed the slippers on the floor by Bella's bare feet. 'Scent, my lady?'

'I do not have any.'

'There was this in the cupboard, my lady.' Gwen produced a gilded flask and took out the stopper. Both women bent over to sniff.

'Phew! Certainly not that, it belongs in a—'

'It certainly does.' Gwen wrinkled her nose. 'One of his late lordship's fancy pieces left it, I've no doubt. I'll pour it away outside, shall I, my lady? The flask is pretty, though.'

'Yes,' Bella said. *Fancy pieces?* They were back to the orgies again. Would Elliott like this scent? She decided she did not care whether he did or not, she was not going to wear it. 'Keep the flask, Gwen. You may go now.'

'Thank you, my lady. Goodnight, ma'am.'

Bella sat and wrestled with the images that the perfume and this chamber conjured up. A man would have certain expectations of a woman dressed as she was in a room like this one.

'Arabella?'

Elliott had come into her room without her hearing him. She shot to her feet like a startled partridge with an entire shooting party after her.

'I beg you pardon, but I did knock.' He was smiling slightly at her discomfiture as he stood there in the same blue silk robe he had worn two nights ago. Only there was no glimpse of nightshirt at the throat and his feet were bare. Now under the thick silk he was naked, she realised, feeling as though all the breath had been sucked out of her lungs.

She had to say something. 'I was thinking about clothes and wondering if you would like this ensemble.' She twitched the skirts a little. 'I think the colour very pretty, don't you.'

'I think the wearer very pretty too,' he said, walking up to her and putting his hands on her shoulders.

'Oh, Elliott, you know I am not!'

'I must confess that cold, hungry, frightened and feeling sick, you can look a trifle drawn and wan,' Elliott admitted. 'I did not see the true you. Our wedding day was a revelation and I should have told you so. Now I see big hazel eyes, with long lashes, perfect skin, a mouth that was made for eating strawberries—'

'It is too wide.'

'All the better for kissing. Your nose—'

'Is too long and straight.'

'All the better for looking down in a provocative manner. Your hair—'

'Is perfectly straight and mouse-coloured.'

'A very pretty mouse, for all that. And when I see it loose…' his hand sifted through the weight of it on her right shoulder '…I think of all kinds of things I would like to do with it.'

Bella could not think what Elliott meant, although from the glint in his eyes whatever it was involved sex.

'Oh, yes, and you blush delightfully.' He watched her for a moment. 'Arabella, I would like us to be…open with each other in bed. More relaxed. I want you to feel free to express what you feel and need.'

'Yes, so do I, Elliott.' It was a lie. In fact, it was a wonder he did not hear her knees rattling together like castanets, but she could not go on like this. She had made her wedding vows and she must keep them.

'Good,' he said, his deep voice huskier than usual as he bent his head. She thought he was going to kiss her, but he held her a little away and brushed his mouth against her throat, nudging gently until she tipped her head to give him better access.

Then his mouth trailed down to the edge of the négligé and his fingers found the ribbons and tugged until it opened. 'Ah,' he murmured, the vibration quivering against her skin. Bella swallowed, fighting to stand still as his lips followed the curve of her breast and his hand cupped the weight of it. Then the flickering exploration of his tongue found her nipple through the gauze.

'Sweet.' The satisfied sound seemed to come from deep in his chest as Elliott settled her firmly in his arms and began to torment the tight bud with tongue and lips and teeth, tugging and sucking and nipping, saturating the fabric until it might as well not have been there.

Elliott! Waves of sensation, not quite pain, too much for pleasure, pulsed through her. He had not done this before, only kissed her mouth and caressed her body gently with his hands.

Rafe had not touched her like this. He had handled her with what she had thought was the impatience of desire, squeezing her breasts, hurting with a pain that was nothing like this exquisite torment. Elliott moved to the other nipple as Arabella writhed in his arms. The négligé had gone, somehow, and so had the nightgown, slithering down to his imprisoning arms where it caught, the silken folds brushing and teasing around her legs.

'Elliott.' She managed to say it out loud this time. A protest, a plea, a gasp of embarrassment? All three, perhaps. Arabella could not understand what he was doing to her body, but it was sending her rapidly past the point where shyness was even an option. 'Elliott, what are you *doing*?'

He looked up, his lips curving. 'Making love, Arabella.'

'You are making me…I do not know. I want…'

'This?' He kissed her on her mouth, one hand still cupping her breast, his thumb fretting hard over the impossibly tight knot of the nipple while his other smoothed down over her hip, pushing the nightgown aside. She became aware again that his hands were hard, as though he worked with them.

His mouth was demanding, his tongue thrusting, insistent that she open to him, insistent that she tangle her own tongue with his. He sucked it into his mouth, holding her when she would have withdrawn, nervous of this intensity and the knowledge of where it was leading, then nipping at her lips with tiny, biting kisses.

In the pit of her belly there was heat and an ache and a pulse that had her pressing against him in a blind search for relief, only to find that she was straining against the blatant jut of his erection through the heavy silk of his robe. But there was no room to withdraw her body, hardly any room in her head for the confusion of thoughts. How could she feel like this for a man she scarcely knew yet and did not love? Was she utterly wanton or was Elliott a warlock, conjuring lust out of her ignorance and shyness? But perhaps, just perhaps, it would be all right…

He moved, scooped her up and laid her on the bed, naked, exposed and quivering with shock. 'Don't cover yourself,' he ordered, his voice almost harsh, as she reached for the covers to drag them across her body. He kicked off his slippers, shrugged out of his robe, then stood, his hands on his lean hips, looking at her. And Arabella stared back, seeing him naked for the first time, breathless with discovery and terrified desire.

Chapter Fourteen

❧❧❧❧❧

Rafe had taken her virginity in the hayloft of the parish tithe barn. It had been shadowed, the gloom pierced by shafts of sunlight where roof tiles had slipped, the light full of floating dust motes. Bella had hardly been able to see his face, or the details of his body as he stripped her, undid his breeches and pushed her on to his coat spread on the pile of loose hay. He had kissed her, ravished her mouth, handled her breasts with avid hands, pressed her legs apart and taken her with the unsubtle urgency of need.

She had not seen then, not really understood his body, but now, in the warm glow of a dozen candles, she could see very clearly the anatomy of a fully aroused man. It took her breath away with a mixture of fear and desire and shock at just how beautiful Elliott was. How hard and lean, how fit. How did he get those muscles, that flat belly, those calloused hands?

He knelt on the bed beside her, his hands skimming down over her body, making her catch her breath. Then he placed his hands on her thighs and eased them apart and she shut her eyes, shamed by the heat and dampness that betrayed her arousal.

'Arabella, look at me.' She felt his weight coming down over her and shifted her hips instinctively to cradle him. Of their own accord her hands curved over his shoulders, and she made herself open her eyes. She thought she was a little more relaxed this time—did Elliott notice? His face was shadowed as it hung over her, the candle flame sharpening the cheekbones, sending blue sparks from his eyes. The image of Rafe slid over his features like a mask and she closed her eyes again to shut it out. She would not let that spectre ruin this, not now. 'Bend your knees up to try and relax,' he urged and she struggled to obey, feeling him nudging closer into her slick, hot folds. 'We have as much time as you need.'

Now. I must not cry out however much it hurts. I must try to forget that, caress him, discover what he likes, stop being so passive...

'Arabella!' Elliott's voice was so sharp that her eyes flew open. She found his intense gaze locked on her face. 'Why are you crying? What is it?'

'I...I'm not.' He rolled off her and she rubbed her hand across her eyes. It came away smeared with moisture. 'Oh. I am sorry, I did not mean to. I was trying so hard not to—'

'Hell and damnation.' Elliott sat up. 'No, I'm sorry. I did not mean to shout at you, let alone swear. Arabella, I thought you were responding to me.'

She felt her face flame. 'Yes. I was. I was determined. It is just...' How could she explain her cowardice? It was her *duty* to lie with her husband. And she wanted to. She could not allow the fear and the pain to prevent her. Every other wife managed it. Perhaps they allowed themselves to be swept up in that turmoil of feeling before *it* happened. If only that was all there was to it, that heat and desire and longing.

But she owed Elliott an explanation and then, no doubt, he would do as his brother had done and ignore the cries she tried to stifle and take her.

'Arabella?' He reached out and touched her face, his big hand gentle as the fingertips caressed her cheek. 'Tell me.'

It was so difficult. His tender gesture made it worse, somehow. She did not deserve that he touch her like that, reach out for her when she was rejecting him. 'I can't explain,' she blurted out. 'I cannot…'

The soft light faded from his eyes. 'You must try, Arabella.'

'I *am* trying so hard,' she protested. 'You don't understand. Let me—'

'I understand perfectly well that you are not ready to be my wife, despite what you say,' he said harshly, getting off the bed and scooping up his robe. 'When you are, then perhaps we will have a marriage. Until then, Lady Hadleigh, I will not trouble you.'

The door to his dressing room clicked shut with controlled care. He was angry, she realised. Very, very angry. She had made him think she was ready and she had not had the courage or the self-control to convince him when it came to it or the words to explain what had happened before.

It hurt, apparently, when a man was very aroused and

then denied satisfaction, so she had gathered from Polly the vicarage laundry maid's cheerfully robust chatter. So there was physical discomfort for Elliott to add to the realisation that he had married a woman who could not even be relied upon to do her marital duty.

I cannot bear this, Bella thought. She sat up and looked at the closed door. *Sooner or later we must talk. After all, he knows now how useless I am in bed. I must get it over now.*

'Damn and blast and bloody hell!' Elliott belted his robe, stalked across his bedchamber and splashed brandy into a glass. Arabella had been ready for him, her body had shown that. She had finally responded to his lovemaking with a sensuality that had surprised and delighted him—and then she had become stiff as a board and started weeping. He added a few more choice epitaphs and swallowed a mouthful of fine French spirit as though it were cheap ale.

She was *trying so hard*. Her words jabbed into his brain like hot pins. He had almost forced himself on her. And he had been angry with her. Called her *Lady Hadleigh* in that cold, hard voice. *Damn.* He had made a mull of this and it was not going to be easy to make it better, restore her confidence in him. Why couldn't he have married a trusting little virgin who would be easy to tutor, or a widow who knew what she was doing? *Because this is your duty*, his conscience told him. He had not chosen this wife, but she was the one he had and he must make the best of it.

Elliott went back to the door and leaned against it,

listening for the sound of sobs. But it was too well made for sound to carry. And what if she *was* in there, weeping her heart out? She would not welcome attempts at comfort from him, of all people.

Against his shoulder the panels moved. Startled, he looked down and saw the handle turn. He stepped back as the door swung open. 'Please, Elliott,' Arabella said, standing shivering in her flimsy scrap of a négligé. 'Please do it.'

'Do it?' He must be gaping like an idiot. Elliott took her hand and drew her into the room, closed the door and snatched up a blanket that was draped over the back of a chair. 'Here, you are cold.' He tried to wrap it around her shoulders, but she wriggled free, walked to his bed, threw off the négligé then climbed on to the wide expanse of green satin and lay down.

'Elliott, I am determined. I must accustom myself and learn. Please—' She gave a gasp as her head met the pillow and she looked up at the mirrored underside of the canopy. 'That is indecent!'

'*I* didn't put it there,' Elliott said, goaded. 'Arabella, I am not going to *do it* with you on the verge of tears and lying on the bed like a virgin sacrifice in some pagan temple.'

'It is my duty,' she said. 'And—'

'Well, you certainly know how to reduce a man to the state where he couldn't if he wanted to,' he interjected bitterly, aware of his aching erection subsiding in discouragement.

'*Please*, Elliott, let me say this,' Arabella said with a desperate earnestness that cut through his own preoccupations and silenced him. 'I know I am a coward. It will hurt, I expect that, but it was a little better last time. And the more I think about it, the worse it is going to be. So, really, I would much rather you just did it again now. I will get accustomed, honestly I will.'

'Hurt?' He stared at her, then picked up the blanket and laid it over her cold white body. The brandy was still on the nightstand. He took another swallow, handed her the glass and sat down on the end of the bed. 'Drink. Arabella, were you so stiff because you expected it to be very painful? Is that why you were crying? Did I hurt you on our wedding night?'

'Yes, but it was not your fault.' She sat up, dragging the blanket to cover her breasts. 'I am such a coward. I knew it would hurt. It was just that the first time…I hadn't expected it to be so bad, you see. And so much blood was frightening.'

Dear God. Elliott closed his eyes. *You selfish, randy, thoughtless swine, Rafe. A notch on your bedpost, that is all this girl was to you. A virgin and you brutalised her for sport as though she was a hardened whore, left her torn and pregnant.* Had he damaged her permanently?

'Have you healed?' he asked gently when he managed to open his eyes with some confidence that the blazing anger would not show in them.

'Yes,' she said. 'I did. I am fine now, truly, Elliott.' The wide hazel eyes fixed on him, determined, and, through the fear, trusting. 'It really was not so bad the other night.'

If Rafe had come back to life and walked through the door at that moment, Elliott realised, he would have punched him on the jaw. 'Not tonight,' he said, making up his mind. 'You are cold and upset. I am…tired. But I promise you that next time it will not hurt. Not at all. And you will enjoy it.'

'Enjoy it?' She looked so bemused by the concept that he almost laughed.

'You have my word.'

'But you do not understand.' She bit her lip, then took a deep breath. 'You see, even before he…before I was expecting it to hurt, I was no good. I am clumsy, you see. Inept. Probably frigid.'

'*What?*'

'I am very sorry. I am trying, but it is difficult, knowing that whatever I do you will be disappointed. I expect you had a mistress who was very skilled and beautiful—that's why I wouldn't mind if you went back to her.' He saw her throat move convulsively as she swallowed. 'Well, no, I *would* mind, but I know it is my fault so I would never reproach you.'

'Who told you that about yourself? Rafe, of course.' The anger became a red haze, then he saw the look in her eyes and made himself be calm.

Bella saw the fury in Elliott's eyes subside and drew in a shuddering breath. She must not cry, that would only make him angry again. She had told him, confessed to her failure as a wife and now he had the worst confirmed. No, not quite that—soon she would be as big as a whale, even clumsier. He had been kind about her looks, but then he was a kind man and had been trying to put her at her ease.

'Arabella,' Elliott said, 'Rafe was selfish, grasping and insensitive. He set out to seduce you with every intention of abandoning you, right from the first. He did not care about you, not one iota. When he had what he wanted, the last thing he needed was a woman who thought herself in love, who expected things from him, who clung. And the easiest way to prevent that was to be as cruel as possible, to hurt your heart and your mind as he had already hurt your body by his heedlessness.'

'He was lying?' But Rafe had lost his temper with her—could that have been feigned?

'Yes. That is what Rafe did. I do not. I will not lie to you, Arabella. You are not a classical beauty, but I think you lovely, graceful and charming. I desire you. When I tell you that you must believe me or call me a liar.'

'Oh.' *Lovely?* 'I believe you, Elliott.' The truth was in his eyes. 'But—'

'You were a virgin. Of course you had no idea what to do, how it would be—how it should have been. It was up to him to be gentle, to be thoughtful, to show you with patience what your body needed and how you could please him too.'

'I should not have known instinctively, then?'

'No, of course not. Your body knows some things, but your mind does not. Can you swim?'

'Yes. Mama taught us in the millpond, long ago.' *When Papa had been away one long hot summer. Mama and Meg and little Lina...*

'Did it take a little while to learn?'

'Of course.'

'And what would have happened if she had grabbed you and thrown you into deep water?'

'I would have panicked, flailed around and

drowned, I suppose. Elliott, do you mean that making love is the same?'

'Yes.' He leaned back against the bedpost, careful not to touch her, she realised. 'Just the same.'

The relief was incredible. It had not been her at all. The concept that she might be able to please her husband, that making love was something that might give her pleasure, was breathtaking. 'So, kissing is like paddling close to the shore?'

'It can be. It can be like diving into deep water, too. Arabella, we can take all the time you need to learn. All I ask is that you are honest with me and tell me how you feel.'

'Could we start now?' she asked, greatly daring. 'Can I try to make love to you?'

'Yes.' It sounded as though he was having trouble breathing.

Before she could think about it too much Bella wriggled out of her nest of blankets and down to the end of the bed. 'Then you must take off your dressing gown.'

'You do it.' That was daunting. Bella tugged at the knot, then pushed the robe back over his broad shoulders. 'Would you like me to lie down?' Elliott enquired, the corner of his mouth twitching.

'Yes, please.' He was teasing her a little, but he was not laughing at her. Confronted by six foot and several inches of large naked man, Bella wondered where she was supposed to start. The top seemed safest and she knew that kissing was something she could do.

She lay down along Elliott's right side, put a tentative hand on his shoulder and leaned across to kiss him on the mouth. It was disconcerting to be on top and to feel the heat of his body below hers, the spring of hair tickling her breasts, but it also felt safe not to be trapped under a man's weight. Elliott had kissed her neck, her shoulder; perhaps he would like it if she did the same to him.

Bella let her mouth roam and discovered that he tasted good, smelt better and that there was a pleasure to be had in the feel of satin skin over hard muscle. Elliott appeared to like what she was doing too, until her hand carelessly brushed his nipple. Instantly it hardened under the palm. 'Oh. I'm sorry—'

'Don't be,' he said, touching her in the same way. 'You see? You could use your mouth,' he suggested.

Breathless, she slid lower, licking and kissing. How odd that to pleasure him—and the way his body tensed told her that she was doing that—gave her pleasure too. Her breasts felt swollen and acutely sensitive as they moved against Elliott's body and she felt a growing ache of pleasurable need low in her belly.

Now she was lower down his body her left hand, the one that was not pressed against his heart, was lower too. It brushed coarse hair, then hot hard flesh and Bella froze. Elliott simply took her hand in his and curled it around his erection. 'Hold tight,' he said, the lightness in his tone suddenly changing as she took him at his word. 'Ah, *yes*. Arabella…'

She looked up. His eyes were closed, his head thrown back on the pillow as if he was in pain, but the low growl that came from his throat was one of pleasure and when she let him show her how to move her hand it became a gasp.

I am touching my husband and he is enjoying it. I am not inept, not clumsy. It felt so good, so right, but she had no idea what to do next. 'Elliott?'

He opened his eyes and looked at her, the deep blue almost black, the lids hooded, his lips slightly parted. For a long moment they looked into each other's eyes and then he rolled, taking her with him until she lay beneath him. 'Slowly, this time,' Elliott murmured and began to enter her.

It was slow, and for the first time Bella discovered that there was pleasure, that her body would open to caress his and that she could move to find the right angle to cradle him. And then, mysteriously, it was too slow and she wanted him, wanted that hard, possessive thrust. 'Elliott, please?'

The dark eyes smiled into hers as he moved, took her fully, and set up a rhythm that rocked her up, up into a place that was full of sensation, tension, aching need. She felt his hand slide between their bodies and touch her and the tight knot unravelled into sensation so acute that everything went black, she lost herself and fell.

And Elliott caught her and she felt him cry out and go rigid and then there was peace.

Bella found herself again, tucked against Elliott's side, her cheek on his shoulder, his arm around her.

'Arabella?'

'Mmm?'

'Do you need me to tell you that you have pleased your husband?' She could not see his face, but she could hear he was smiling.

'I do not think so,' she said, her own smile ending in a kiss against the smooth skin below his collar bone.

'Would you like to go back to your own room?'

Oh. No, I would not. I want to stay here with you and perhaps… But it was not fashionable for wives and husbands to share a bedchamber and no doubt Elliott wanted his privacy and his rest now. After all, what had been a miracle for her was simply what he would expect as the minimum from a lover. He had been very patient with her.

'Thank you, I think I would.' Bella made her voice as polite and distant as she could. She must not spoil all that had been gained tonight by seeming needy or clinging.

Elliott was still for a moment, then he got up, lifted her in his arms and carried her through to her own bed.

'Goodnight, my dear,' he said as he bent and kissed her, and was gone.

Chapter Fifteen

⟨ornament⟩

Elliott built on the lessons of that revelatory night during the next week. There were kisses when he came upon her alone, on the mouth, the hand, the nape of her neck if he surprised her, and at night long, passionate kisses when he came to her room and showed her how to listen to her own body and to read his. But he left her afterwards alone in her bed. She wished he would stay so that perhaps they could talk, relaxed and intimate together. She could tell him her feelings and perhaps he would reveal more about his hopes and fears and plans. But viscountesses did not hang upon their husbands' sleeves and expect to behave as though they were partners in a love match.

And it was wrong and ungrateful to expect more than Elliott had already given her.

'My lady?' Gwen asked, her hand with the hair-brush suspended as she saw the expression on Bella's face in the glass.

'Oh, nothing. Just a foolish thought about something

I have no courage to do. I will go out and visit tenants today again, so my walking dress, if you please.'

The visiting was going well, she thought as she sat in the gig, one of the grooms at the reins and Gwen beside her. She would like to learn to drive, but Elliott would not hear of it, not while she was pregnant. And even on the estate she must take Gwen as well as the groom.

'You are mollycoddling me,' she had said, trying for a light tone, hoping he might say that he would come and drive her himself so they could be alone and she could watch him at work.

'I am trying to look after you,' was all he would say before he strode off. Breakfasts were becoming increasingly precious. Dinners were formal, just the two of them. More lessons in conversation, table manners, formality that continued into the evening and careful discussions of neutral topics over the tea tray, with the pulsing awareness of the bedrooms upstairs always at the back of her mind. And then the wonder of lovemaking and the lonely comfort of a luxurious bed.

'Mrs Trubshaw's, my lady,' the groom said, pulling up in front of a cottage with a sagging roof and an overgrown garden. 'You said you wanted to start here today.'

'Thank you, John.' Bella got down and made herself think about something she did have some control over. Mrs Fanshawe had told her all about the Trubshaws. Father had run off when pursued by the gamekeepers for poaching and had not been seen for seven months, the eldest daughter had a wasted leg and could only get around on a crutch, the son was rapidly heading along

188 Vicar's Daughter to Viscount's Lady

the same path to crime as his father and Mrs Trubshaw was pregnant with the baby due at any moment.

'A challenge, this household,' she murmured to Gwen, who was carrying the basket Bella had packed that morning. Cheese, bacon, butter, some clothing, baby blankets and money should all help, but only in the short term.

The boy answered the door, dragging it open and staring sullenly at the visitors. 'Good morning. Is your mother at home?'

'Aye. My lady,' he added as Gwen raised a hand to cuff him. Bella took a deep breath of fresh air and walked into the smelly, stuffy cottage.

'That is a list of the repairs that I can see, so far.' Arabella pushed the paper across the desk to Elliott. 'I've been to the cottages where Mrs Fanshawe said the family's need was greatest, so I may not have seen the worst of the buildings yet.'

Elliott picked up the list and studied it. Not only were faults listed, but often their cause. *Damp walls with plaster peeling: dense shrubbery too close and broken guttering*, he read against one entry. 'You would appear to know what you are talking about,' he commented. 'I will get Turner on to these repairs at once.'

'It is merely a matter of observation,' Arabella said. He could tell she was nervous of his reaction; her hazel eyes were fixed on his with too much concentration. He had hoped, now that their lovemaking was pleasurable and relaxed, that she would relax with him during the day also, but somehow, with those fears laid at rest, she was more, not less, distant. It was as well; this was exactly the kind of companionable, undemanding marriage he could expect from a wife who had been raised for it. 'And here is the list of men and boys wanting work.'

'I'm thinking of re-laying the carriage drive and there is almost half a mile of wall needing repair, so I should be able to give most of them some labouring, if nothing else.' Elliott took the second piece of paper, reached to put it on another pile then focused on one name. 'Young Trubshaw?'

'He is only thirteen,' Arabella said. 'With his father gone he needs to be working, not hanging around getting into trouble.'

'He does that. I'm not sure about him. Are you a soft touch for a pair of big brown eyes and an air of spurious innocence, Arabella?' Her earnest look made him want to go around the desk and kiss her.

'Willie Trubshaw looks about as innocent as a weasel,' she said, making him laugh. 'And I prefer blue eyes,' she muttered.

'Are you, by any chance, flirting with me, Lady Hadleigh?' Elliott enquired, keeping his tone light despite the way his breath hitched suddenly, inexplicably.

'I wouldn't know how,' she admitted with a candour that made him laugh. 'But I am certain you could teach me.'

'I don't think you need lessons, I think you have the instinct,' Elliott said, wondering if locking the study door and taking her here, now, on the hearthrug might not be thoroughly satisfactory. 'And you are blooming, my dear.'

And that was no lie. Her bosom was delightfully rounded, the colour was in her cheeks, her hair was glossy and the slight curve of her stomach was unexpectedly attractive. He glanced at the hearthrug, his whole body tightening in anticipation.

'Oh.' Now she looked apprehensive at what she must be able to see in his face. Elliott got a grip on his desire. This was no way for a sensible married man to behave, and his wife was not a lightskirt to be tumbled on the rug.

He glanced at the pile of letters and invitations on the corner of the desk. His friends were seeking his company, writing to congratulate him on his marriage, inviting the Hadleighs to stay, hinting that they would be only too delighted to make her ladyship's acquaintance.

Under normal circumstances, and with any other bride, he would have happily invited a houseful of them. After a couple of weeks of marriage he would have had no qualms about leaving for a day or two to attend a boxing match or a race either. But the thought of inflicting a houseful of sports-mad, fit, exuberant, sophisticated men on Arabella was ridiculous: she would be terrified of them. They would cheerfully flirt with her, which would alarm her, talk about people and places she had no knowledge of and fill the house with noise and activity when she ought to be resting.

Elliott shovelled the whole lot into a drawer. 'Just do not overdo it, my dear,' he said and she nodded, apparently meek. How relaxing life was now that he had a compliant wife, regular sex and he was getting a grip on the estate and Rafe's chaotic affairs. Why, then, did he feel that something was missing?

* * *

'I thought you might like it if we took the gig and a picnic and went and explored the estate today,' Elliott said at breakfast the next day. Bella looked up, startled, from thoughts about how successful her breakfast strategy had been. She had hardly dared hope she could lure him away from his study every morning, but the delights of a proper cooked breakfast did not seem to have palled on her husband yet. If she could just get him into the habit, she thought, he would begin every day with a proper meal. Men were, in her limited experience, creatures of habit. Perhaps one could train a husband? Her mouth twitched at the thought of trying to tame Elliott.

The pointers had taken up their positions on either side of the fireplace and Toby was sitting on her toes, quivering with eagerness for a titbit. Bella surveyed the room with satisfaction: this was what a marital breakfast should look like. Even her wretched morning sickness seemed to have subsided and it was no longer a matter of willpower to remain in the same room with so much savoury food. *Almost thirteen weeks*, she thought. Her back ached a little and she was sure that at any moment her condition would become obvious to anyone who looked.

'A picnic? I should like that very much.' He smiled at her and she smiled back, a warm, happy sensation that she could not quite put a name to settling around her heart. She loved that smile—lazy and assured and intimate. He really was the most dreadful flirt when he put his mind to it, she thought fondly. Elliott was being so good to her. The odd mood she had sensed in the nursery had not come back, he appeared to be satisfied with her in bed and his teasing kisses kept her in a state of quivering anticipation. She must continue to study to please him; he would not regret his honourable action if she could possibly prevent it.

'I know a very secluded spot,' Elliott began, something warm and heavy in his voice that had her looking at him in wild speculation. He couldn't mean to make love to her *outside*, could he?

'The post, my lord,' Henlow said, proffering a salver laden with envelopes. 'And yesterday's *Times* and *Morning Post*.' He placed a much smaller pile of envelopes beside Bella's plate. 'For you, my lady.'

'For me?' Who would be writing to her here? *Papa.* 'Thank you, Henlow.' She sat regarding the post warily. Her day had hardly started and now she must read her father's justified reproaches. Doubtless he would have disowned her. Bella turned over the top letter, then another and another until she had reached the bottom. She recognised the handwriting on none of them. The relief was intense.

But who were they from? The wax splintered as she opened the first. Madame Mirabelle, *Exclusive Ladies' Milliner of Worcester*, begged the Viscountess of Hadleigh would forgive her presumption in writing to felicitate her ladyship upon her nuptials and entreated her ladyship to summon her to attend upon her at any time with a selection of hats the equal of any to be found in London's Bond Street.

The next was from George Arnold, *Shoe and Boot*

Maker to the Nobility and Clergy, also soliciting the favour of her ladyship's attention. Then there was a haberdashery store, a portrait painter and a furniture warehouse.

Bemused by the notion that her spending power was great enough to attract so much interest, Bella set them to one side and picked up another with a London frank. The one under it was similarly stamped. 'London? I do not know anyone in London.'

'That will be my paternal aunts, Lady Fingest and Mrs Grahame, writing in response to my letters to them,' Elliott said, glancing up from his own post.

Bella opened the first. Lady Fingest expressed herself delighted that her nephew had married and extended an invitation to visit at the earliest opportunity. Her bride gift was on its way and she did trust dear Arabella would find it of use. The second, from her sister, was in similar vein.

'They do not sound at all distressed that you have married a nobody,' she said to Elliott.

'I told them that you were a daughter of the church and a paragon of virtue. I have no doubt that they are so delighted that I am settling down respectably that the fact they have never heard of your parents is a mere detail.'

'But I'm not a paragon,' Bella said miserably after a swift glance round to make sure all the footmen were out of the room. 'The baby—'

'Which is another reason why we are not going up to Town until February. We can but hope that he is a small baby and can appear convincingly premature after an interval of a couple of months. People will do the sums, but by then it will be old news.'

'But Lady Abbotsbury will know and tell them.'

'I am sure she knows—there is nothing wrong with her eyesight or her ability to add up. I expect to get a stiff lecture and then to be forgiven. She likes you—she will not want to damage your reputation with the family.'

Reassured, Bella turned to the last letter. 'It is from Mrs Baynton in response to your invitation for next Wednesday. She says they will be delighted. I am so—'

'Hell's teeth!' Elliott flung a sheet of heavy, embossed writing paper down on the table, narrowly missing the marmalade. Bella craned to see it; there was an embossed crest with what looked like a mitre and crossed crosiers. 'Your father has written to the bishop, complaining that I have seduced you away from your home and duty and demanding that he annul the marriage forthwith.'

'He cannot! Can he?' Bella gasped. Twinges of pain shot across her stomach and she flattened her hand to it. 'Elliott?'

'No, of course he cannot. There are no grounds. You were single, of age and of sound mind. We told no lies in obtaining the licence. The bishop expresses himself quite satisfied with our application. However, he wants to talk to me—presumably he is not happy to have an incumbent from another diocese threatening scandal.'

'I am so sorry.' She gazed at him, aghast. 'I never dreamt Papa would do anything but disown me.'

'He has lost his unpaid housekeeper, has he not? And you are out of range—this is the only way to punish you,' Elliott said. 'I will go to Worcester today; Bishop Huntingford invites me to stay until Monday.'

'So long?' She felt bereft. And guilty. So much for being a suitable viscountess.

'I can hardly march in, insist he fits this into his doubtless extremely busy schedule and then bolt back here. If I stay for Saturday he will not want me to travel on a Sunday, so that will make it Monday. But it will give me the opportunity for a discreet word about your father—we will be able to nip any scandal in the bud, do not fret, Bella.'

'What if Papa complains to his own bishop?'

'Then he will write to Huntingford who will reassure him—all the more reason for me to put some effort into it now. I am sure your bishop is only too well aware of the foibles of his own clergy.'

'Yes, I suppose he must be. Oh!' The cramp clenched at her belly again. 'Elliott—'

'What is it?' He was on his knees beside the chair, one arm around her. 'The baby?'

'I don't know. Cramping pains. Not severe,' she said, trying not to panic. 'Twinges under the skin. But I have never felt anything like it before.'

Elliott got to his feet and yanked the bell cord. 'Henlow, send a groom for Dr Hamilton immediately. Tell him it is urgent. He's a good man,' he said, turning back to her.

'I am sure he is.' Bella did her best to smile. 'I will just go up to my sitting room.'

'You will go to bed.' Elliott scooped her out of her chair and carried her across the room. 'We will say you pulled a muscle by standing awkwardly just now. All right? I will tell Hamilton to say nothing that might give the staff any other impression.'

'Yes, Elliott. That would be best.' She laid her head on his shoulder and tried to keep calm while the fear clawed at her heart.

* * *

Elliott paced outside the door, cursing under his breath. He wasn't supposed to be doing this for another six months and here he was, thrown out of his own wife's bedchamber by Hamilton when Arabella needed him.

She had been so brave, only the painful grip on his fingers while she lay on the bed waiting for the doctor betrayed her agitation. 'It is not a bad pain,' she kept reassuring him, as though he were the one to be worried about. 'Only I have no idea whether I should expect it or not.'

Hamilton had come quickly, that was one mercy. If anything was wrong with the baby Arabella would be bereft and he couldn't do a damn thing to help her. He felt frustrated, helpless and angry. Damn Rafe. If he hadn't seduced Arabella she would be blamelessly at home in Suffolk, he would be engaged to Freddie and in control of his life and not pacing…

'My lord?' Dr Hamilton came out smiling and Elliott released the breath he had held from the moment he saw the door handle begin to turn. 'All quite normal and nothing to be alarmed about. It is a pity Lady Hadleigh has no female friends or relatives to confide in.'

'Yes,' he agreed. 'I am as ignorant on the subject as she is. However, I hope Mrs Baynton and she will form a friendship. I am sorry I had you over here on a wild goose chase, Hamilton.'

'Not at all. As well to be safe, not sorry, my lord. Your wife is in excellent health, I am glad to say. However, if you would like me to call every few weeks or so, I would be more than happy to do so.'

'Thank you.' With Anne Baynton and Dr Hamilton both aware of Arabella's secret she should worry less, he was sure. 'I will be happier when we can abandon this pretence about the pregnancy,' he added.

Hamilton nodded. 'It will start to show in about another week,' he said. 'Perhaps if I call in a fortnight, just to check things out?'

'Thank you,' Elliott said, shaking hands. 'I must confess to finding this a somewhat unnerving experience.'

'Oh, it gets better after the third one,' the doctor said, still obviously amused by Elliott's nerves. 'I'll show myself out, my lord.'

Elliott went to open the door into Arabella's room and stopped, his hand on the handle. All he had cared about, he realised, was Arabella. He had not worried about the child, only the effect it would have on her if she lost it. The treacherous thought had even flashed into his mind that if she did miscarry, then they could have another. *His* son. *What kind of wretch does that make me?* he wondered, resisting the impulse to kick the door panel out of sheer self-disgust. The child she was carrying was his blood, his nephew—somehow he was convinced it was a boy—he should be prepared to do whatever it took to keep it safe.

It was his duty. Elliott fixed a smile on his lips and opened the door. *Duty. And what a cold word that is.*

Arabella was sitting up in bed, looking relaxed, and he felt his smile relax, too, into something almost genuine. She was such a trouble to him, yet he could not resent her.

'I am so sorry to cause a fuss,' she apologised.

'Doctor Hamilton was very kind and explained that it was quite normal to have those little cramping pains at this time. He says it is my body adjusting itself to the growing baby.'

'You were not to know, it must have been alarming.' Elliott sat on the edge of the bed and held her hand. 'And now you had better stay in bed for the rest of the day, nursing your fictitious bad back.'

'I suppose I had,' she agreed ruefully. 'I will plan what to do with the decoration of this room. I have to admit to becoming very weary of pink and frills, which, when you consider that at the vicarage I had a room half the size of my dressing room here, with faded chintz curtains and a rag rug on the floor, is very ungrateful of me.' Her mouth thinned as she looked around. 'I suppose Rafe had a very conventional view of female tastes.'

'Of some female tastes, certainly,' Elliott said drily.

'That is true.' He saw her give herself a little shake as though to push away an unpleasant memory. Then she frowned; obviously another troubling thought had arrived. Elliott made a conscious effort not to frown too. This marriage business, this being aware of another person's feelings and moods and fears all the time, was unsettling. He had not realised how much a wife would take over his thoughts.

'I wonder how Papa is managing without me,' Arabella said.

'Doubtless he will hire a housekeeper. He will be able to select one to suit his temperament.'

Arabella chuckled. 'How very gloomy.' Elliott

watched her face as sadness took her again. He wanted to make it go away, but couldn't think how to. 'He wasn't always like this, you know. When we were little he was pious, of course, and quite strict, but there was laughter. I can remember flowers in the house and Mama singing and reading books that I am certain were not volumes of sermons.'

'What happened?'

'She died. She went to visit her sister in London quite unexpectedly, for I can recall Papa was out and when he came back and she had gone he was furious. And then, a few weeks later, he told us she was dead of a fever.' She frowned. 'That must be the aunt Lina ran away to—she had found a letter from her, but all that was left in Lina's room was the torn bottom edge. Her name was Clara.' Arabella bit her lip, deep in memory. 'Mama said she would send for us to visit our aunt, too, so we must not cry. And there was a carriage outside, but I do not know who was in it.'

'And your mother's body was returned home. What a terrible thing for three little girls,' Elliott said, a suspicion beginning to grow in his mind.

'No. That was so sad too. Papa told us she had been buried in London. I do not even know where her grave is.'

'And it was after that your father became stricter, obsessed with sin, especially female sin?'

'Yes. I suppose her death made him…strange. The responsibility of bringing up three motherless daughters, perhaps.'

'Or three daughters whose mother had run off with

another man?' Elliott suggested, thinking aloud and not watching his words.

'Run off?' Arabella pressed one hand to her mouth as though to shut off the words. 'Mama left him? Oh, no!'

Chapter Sixteen

∼∽∿∼∽∿∼

The words were out now, he could not take them back. 'I think she must have run away, don't you? I imagine you never thought to consider the evidence as an adult, but she left when he was out, there was a carriage waiting for her. If that was your aunt, why not come in and see her nieces? Why leave when your father was away from home and promise that she would send for you? Why did your grief-stricken father not want her body returned home?'

'But she never sent for us,' Arabella protested. 'And she would have done.'

'How do you know? Would he have let you go to her and another man, do you think? How old were you?'

'Seven,' she murmured. 'No, you are right. I would never have known if she had tried to make contact. Like Meg and Lina now—I am certain they will have written and that he destroyed the letters.

'He kept us close, I remember that. It seemed an age before we were allowed to go out without Cousin

Harriet: she lived with us until I was seventeen.' She stared at him, eyes wide. 'Oh, poor Mama. She must have been desperate to have left us.'

Elliott caught her hands, which were clenched in the bedclothes, and stroked until the stiff fingers relaxed into his.

'How could she bear to leave her own children?' she wondered and she put her own hand, bringing his with it, to lie over her belly.

Shaken by the emotion he could feel coursing through her, Elliott made himself keep still. 'I am sorry, Arabella. I should have thought before speculating aloud. I did not mean to upset you.' And upset her he had—her expression was tragic. 'She must have been desperate, I agree. And she thought you would be able to join her later.'

'Mmm.' She nodded, deep in thought. 'How will I tell Meg and Lina? If I ever find them. Oh, Elliott, I do miss them so.'

'Ah, Arabella.' Elliott pulled her into his arms and she clung while he rubbed her back gently, wondering how he could ever make this right for her.

'I will check the Army List while I am in Gloucester,' he promised. 'The local militia headquarters will have the current edition. We can find where Meg's husband is based.'

'Oh, thank you. His name is James Halgate. I don't know which regiment he is in, but he went to the Peninsula, I know that.' She emerged, tousled, her nose pink, her eyes wet. Elliott was surprised to find himself still sitting there; the prospect of any woman weeping on his shoulder would have sent him running just a few weeks ago. Arabella took in a big, shuddering breath. 'I'm sorry, I am making such a lot of work and worry for you.' Elliott shook his head in denial. She was indeed a worry, but he wanted to help her. He wanted his wife to be happy.

'And now two of us have run off with men and the third has gone and Papa suspects there must be a man involved there too. How right he has always been about us,' she said with an attempt at lightness that made his heart contract with sympathy. 'No wonder he is writing intemperate letters; he must be beside himself.'

Elliott thought of the plan he had conceived of asking his new father-in-law to stay at Hadleigh Old Hall, once his initial fury had subsided. Now, however he might pity the man, he was not going to allow him anywhere near Arabella. His wife's desertion had obviously made a domestic tyrant out of a strict father; the loss of all three daughters could well have unhinged him.

'May I be frank with Bishop Huntingford? I think it might help head off any future problems if he understands that your father is not entirely rational on some subjects.'

'I suppose so—so long as it would not get back to his own bishop. I would not want his living to be in any danger. I have had no letter from him myself. I am not surprised, I confess.'

Bless her, Elliott thought, squeezing her hand. *The man makes her life a misery and she still worries for him.* What a very warped model she had of men and how low her expectations must be. She seemed to be learning to trust him—but what would she think if she realised how he was increasingly feeling about the child she carried? 'Of course, I will ask for his assurance of strictest confidentiality before I say anything.' He got up and walked to the door.

'Thank you,' Arabella said, her smile making something inside him twist with guilt. 'You look after me so well, Elliott. I feel safe with you.'

'I will see you later,' he said from the doorway. 'I'll tell Gwen to make sure you rest.'

The day passed surprisingly quickly, Bella found. The morning she spent deep in thought, trying to recall every nuance, every clue of the days and months before and after her mother's departure. Elliott's interpretation made more sense, the more she thought of it. She could vaguely recall the arguments, her mother weeping at night. Her eyes had been red when she hugged them goodbye. *How miserable she must have been to have left us,* Bella thought, her hand straying to stroke gently over her own child. *And who was the man?* Perhaps Mama was still alive somewhere. But instinct told her not. It was hard not knowing. Harder than believing Mama had died all those years ago. That had been a tragedy, but now, from the vantage point of her own bitter experience, her heart bled for her mother's unhappiness and desperation.

If only she could talk to Meg and Lina about this. If only she could be certain they were safe. Bella closed her eyes, mourning her mother all over again, imagining her, for the first time, as a young woman in love and bitterly unhappy. Who was she to judge her after what she had done herself?

She felt strangely better after that and sent Gwen for paper and pencil so she could lie in bed making lists of things to be done to redecorate her suite and the nursery. And Elliott's rooms—was he content to simply walk into the chambers his brother had occupied?

'Have you used every sheet of paper in the house?' Bella looked up and realised that the bed was strewn with lists and sketches. Her husband was standing in the doorway, his shoulder against the frame, his coat hooked on one finger over his shoulder. His shirt was open at the neck, rolled up to his elbows and filthy. His hair was in his eyes and there was a long graze up the length of his right forearm. He looked utterly male and quite breathtakingly virile.

Bella swallowed hard. 'What on earth have you been doing?' She tried to sound like any wife confronted by a filthy, sweaty man who had wrecked his clothes and who had arrived home late for dinner and in dire need of a bath. But she could not feel anything but shamefully aroused by the sight.

'We're building a new sawpit.' Elliott sauntered into the room, shedding sawdust as he came and bringing with him an intoxicating scent of resin and fresh sweat. Any proper lady would shriek and order him from the room—Bella wanted to strip all his clothes off.

'And I suppose *we* is the royal *we*, and means quite literally that you are involved,' she said severely. 'You have men to do such things, surely?'

'I enjoy it,' Elliott said, unrepentant.

'And I suppose it was necessary for you to try it

out from *inside* the pit,' she said with a sigh. 'Look at the floor.'

He regarded the trail of sawdust. 'It is good for cleaning the carpet.'

'That is damp tea leaves, not sawdust. Do *not* sit on the bed!'

Elliott grinned, leaned down and kissed her. 'How are you now? Any more cramps and twinges?'

'A few, but, now I know it is only to be expected, they are not so bad. I was just worried about the baby.'

'I know you were.'

'Looking at you now, I can only hope it is a boy. The pair of you would have such fun together.'

His face clouded, then he smiled, leaned in and kissed her again, hard and fast, before he straightened up and made for his dressing room, much to her regret. 'I am not fit for respectable company. I will go and bathe and take dinner up here, shall I? You can have yours in bed and tell me what you have been getting up to all day.'

'Plans for my rooms and the nursery,' Bella admitted, part of her mind troubled by that sudden chill in his expression. 'Elliott, how much may I spend?'

'As much as you wish.' He paused at the door, the smile gone again.

'But you said there were many things wrong with the house and the estate. I do not want to spend money on inessentials.'

'There are many things to put right.' For a moment Elliott looked almost grim, then the smile was back. 'But nothing so dire it will condemn you to pink frills.'

'Thank you. Elliott—will you get me some fabric

patterns in Worcester if I tell you what colours I am looking for?'

With a groan he vanished into his dressing room and his voice drifted back to her. 'Bishops and silk warehouses. No one warned me marriage would be such a trial.'

There was the sound of Franklin, his valet, asking a question and Elliott laughing in response, then the door closed behind him, leaving Bella prey to disturbing imaginings of bath tubs and Elliott's hard-muscled body dripping with water.

When her husband returned clean and elegant in evening dress, Bella was almost disappointed. And uneasily confused by her own responses. She was married to Elliott, she was trying to be a dutiful wife. And yet—what she felt for Elliott was not dutiful. She had a lowering suspicion that it was, in fact, lust, plain and simple.

Elliott wanted her to enjoy their lovemaking, but a decent married woman was not supposed to take such pleasure in sex, was she? And certainly not with a man she did not love, however much she liked and respected him. Giving her pleasure seemed important to Elliott. She suspected he would think less of himself if he did not. But did her growing enthusiasm make him respect her more, or less? *Is he going to stay tonight*? she wondered as he directed the footmen to set up a table for him by her bed and organised her own tray.

They spoke of sawpits and farm improvements, colour schemes and fabric swatches, the Bayntons' visit and whether the new blend of coffee was entirely to

Elliott's taste. Bella found herself relaxing, confident that she could contribute something on all these subjects, even if it was only by asking questions and giving encouragement when Elliott spoke of the estate matters.

Dinner was good and the glass of claret he coaxed her to drink, smooth and full. By the time he lifted her tray away and rang for the dishes to be cleared she was hiding a yawn behind her hand.

Or, trying to hide it. Not a lot escaped Elliott's eye, as she was beginning to discover. 'You are tired, I will leave you to sleep.'

'No! I mean, how can I be tired? I have done nothing all day,' she protested.

'You had a scare, a revelation about your mother that can only have been emotionally draining, you have been working hard, even if you have been lying in bed, and now you have eaten a very good dinner. I am surprised you are not asleep already.' He was on his feet and not, she realised, in order to take his clothes off and join her in bed.

'You aren't coming to bed with me?' She knew she was blushing, yet she still found the courage to ask because the disappointment was intense.

'I want your full attention when we are in bed together, and for you to be very much awake,' Elliott said, his eyes darkly intense as he looked at her. 'I will be gone early tomorrow.' He came and ran the back of his hand down her cheek, making her shiver. 'I will see you Monday afternoon, assuming I am not trapped in the drapers' and the upholsterers' shops. Sleep well, Arabella.'

* * *

On Saturday Bella realised that not only was she thirteen weeks pregnant but it was finally beginning to show in more than her mood or the state of her insides. Her waist was definitely thickening and her stomach was more rounded she discovered as Gwen tugged on her corset strings.

'Not too tight, please, Gwen.'

'Yes, my lady. With your back it's best to be careful.'

Had she guessed? It was going to be impossible to keep the secret for much longer, not from a bright young woman in such a close relationship with her. Oh well, all the staff and most of the neighbourhood would know soon enough that the new Lady Hadleigh had anticipated her marriage vows. Would they think of Elliott admiringly as a bit of a dog or would they disapprove, look down on him because of her folly?

But there was nothing she could do about it except be a model viscountess. Today, Bella resolved, she would talk to Cook about the meals to be served when the Bayntons came to visit. It would be wonderful to have another woman to talk to. Bella found she was missing Lina and Meg in ways she had never imagined.

But Cook and Mrs Knight seemed more than capable of looking after the arrangements and Bella felt rather at a loose end. She should have asked Elliott which of the remaining tenants he wished her to call on as a priority.

But she could call at the Dower House and thank Lady Abbotsbury and Miss Dorothy for their hospitality. And she could take flowers, if she could find any. The lawns around the house were bare of ornamental beds.

'Is there a flower garden, Henlow?' she asked the butler who was supervising two footmen as they moved a vast and ugly epergne that Elliott had banished from the dining room.

'Of sorts, my lady. It is not what it was in his lordship's mother's day.' He opened the front door. 'Shall I show you, my lady?'

'Thank you, but I will explore a little by myself. Just give me directions and tell me the head gardener's name.'

'Johnson, my lady. A cantankerous old man, I am sorry to say, but a good gardener. If you go left around the side of the house, follow the high brick wall along, there's a green door.'

Bella tied on one of her old straw bonnets and set out with Toby at her heels, trying to make herself believe that she was now mistress of all she could see. Mostly, on this side of the house, it appeared to consist of an overgrown shrubbery, expanses of rather lumpy lawn and trees that to her inexpert eye needed pruning. The long wall looked promising, she decided—surely it must shelter a walled garden?

The green door was unlocked and Bella opened it. The terrier shot through the gap as she peeped in. What wonders would it reveal?

'Vegetables,' she said flatly, knowing that as mistress of the house she should be pleased at the expanse of well-tended crops, the peach house, the cold frames and the orderly stacks of manure and compost.

'Aye, and good vegetables they do be and if that pesky dog digs up my asparagus bed again I'll take the rake to 'im.'

She turned and found a red-faced old man glowering at her. 'Good morning. You must be Johnson. I am Lady Hadleigh.' He grunted and made a move as though to lift his battered billycock hat. 'This is a most admirable vegetable garden and I look forward to seeing round it another day, but just now I am in need of some flowers for Lady Abbotsbury.'

'Had the flowerbeds all turfed over, 'e did,' the old man said dourly. 'Said it was a waste of money employing men to grow flowers. Can't eat 'em and the wages cost 'im.'

'What happened to the gardeners, then?' Bella asked. It was presumably Rafe this grumpy old man was referring to. How like him to sacrifice both beauty and other men's livelihoods to fund his own pleasures.

'Labouring they are now. Right waste of trained men, it is.'

'I will speak to his lordship.' Perhaps Elliott would think the wages justified. She hoped so; she did not like to think of hard-working men out of a job for no fault of their own. 'So there are no flowers at all?'

'There's the rose garden. I sees to that. Out of sight, out of mind, so 'e left it be.' He stomped off round the brick path without waiting to see if she was following him. Bella had heard that the head gardeners from big houses were a law unto themselves and even refused to let their mistresses cut flowers if it spoiled their borders, but this one amused her rather than offended. She liked his fierce defence of his domain and his concern for his men.

It was early for roses, but the shelter of the red-brick enclosure, and the care they had been given, had coaxed several bushes into flower and their scent filled the air.

She saw small glasshouses as well, which held the flowers that had been used for her wedding. There were plenty to pick for the ladies at the Dower House, and for the main house as well. One particularly vivid bush caught her eye, the blood-red petals almost throbbing with velvety passion. That was how she had always imagined love would look, she thought, rubbing one soft petal between fingers and thumb.

'This is beautiful,' she told Johnson and thought she detected a slight softening of his expression. 'They do you credit. I would like to pick some now—could you get me a knife and a basket?'

'I'll cut these, my lady, and bring them round. You'll not be wanting to get your hands scratched.'

Bella watched him, drinking in the perfume and the peace and the sounds of bird song. 'How many men do you need to get the gardens back to how they were in his lordship's mother's time?' she asked.

'Four more,' he said without hesitation. 'And a new heavy roller for the lawns.'

'I will see what I can do. But I cannot promise, his lordship has much to be seeing to.'

'Aye, 'e will have.' The old man laid a tight-furled rosebud carefully in the trug and pushed back his straw hat. 'Glad to 'ave 'im, we are. I recall when 'e were just a nipper. Good lad. Not like—' He recollected who he was speaking to and bit off the words.

'Speaking of lads,' Bella said, not wanting thoughts of Rafe to blight her day, 'have you any need for a gardener's boy? Because young Trubshaw needs some honest work.'

'That hellion?' Johnson scratched his head. 'Reckon I can work 'im 'ard enough to take his mind off mischief.'

'Thank you, Johnson,' Bella said with real gratitude. At least one of her worries was solved. She just wished all of them were so easily dealt with.

Chapter Seventeen

Next morning Bella drove to church after breakfast. Lady Abbotsbury's carriage pulled in behind hers as it set off, leaving Bella feeling rather shaken that the formidable dowager was yielding precedence to her. Was she ever going to get used to being a viscountess? And would she learn to behave in the manner Elliott should expect from her?

Another carriage was stopping just as the footman helped her down. Daniel strolled over, raising his tall hat. 'Good morning, Cousin Bella.'

'Good morning. It is delightful to see you, of course, but isn't this rather a long way from your home for morning service?' She accepted his proffered arm and, once Lady Abbotsbury and Miss Dorothy had descended and joined them, they walked towards the porch. Bella did her best to smile and nod and exchange greetings. Presumably most of the people hailing her had been at the wedding, but she could recall few of them.

'I knew Elliott was away from home so I thought I

should escort you,' he said. 'It is merely ten miles and a pleasant day.'

'But how did you know he was not at the Hall?'

'Oh, I saw him late yesterday in Worcester,' he said with a grin. 'He didn't see me, and I feared being dragged into the upholstery warehouse to give him moral support, so I cravenly hid, but I thought it unlikely that he would be home today.'

Daniel showed her to the family pew, helped the other ladies with their things, found the first hymn for everyone and generally made himself useful. 'There's the family chapel,' he murmured, nodding to where the top of several ornate monuments could be glimpsed over the high box pew. Bella did not turn her head to look.

Mr Fanshawe's sermon was well delivered and thought-provoking and helped her focus her mind on the prayers without thinking of the last church service she had attended with her father in the pulpit. At the end of the service the verger appeared to open her pew door for her and preceded the Hadleigh party down the aisle, making great play with his long, silver-topped verge. Bella fought an inclination to giggle at the thought that she, plain Miss Shelley, was receiving all this attention, but she had herself under control in time to shake hands with the vicar at the door.

'I wonder if I might call and ask Mrs Fanshawe's advice on where the greatest need is in the parish,' she said.

'How very thoughtful. My wife would be delighted. There is only so much we can do, you know. I am sure you will be a most beneficial influence in the parish,

Lady Hadleigh.' He smiled and moved on to the next parishioner in line.

'Do you want to see the family chapel while we are here?' Daniel asked. He seemed to take her silence for consent and steered her back into the church and down the side aisle. 'Here we are and that...' he gestured to where a large slab in the floor was highlighted by the lines of fresh mortar around its edge '...is the entrance to the vault.'

Bella took a deep breath. Whatever she did, she must not express any emotion. 'Where will the memorial tablet go, do you know?' she asked, reading some of the inscriptions she could decipher and which were not in Latin. There was a florid monument from 1707 with the viscount of the time depicted in Roman general's uniform that contrasted oddly with his full-bottomed wig and a charming table tomb with a fourteenth-century Calne and his wife, he with his hound and she with her lap dog at their feet.

'There, where the board has been set up, next to his parents' memorial.' Daniel pointed to a bare patch of wall where a rectangle of painted wood had been placed. When she came closer she saw it was a coat of arms.

Now she was here she was surprised to find how little emotion she felt. The man she thought she had loved had squandered his life, hurt many people, betrayed trust and his duty and now he was gone, leaving only Elliott, the brother he had spurned, to mourn his loss. Poor man, she thought, startled by the pity that overtook the hurt and anger that had been inside her. *So arrogant, so proud—did you sense that your brother is worth six of you? Why didn't I meet Elliott Calne first and fall in love with him? Or perhaps I have.*

The thought was so unexpected, so sudden, that she gasped and sat down in the nearest pew with a bump.

'Bella?' Daniel sat down too. 'Is something wrong?'

'I was thinking of Mama,' she lied. 'I do not know where she is buried and I wish I could leave flowers on her grave, visit it from time to time.' Using such an excuse stung her conscience. *Forgive me, Mama*, she thought. *I had to tell him something.*

'But you are thinking of her,' Daniel said. 'That is all that matters.'

'Yes, you are right, she is in my heart.' She took her handkerchief, a very pretty scrap of Swiss lace that Elliott had picked out for her when she had been buying her reticule, and dabbed her eyes, pretending tears.

Am I in love with him? It was too difficult a thought to come to terms with here, now, with Daniel, unwittingly tactless at her side.

'I am sorry to be such a watering pot,' she said with a smile. 'The monuments all look very handsome against the grey stone, I think. Will you come back for luncheon?'

'If it would be no trouble.' Daniel walked her back, handed her up into her carriage then followed in his. Bella regretted her polite invitation the moment she made it. Now, instead of the simple luncheon she had intended to eat on the terrace and the opportunity to try to come to terms with what she actually felt for her husband, she would have to sit inside in the small dining room and make conversation while Henlow and

at least one footman danced attendance. She just
wished Elliott would come home.

Elliott studied the stonemason's notes. The man was
right, he was almost certain. If the memorial slab was
made a little narrower and taller and the angles at the
top replaced with a wreath, then it would sit more har-
moniously next to his parents' monument. It would be
the work of a moment to look again at the chapel and
then he could get home and see Arabella, put her mind
at rest about the bishop before he broke the news about
her brother-in-law.

He wondered how she was and hoped she would
have sent for the doctor if she had felt unwell again. He
wondered, as the carriage drew up at the churchyard, if
she was thinking of him.

He strode down the aisle, hat in one hand, notes in
the other and into the Calne chapel, put down his hat on
a pew and studied the wall. Yes, he would write and order
the changes. His eye was caught by something close to
his foot, a scrap of white, and he bent to pick it up.

The very new, very pretty handkerchief embroidered
with lily of the valley in whitework was one of the set he
had given Arabella in Worcester. Arabella had been here.

She had sat here, amidst his ancestors, carrying the
child who could well carry on the line. She would be
hoping for a boy, he thought. It was the natural wish for
every wife with a title and an inheritance to secure for
her husband. It would not occur to Arabella that her
husband could be so dishonourable that he hated the
idea of her with his brother's son in her arms.

I hope she found peace here, Elliott thought as he took up his hat and strode out of the church, the heavy door closing with a bang behind him, *because it gave me none*.

'I'll walk,' he said to the coachman. 'Tell her ladyship I will be home after luncheon.' He strode off in the direction of the village before the man could respond. What he wanted was not a civilised noon meal with his wife. He wanted to get drunk and hit someone.

He probably needed someone to hit *him*, he acknowledged furiously as he vaulted the fence into the lane— a fight would be deeply satisfying. He felt betrayed, which was nonsense, illogical. It would be satisfying to be able to shout at Arabella, rant at her for her actions, her pregnancy. He had felt none of that when she first told him, only anger at Rafe and pity for her.

But the child had not been real to him then. Now he could see the changes in Arabella, saw the consequences in the doctor's visit, her desire for the nursery. She had ordered the cradle to be polished—for Rafe's son.

Elliott reached the village duck pond and kicked a stone into it, sending three ducks and a coot panicking to the far shore. Two small boys, who doubtless should have been doing something useful for their mothers, looked up from where they were fashioning a fishing pole from a length of twine, a bent stick and a pin with a wriggling worm, dismissed him as no threat to their truancy and went back to their task.

Elliott sat on a log, ignored the effect on his elegant pantaloons, and watched them. They were about six, he supposed, grubby, ragged, gap-toothed and utterly absorbed in their adventure. He wanted a son like that.

He wanted Arabella to have a son, *his* son. They would go fishing together, play truant from the tutor together. He would teach him to ride and shoot and care about the land. His son, a boy with Arabella's hazel-green eyes and his own dark honey hair.

Damnation. He had no right to be thinking like this. It had been no problem at first. It was as he came to know Arabella, to like her, to realise she was not just his wife in some abstract sense, but a person who mattered to him—that was when the fact that the child she carried was not his began to hurt.

He hated himself for it, he decided as he stood up and circled the pond. If she knew, she would despise him for feeling like this after all his talk of honour and duty. Elliott dug into his pocket, found two sixpenny pieces and tossed them to the boys as he passed. Their gasps of delight made him smile, albeit grimly, as he headed for the Calne Arms.

Bella finished her luncheon and went back to contemplating the pile of parcels the footman had brought in from the carriage. She supposed they must be for her—who else would Elliott be buying hats for?—but she did not like to open them. The thought that he had been choosing gifts for her made her happy, but she dare not cling to the hope that the gesture meant more than the kindness he had shown her all along.

She wanted to see him, to hear his voice, discover whether the pleasant ache in her heart was truly love. She feared it was. The misery of loving and her love not being returned warred with the happiness the emotion brought her. Elliott had already been so kind, had sacrificed so much, been so patient, she could not burden him with her feelings, feelings he would not return. And why should he believe her, even if she told him that she loved him? She had fancied herself in love with his brother—Elliott would think her fickle, would question her judgement.

But where was he? It was two hours since the carriage had returned and the footman said his lordship had apparently finished his business in the church and had walked off towards the village.

The clock struck three and she found anxiety had turned into worry and worry into anger. He had been gone for almost three days, he must know she was anxious, and yet he had not even put his head round the door, just sent a message and a pile of shopping.

Bella seized the nearest thing, a hat box, and yanked at the ribbons. It cost her a broken nail before she could open the knot she had jerked tight. Inside was the most frivolous villager hat with a big knot of green ribbon over one ear. She tossed it aside and tore open another that proved to contain a stack of fabric samples. They spilled at her feet as she looked at the next. Elliott, it seemed, had indulged himself by buying her fine lawn chemises.

'Hah!' Bella dropped them back on to the tissue paper from where they slid on to the floor. What did he care about her underwear? He didn't even come straight home to see her.

'Don't you like them?' She spun round as the deep voice from the doorway made her breath catch. Elliott lounged there, looking very slightly dishevelled. She was not sure whether she wanted to slap him or kiss him. Possibly both.

'You've been drinking,' she accused.

'Not much,' he said, wandering into the room. 'Not enough. A pint of knock-me-down, but I'm still standing.' His eyes were shuttered, wary, a strange contrast to his careless slouch and loosened neckcloth.

'Why did you not come home?' she demanded. 'Look at the time! Your luncheon has gone to waste, I was worried…'

'Are you turning into a shrew, wife?' Elliott picked up the bonnet and reached out to drop it on her head.

Bella slapped his hands away and the hat went flying. 'Where have you been?' He frightened her like this.

Elliott picked up the hat and laid it back in its box with exaggerated care. 'In the inn.'

'Is it muddy in there?' Bella demanded, gesturing at his boots.

'No. I walked round the pond, I seem to recall.'

'I was worried,' Bella repeated, laying a hand on his forearm. Elliott looked down at it and she lifted it away.

'The footmen would have told you I was in the village,' he said. 'Must I account for my movements to my wife now? What do you think I was getting up to? Debauching local innocents?'

That hurt, as it was obviously meant to. 'No,' she countered sweetly. 'I assumed you were getting drunk in the local tavern and perhaps getting into a fistfight.'

'I would have enjoyed that. As it is, I am not drunk, I have not fought anyone and now I am home. How have you spent the time?'

'I went to church and then I went to see the family

chapel. Daniel showed me. I was upset because—'
Because I realised I loved you. 'And then I came home and
entertained Daniel for luncheon. He is being very kind.'

She stalked over to the bell pull and yanked it. 'I
suppose you would like some luncheon now?'

'You rang, my lady?' Henlow appeared, calmly
oblivious that the drawing room was a litter of packages
and underwear, his mistress was standing, elbows
akimbo, in the middle, and his master was mired in mud.

'Thank you, Henlow,' Elliott said. 'Her ladyship has
changed her mind.' The butler bowed himself out, still
expressionless.

'I am not hungry,' he snapped before Bella could
catch her breath and call the butler back.

'What is the matter with you?' she demanded. She
was not scared of him, not exactly, but she was scared
for *them*. This was not the Elliott she had come to know.
His eyes were fixed on her midriff and she realised she
had laid a protective hand over the swell of her belly.
'Don't shout at me, I am certain it upsets the baby.'

'I am so sorry,' Elliott said, not sounding so in the
least. 'I should not have forgotten that everything
revolves around that confounded child.'

'Elliott! How could you? Our baby—'

'Rafe's son,' he fired back and then caught himself,
his face pale and his eyes dark with emotions she had
never seen there.

'But you married me because it might be a boy,'
Bella said, struggling to understand. 'You said it must
be the heir if it is a boy.' And then she recalled the
shadow that had crossed his face when she had teasingly

remarked that she hoped the baby was a boy because they would have such fun together. 'You resent it, don't you? Elliott, it is an innocent baby. If you are angry, be angry with me, not the child.'

'I am not angry with the child, or with you,' he flung at her over his shoulder as he kicked aside some fallen underwear on his way to stand and stare out of the window. 'I am not even angry with Rafe although, God knows, he deserves it. I am furious with myself.'

'With yourself?' Bella stared at the broad shoulders, braced as though he expected her to throw things at him. 'You mean, because you want it to be *your* son? But you said—'

'I know what I said. I know what I should think. I know what is the right and honourable way to feel,' he said without turning around. 'So that makes me dishonorable and wrong, does it not?'

'Oh, Elliott. No.' Bella wrestled to find the right words. *What have I done to him?* 'It just makes you human. I should have realised, I should have thought.'

'Don't blame yourself,' he said, his voice flat. 'I don't want your guilt to add to mine, thank you.' She stood and stared at him. He was dishevelled, he smelt of the ale house as he stood there shedding mud on the Chinese carpet, and she loved him. And now he showed her the truth of what she had done by imagining she loved his brother.

This was not simply inconvenience and expense and the end of any choice for him in who he married. This was pain and guilt for him and the loss of a father's love for her child.

Chapter Eighteen

'Elliott, I do not know what to say. I do not know how I can ever make this right.'

He turned and smiled at her. It was quite a successful smile, all things considered, and it reminded her, with a jolt, of all the reasons she loved him and why this hurt so much. 'There is nothing you can do, Arabella. I am just going to have to learn to deal with it.'

And so must I. And the child will know, somehow, that something is wrong, that something is missing from its life. There will be two of us, hoping for his love.

'Elliott, will you promise me something?'

'I will try,' he said, his eyes wary. 'I am not going to promise something I cannot hold to.'

'Be honest with me from now on. Tell me what you feel, what you need.'

He watched her for a long few seconds and then shook his head. 'No, I am sorry, my love, I cannot promise that. I can promise to try, but that is all.'

'Then that will have to do,' she said. *My love. It is*

just an endearment. I am a fool to hope that one day you will call me your love, and mean it from the bottom of your heart. Something flickered in his eyes and was gone. 'What is it?'

Elliott shook his head. 'A thought that you do not want to hear.'

'Tell me.' Bella went to him and caught his hands in hers. 'Please.'

'I want to make love to you,' Elliott said. 'Don't ask me to explain why, now of all times. I know you won't—'

'Yes,' she said, confused, but trying to understand. He needed to prove that she, at least, was his and no longer another man's. 'You are my husband and… Elliott!' He scooped her up and was halfway up the stairs before she got her breath back. 'Put me down…the servants will see…you're drunk!'

'They are paid to be blind, Arabella. And I am stone-cold sober.' He shouldered open his bedchamber door, laid her on the bed and went back to close and lock the door.

Bella sat up and watched as he tossed his coat and waistcoat on to a chair, unwrapped his neckcloth and began to unfasten his shirt. *I have seen him naked*, she told herself, forcing her fingers to unclench from the bedspread. But she had never seen him undress like this, stripping away his clothes, tossing them aside as though all that mattered was to get to her.

'Your boots,' she managed, hearing the way her voice quavered.

'Don't worry, Arabella, I'm not the sort of husband who comes to bed in his boots and spurs.' He sat on a chair and dragged them off, pulling the stockings with them. Which left him, in broad daylight, in nothing but his breeches. He was very obviously aroused as he stood up and advanced purposefully on the bed. And so was she, with thudding heart, shortness of breath and the embarrassingly insistent intimate pulse between her legs. She ought to be alarmed, she knew. This was her husband, but in a mood she had never seen him before.

Elliott put one knee on the bed and began to unbutton her simple afternoon gown. He bent and kissed her neck as he pushed off her gown. 'And there is absolutely no hurry.'

It took at least fifteen minutes to remove her petticoats, her chemise and her stays. Every tape, hook and button appeared to require a kiss or a nibble or a touch of his tongue. Bella closed her eyes and wondered if this was a branding, whether he was marking her entire body as his. She was uncertain, but she was also aching and needing and hot and restless. Her breasts were swollen and tender, the nipples hard, wanting his mouth to cover them.

Finally all that was left were stockings and garters. Bella opened her eyes, found Elliott kneeling at her feet and closed them again as he began to untie the ribbons, peel down the stockings, his mouth following the silk to her instep. And then, to her utter shock, he took her toes in his mouth and sucked.

'Elliott!' She sat bolt upright, outraged. He looked up, his eyes challenging her to protest again and he kept right on sucking and nibbling until she flopped back, beyond any resistance or shame. Then the other stocking, the other toes, before his hands slid up to press her thighs apart and he began to torment the soft skin behind her knees.

Bella reached for him, wanting to touch, but he evaded her easily. 'Relax,' he said harshly.

'Relax?' Impossible. There was too much to think about, to worry about. Then she arched off the bed like a bow with shock and delight as he pressed her thighs wider and licked right into the hot aching core of her. Thought became disjointed, feeling was everything— and she burned and throbbed and became liquid with desire. She felt him slip a finger, then another, inside her and felt only the delicious sensations, the urge to close around him, draw him deeper. But his tongue would not let her focus, concentrate, everything was blurring, dissolving and then splintering.

There was a scream and she knew it came from her own throat. Elliott shifted his weight over her and she anchored herself to his big, strong body and held him close. Then, slowly, while her body was still rippling and quivering with delight, he slid into her, inexorable, delicious, until he filled her and she could embrace him with all of herself.

'Arabella?' She took one hand from his shoulder and used it to pull his mouth down to hers and kissed him as he started to rock gently, gently inside her. When it changed she did not know, but she was thrusting up to meet him, digging her nails into the tight buttocks to bring him closer still, desperate for him and the building, dizzying sensation that swept over her.

She heard him groan as her body rippled around him

and then he thrust hard and cried out and she felt the heat inside her as he came. And then he was lying on her, heavy and hot and male, and she tightened her arms around him and thought she would never let him go.

Elliott was awake, she could feel the slight tension in his body as he tried not to move and wake her. Bella smiled, her cheek against his chest, and fluttered her eyelashes so they tangled with the dark springing hair.

'Awake?' he murmured and she nodded, tilting her head to look at him.

He looks at peace with himself again, she thought. *Sleek, satisfied male. My male.*

'It was good for you?'

'Are you fishing for compliments?' Bella asked, coming up on one elbow to study his face. 'It was wonderful and you know it. Elliott, we must talk about the child.'

'No. There is nothing more to be said.' The warmth cooled as though a current of air had passed over their hot skin. 'Bella, there is nothing you can do about this. I will just have to come to terms with it in my own way.' Elliott pulled her in close to his side again. 'You are very beautiful, you know.'

He is avoiding it now. He only spoke of it before because he lost control of his temper. Now he is going to try and make me think he can forget. But there was no point in angering him again, not after that perfect lovemaking. She made her voice light. 'Liar. You told me I was not.'

'I was wrong. You are graceful and charming and pretty always, but when you are on fire in my arms you are beyond beautiful, every inch of you.'

And he has explored every inch, there cannot be anywhere his mouth and hands have not been.

'I will be fat soon,' she lamented. 'My waist is thickening already. And look.' She rolled on to her back and ran her hand over the curve of her belly. *Oh Lord, of all the stupid things to say.*

'You are blooming,' he contradicted her, pleasantly enough, but the intimacy that had briefly blossomed was gone again.

Bella wriggled up against the pillows and pulled the crumpled bedspread around her. There seemed to be nothing to do but change the subject. 'Tell me about the bishop.'

'He was very understanding. Tutted a bit over the baby, but gave me no lectures. And he was not surprised when I told him about your father's mental state; he had thought his letter intemperate considering your age. He will say nothing to your father's diocese and will write back to him to say the marriage is legal and has his approval.'

Bella let out a long breath. *Thank goodness.* The thought of the scandal and the embarrassment to Elliott if the bishop had not been sympathetic had been keeping her awake at night. If only her father would come round and accept this marriage. She did not hope for his forgiveness, just his indifference.

'Then I did your shopping,' Elliott continued, playing with her hair.

'I asked for fabric swatches, not underwear and hats,' she said, letting her fingertips trail down his ribs. 'But they are very lovely. Thank you.'

'My pleasure. And what have you been doing?' There was that constraint again; he was avoiding telling her something.

'Exploring, getting to know the staff and my way around. I visited the gardens. Elliott, did you know Rafe dismissed the assistant gardeners who used to help with the ornamental work? Old Johnson says they have only been able to get labouring jobs and he has had to grass over most of the flowerbeds. Can we afford to employ them again?'

'If you want.' He was still sprawled against the pillows, looking up at her. 'And what else did you do?'

'I visited the Dower House and I went to church on Sunday—Matins. That was when Daniel arrived. He said he saw you in Worcester so he came to escort me in your stead.' There it was again, that shuttered look. 'Elliott, what is it you are not telling me?'

'You can read me like a book, it seems. I went to the castle and I looked at the Army List. Arabella, there is no gentle way to say this—your brother-in-law, Lieutenant James Halgate, is dead, killed at Vittoria in August 1812.'

'James? Oh, no.' James had been so alive, so vivid, so dashing, it was hard to believe. 'But that is almost two years ago. Where is Meg now?' Bella stared at him as though he could conjure the answer out of thin air.

'I am sorry, I have no idea. I asked the militia commander who we should contact in London to find out about the widow's pension, so we can do that. We will find her. And your other sister.' Elliott pulled her to him in a hard hug. 'I promise.'

'Thank you. You are so kind to me,' she murmured against his shoulder, grieving for James, aching for Meg.

'You are my wife, Arabella,' Elliott said. 'Of course I will help. Your sisters are family now.'

Not, I love you Arabella, I will do anything for you. *Oh, Elliott. So kind, so supportive to his unasked-for, inconvenient, wife and the child he does not want.*

'I am so happy that Elliott has come back here to live,' Anne Baynton said, as they braced themselves against the jolting of the carriage. The two women had decided upon a day in Worcester shopping while their husbands looked at woodland and then, Bella suspected, spent the rest of the time enjoying a holiday from domestic life. Goodness only knew, Elliott deserved one, she thought.

Bella smiled back. It was good to have a friend, one that she would be able to confide in and to share the joy of her baby with. Nothing and nobody could replace Meg and Lina, but she had liked and trusted Anne from the start. 'I thought that Elliott did not come here often since he left to go to university,' she ventured.

'He did not.' Anne pursed her lips. 'He and John knew each other as boys, but when Rafe inherited we only saw Elliott in London during the Season or when we visited Fosse Warren.'

'You knew Rafe, of course.'

'As much as we cared to.' Now Anne's expression

was positively disapproving. 'As neighbours, merely. I must confess to not liking his way of life.'

Anne had already confided that she was with child again. Bella plucked up her courage. 'May I tell you a secret?'

'How secret?' Anne asked, her smile reappearing.

'You may tell Mr Baynton, but that is all.'

'Very well, my lips are sealed, but tell me at once, I cannot wait.' Anne leaned forwards, eyes sparkling.

'I am expecting a baby.'

'Wonderful!' Anne leaned over and squeezed Bella's hand. 'I must confess to guessing that you were. Your figure, if you do not mind me saying so, has changed since the wedding! When is it due?'

'Early December,' Bella said. Anne froze halfway back against the squabs, her mouth forming an O as she did the calculation.

'Yes, I am afraid things were anticipated more than a little,' Bella admitted.

'But it is very romantic—a clandestine love affair! And how dashing of Elliott, the sly dog!'

'Oh, please do not tease him about it!' Anne smiled and shook her head. 'I so dread the gossip when I cannot hide it any more—which will be any moment now. My father did not approve—he thinks aristocrats are immoral—so it was all rather difficult, which is why we…which is why I ran away.

'My mother died years ago, and my sisters have left home and I— Anne, I would so much value your advice. I have no idea what to expect and I want to be a perfect mother.' She swallowed, suddenly emotional. 'You see,

I keep bursting into tears at the slightest thing. And I made Elliott alarmed and he called the doctor about something perfectly normal…'

'Oh, my dear, of course you can talk to me. I was so lucky, I had Mama close by and my two older sisters both have children. But even then there was much to ask about. Now, I must have a boy and you must have a girl and then we can plan a marriage that will embarrass them enormously when we tease them about it in twenty years' time!'

Perhaps that was her best hope, a daughter. Surely Elliott would love a little girl and then his own son— their own son—would be the heir. But it seemed wrong to wish the child to be anything but who it already was. He or she should be loved unreservedly for themselves.

But that nagging anxiety apart, this journey to Worcester was a far happier one than her trip with Elliott to meet the bishop, Bella mused when the pair of them sat back to draw breath after her long list of questions and worries had been discussed. She was married now, the baby's future was at least secure, things with Elliott were as comfortable as she could hope, given that she was in love with him and he was simply being kind and doing his duty.

In the bedroom *comfortable* was not quite the word, she thought, suppressing the smile that tried to escape every time she thought about their lovemaking. If it were not for the fact that she was terrified of losing control and blurting out her feelings, Bella thought that aspect of her marriage was almost perfect. Except, perhaps, that she wanted to do more, be more adventurous. Elliott appeared to like her touching him, but what if she tried to kiss him as he kissed her, intimately, and gave him a disgust of her for being wanton, just when he had begun to forget, she hoped, how badly she had behaved with Rafe?

And she wished he would invite his friends to stay, or that they could go on visits. Or even tell her more about the estate and how she could help. When she asked he fobbed her off with concerns about her strength, her health, and she wondered if he thought she would blunder out of ignorance or try to interfere with what he saw as his business. She wanted to be busy, and of use, and sometimes she felt a little lonely.

At three in the morning when she lay awake and her worst fears came to haunt her, she wondered if Elliott was ashamed of her. She was no beauty, whatever he told her, she had brought him no useful alliance, nor a dowry, and she had no idea yet how to go on in society. And there was the pregnancy, of course.

But she must not be gloomy now, not with her new friend to bear her company and the prospect of an entire day shopping in front of them. 'I have chosen the fabrics for my suite,' she said, taking the samples from her reticule and showing Anne. 'And I must visit the dress-maker to have some gowns altered and new ones made.'

'And we can look at things for the nursery,' Anne suggested. 'John asks what I can possibly want to buy, for everything I had for Prunella is wrapped up in the attic, but men never seem to understand about shopping.'

'Elliott does, I think. At least, he seemed to enjoy buying clothes with me,' Bella ventured.

'All of them frivolous and most of them for the boudoir, if I can hazard a guess,' Anne said with a grin. 'That is characteristic of new husbands; it does not persist, or apply to everyday articles, I am afraid.'

But even selecting new sheets for the servants' rooms or choosing between one style of sensible walking boot and another had charm when it was done in company with a friend who had a lively sense of humour and excellent taste.

Chapter Nineteen

Bella perched on a rather high stool at the counter of Messieurs Wildegrave and Harris, Linen Drapers, and decided on eight cotton towels at sixteen pence each instead of the cheaper ones at twelve pence. They would wear better. *Ten shillings and eight pence*, she wrote against that item on her list.

'This poplin would be very suitable for the linings, Lady Hadleigh,' the assistant said, placing a large roll on the counter before her.

'Yes, I—' There was a muffled exclamation beside her and Bella turned to see an elegant lady in her forties, accompanied by a pretty blonde. They were both staring at her.

'Lady Hadleigh?' the older woman said in tones of disbelief.

'Why, yes.' Bella stared back. She might not be entirely up to snuff in all matters of etiquette, but this abrupt question from a stranger was certainly not normal polite behaviour. 'I am sorry, ma'am, but you have the advantage of me.'

'Rafe Calne's widow?' the woman demanded. 'I had no idea—'

'No! Elliott's Calne's wife.'

The younger woman gave a little gasp. 'Elliott is married?'

'Yes, he is.' Bella was beginning to feel both embarrassed and irritated. People were looking, the sales assistant was standing there with his mouth open. 'The announcement was sent to the newspapers.'

'We have just got back from visiting Aunt Marjorie who is sick,' the younger woman said. 'She does not approve of newspapers—'

'Frederica.' Her mother silenced her with a gesture. 'The engagement must have been of short duration.'

'Madam, I have no idea who you are,' Bella said, sliding off the stool where she was feeling at a decided disadvantage. 'But—' Her skirts pulled tight across her stomach for a moment as she got down. Both women's eyes fixed on her midriff just as Anne came round the corner with her hands full of fine wool.

'My dear Lady Hadleigh, do look at these charming baby shawls. I think we should both purchase one.' She stopped at the sight of the group at the counter. 'Lady Framlingham. Lady Frederica.' Her expression became perfectly blank for a moment before it was replaced with a charming social smile. 'You have met my friend Lady Hadleigh, I see. Arabella, have you been introduced to the Countess of Framlingham and Lady Frederica?'

'No.' Bella held out her gloved hand. Something was

very wrong here; the countess had reacted badly to the news that Elliott was married before she had realised that Bella was with child.

Lady Framlingham looked down her nose and merely touched the tips of Bella's fingers with her own. 'You have known Lord Hadleigh for some time,' she stated.

Bella told herself she was imagining the emphasis on *known*. 'Since February,' she said. She could hardly tell the truth and say she had known him barely two weeks, not with her pregnancy obvious.

'I see. I felicitate you upon your marriage,' Lady Framlingham said.

Bella looked at the slim, elegant young woman at her mother's side. Suddenly she felt clumsy and ashamed of her own burgeoning body, as though the visibility of her pregnancy was a badge, marking her out as wanton and unchaste.

'Come, Frederica.' Lady Framlingham swept out, her daughter at her heels. The young woman looked back at Bella for a moment, her eyes wide and questioning.

'Anne? What on earth?'

'Let us finish our shopping,' Anne said, the fixed smile still on her lips. 'It is time for luncheon, I think.'

It was not until they were both seated in a private parlour at the Royal Oak, food on the table and the door firmly closed, that Anne's smile slipped. 'Elliott was invited to the Framlinghams' house party. He cried off, of course, when Rafe died.'

'Well, what is that to cause Lady Framlingham to look

so disapproving?' Bella demanded. 'She cannot expect
him to join a house party under those circumstances.'

'No, of course not. Not even one where she was expecting him to make an offer for her daughter,' said
Anne bleakly. 'It never occurred to me. There were all
those rumours about him and Lady Freddie, but all the
time he and you…'

Bella's stomach seemed to have become totally
hollow. 'Elliott was committed to her?' she demanded.
He had told her he had no one. He had—

'No. I am sure he was not. But it was becoming
obvious that he was thinking of settling down, making
a choice. He attended many of the come-out balls, he
was seen at Almack's and he was on very good terms
with Lady Freddie. Perhaps we all had it wrong—we
must have—and all it was, was friendship.'

But the pretty blonde had been startled and bemused.
Was that the reaction of someone on hearing that a
friend had married unexpectedly?

'Elliott is not the sort of man who would court two
women at once,' Anne said with compete confidence.
'He is far too honourable for that.'

'Oh, yes,' Bella agreed. 'Elliott has a highly developed sense of honour.' Why had he chosen to do as he
had? Because there truly was no relationship between
him and Lady Frederica or because righting Rafe's
actions was the correct thing to do for the family honour
in his mind and the feelings of the two women involved
were secondary to that?

He could have married Lady Frederica, that
charming, well-bred, *virginal* young woman who was

everything a man in his position would want. And now he had her and she had not even given him her untouched body to make his. She rested her hand on her belly, hating how she felt about the evidence of her child now.

'Would you mind if we go home after this?' she asked. 'I feel rather tired.'

'Of course. I am too,' Anne Baynton said. The fact that it was obviously a polite lie and Anne was far from weary did nothing to make Bella feel any better. She set herself to making cheerful conversation—just because her emotions were in turmoil and she was facing another unpleasant confrontation with Elliott, there was no reason to spoil her friend's day.

It seemed she had not deceived Anne one whit. The moment they arrived back at the Hall Anne swept into the study where the two men were talking, kissed Elliott on the cheek and dragged her husband away, explaining that she was so weary that she was ready to drop and that Bella had excused them from staying for dinner.

'What was that about?' Elliott demanded. 'I still had things to discuss with John. Is Anne all right, because she looks absolutely fine to me.' He shrugged, the charming half-smile that always made her pulse quicken visible for a moment. 'But what would I know? I am a man.'

'Quite,' Bella said, trying to decide whether to sit down or stay on her feet. 'I met friends of yours in Worcester today, Elliott.'

'Indeed?' He was frowning now.

One thing I can say about Elliott, Bella thought, *he is sensitive to my mood. I just wish I could read him so easily.* 'Lady Framlingham and her daughter Frederica. They seemed most surprised that you are married. They were also, having noticed my condition, surprised that you had, as Lady Framlingham put it, known me so long. They had not seen the announcement, having been away from home.'

'Ah.' Elliott hitched one hip on to the edge of the table and regarded her, his lean face thoughtful. 'I thought you trusted me, Arabella.'

'I did.' She saw her use of the past tense register. 'You told me that there was no one else. Anne tells me that there were rumours that you were interested in Lady Frederica early in the year.'

'I was, although I thought I had been careful not to make it obvious. If Rafe's death had not intervened and I had accepted an invitation to their house party then I would probably have proposed to Freddie,' Elliott said coolly. 'She is intelligent, amusing, well-brought up and suitable.'

'I can see that. You were aiming high; she is a very good match for a younger son.'

'I have money—that appeals to the Framlinghams. Freddie is a younger daughter. I would have been acceptable.'

'And even more so now.'

'Quite.'

'And her affections were engaged?' Bella asked. 'Was this to have been a love match?'

'Good God, no! We like each other. I think I can say we are friends. Lovers, no, never.' Elliott looked at her steadily. 'I told you I had never been in love with anyone, did I not?'

'Yes, you did. And I should have asked you if you had any prior commitments while I was at it,' Bella said.

'You think I am dishonourable enough to jilt another woman?' Elliott was as tense as she now. But of course, she had impugned his precious honour.

'I think,' she said tightly, 'that you would have done almost anything to put right your brother's actions, whatever the consequences. Consequences like society gossip, a young woman who expected a proposal having the shock of her life when she meets the pregnant wife of the man she looked forward to marrying, a child with a father who cannot love it.' Elliott's face hardened, but she swept on. 'Are you going to write to Frederica?'

'No, of course I am not.' Elliott got up and stood in front of her. 'That would imply there was something to explain. Freddie is no more heartbroken over me than I am over her. And if you think if I made her an offer and I would break my word to her because of some obsession with righting Rafe's wrongs then you do not know me at all.'

'I don't think I do!' Bella flung back. 'I know nothing of your life. You keep me shut up here—today was the first time I have been allowed out—you do not invite your friends to visit—'

'You are not shut up.' Elliott was not shouting by sheer force of will, Bella thought, her own heart thudding. She had never seen him like this, the blue eyes blazing, his face taut with anger. The thought flickered into her head that he looked magnificent. Terrifying, but magnificent. 'I am trying to make sure you rest, trying to allow you time to get used to things. Do you think I

enjoy being stuck here face to face with the mess that
this estate is, with no relief from it? I have a perfectly
good life I could be living, friends I could be with,
another estate, invitations—' He dug into his desk
drawer and threw them on to the surface.

'Well, go and live your other life then,' she shot back.
'Go and do whatever it is you do with your friends—I
wouldn't know, I haven't met them because I am not good
enough to meet them. Go and look after Fosse Warren,
go up to Town and visit the relatives I must not see.'

She was being unreasonable, she knew it. But she
loved him and he would not let her past the careful
kindness, would not share his life with her. He could not
even promise to share his needs with her. Bed was one
thing, but all the rest of what made up Elliott Calne was
a closed book. Why should he open up to her? He had
never wanted to marry her. It hurt so much at the back
of her mind where she tried to hide it that today's humiliating encounter was like a fingernail dragged across
a raw graze.

'Very well, if that is what you want. I will drive over
to Fosse Warren now, there is nothing here that needs
me for a week or so. Turner has his orders.' He picked
up a pile of correspondence from the end of the desk.
'I will not refuse these after all.' Elliott paused in the
doorway. 'And do feel free to go shopping whenever
you wish, my dear.'

Elliott drove away from the Hall and his wife more
confused than he could ever remember being, even when
Rafe had turned against him. She made him so angry,

yet he did not want to feel that way and she did not want to cross him, he knew that. Arabella was trying so hard to be a good wife to a man she did not love…

Ah, is that it, you fool? he asked himself. *You want her to love you.* As if things were not difficult enough already.

That would be a miracle, Elliott decided, turning his team in the direction of Moreton in the Marsh. She had loved one Calne brother and had been utterly betrayed. Why should she ever give her heart to another, who looked so much like her betrayer? And what would he do with a wife who loved him anyway? All that emotion, all that pressure to live up to an ideal and never to hurt her. He would never manage that—he was blundering about now, hurting her over the child, over Freddie. And if she loved, then she would hope he would love her back.

He wanted a wife who would be passionate in bed— he had that. One who would preside over his households with competence and charm. And she was learning very fast to do that. He needed a viscountess to look after his people and she was doing that far better than he could ever have hoped. And, of course, he needed a wife to bear him children, give him an heir.

The leaders pecked and swerved as his hand tightened on the reins and Elliott cursed under his breath. If only this relationship was not entangled with his feelings over the baby. But without the child there would be no relationship.

Love was an emotion for women. It hurt, it complicated matters. Men of his class did not marry for love. *You want her to love you because you think you are better than Rafe*, his conscience jabbed at him. *You need to feel you own her, just as you need the child to be yours. Rafe betrayed you, rejected you and now you want to crow that you have made Arabella happy when all he could do was attempt to destroy her.*

What sort of reason is that for wanting your wife's love? he asked himself. *She is no fool. She likes you well enough in bed, she liked you well enough when she thought you would make a decent father. Why couldn't you have hidden how you feel about the baby? Why couldn't you have explained about Freddie?*

Elliott urged the team into a canter. *Just don't fall in love with her,* he thought. *Don't be so stupid as to risk that. Rafe did not love you, the child most certainly won't—children know when they aren't loved—and Arabella can see you all too clearly.*

He was almost at Fosse Warren when he heard the hooves thundering behind him. He reached for his pistols in their holster strapped to the side of the curricle as he turned to look over his shoulder, then thrust them back as he recognised Peters, the head groom from the Hall, galloping flat out on Ace, Elliott's big black hunter.

'What's wrong?' he demanded as the man reined in beside him. 'Her ladyship?'

'No, my lord.' The man got his breath back and pulled a letter out from the breast of his coat. 'Her ladyship is perfectly well. Only she rang, about half an hour after you'd left, my lord, and gave me this letter. She said it was urgent and I was to give it to you as soon as I could.'

'Ride on to Fosse Warren with me,' Elliott said,

putting the roughly folded letter with its blob of sealing wax into his own coat. What had Arabella to say that was so urgent? *Never come back, I hate you*, probably. Or she had sat down with the dictionary and found the words to tell him just what a stiff-rumped, self-righteous, deceitful husband she had found herself.

He fended off the enthusiastic welcome of butler and housekeeper at the Warren and retreated to his study, thankful for the small, well-worn familiarity of the place.

The hastily melted lump of wax broke into shards under his impatient thumb and he spread the letter out on the desk.

I am sorry, it began with no salutation. *I have been so afraid of exposing you to gossip and censure for what I did. For my sin. And there they were, my worst fear. Not only friends who would be critical of you—but such a beautiful young woman. So eligible. She will know what to do always. She will know how to act and what to say. Not like me. I stood there feeling lumpen and ashamed. Of course you should have married her.*

There is no excuse for me losing my temper. I cannot blame it on my condition—it is my insecurity and guilt. My shame. And I should not take it out on you.

But, Elliott, you should have told me about her. I am your wife and I want to be a good wife. And I cannot if you keep things from me.

Do not worry about me. I feel better now I have written this and I will do my best to have long lists of all the tenants' needs by the time you have exhausted all your invitations and reassured yourself about Fosse Warren.

I will do my best to look after the Hall while you are gone.

It was signed simply *A*.

Elliott looked at the letter for a long time. He was not even making much of a fist at being the sort of husband Freddie, brought up to this life, would have expected. Arabella was lonely and ashamed and feeling guilty. He picked up his pen and wrote.

I will come home tomorrow. I am sorry too, I should have trusted you with the truth. I find I do not want to look at turnip clamps or attend prize fights. I will come home and we will hold dinner parties if you would like that. And we will go on picnics.

    E.

Chapter Twenty

$$\text{\textasciitilde}\!\!\text{\textasciitilde}\!\!\text{\textasciitilde}$$

Elliott returned home the next day and discovered that, for a married man, there were interesting ways to make up after a row. They held dinner parties and a card party, Arabella met all the local gentry and faced down the occasional raised eyebrow at her burgeoning figure. The staff, as he suspected, had already guessed well before they were told that their mistress was expecting a happy event, and were quietly delighted. On the surface theirs was a successful marriage.

Anne Baynton and Arabella became fast friends and, as she became more secure and confident, his wife began to blossom in a way that took his breath when he looked at her.

Arabella grumbled about backache and twinges, about feeling too hot and having to disappear at frequent intervals into the brand-new water closet he had ordered to be installed. But she also grew more passionate and adventurous in bed, which delighted him, although, out of the bedroom, she remained slightly distant and reserved. She had not forgotten what he had said about the child and he wondered if she trusted him after he had concealed the truth about Freddie from her.

And he knew he was not reaching out to her as he should. He did not know how to reach her, how to make her trust him without declarations of love that he was sure she would see through. Would he have fallen in love with her if he had been the one to meet her in that country churchyard, if she had looked at him and seen her Sir Galahad on his black charger?

He liked her, he worried about her, he desired her body and enjoyed her mind. Was that not enough without pining away and feeling the need to write poetry and make flowery speeches? As the weeks passed and everything else became better on the surface Elliott found he could not forget, except for a few hours at a time, that the child Arabella was carrying was not his.

Then one morning in the middle of August he found her, her hands clasped over the swell of her belly, her expression intent and inward looking. 'What is it?' Elliott knelt beside her. 'Is something wrong? Shall I send for the doctor?'

In answer she took his hand and laid it on the curve and smiled at him, her face radiant. 'Feel. The baby is moving.'

And under his hand something shifted, kicked. *Arabella's baby. Rafe's son.* An ordinary miracle that every parent greeted with joy and rejoicing. He felt ill with the violence of his instinctive rejection and furious with himself for feeling that way.

Elliott fought to keep his face clear of expression, but

she must have felt his reaction through her hold on his hand. 'What is it?'

'Nothing,' he lied. He had to hide it from Bella, she needed tranquillity and reassurance now, not this dishonourable rejection that he should be able to overcome. 'I was just worried—doesn't that hurt?' Another kick came right under his palm as though the child sensed him and his resentment of it.

'No. It does feel strange that it is so strong. I expect it will be a little uncomfortable when he is bigger.'

'You are certain it is a boy, then?'

'Not really—I cannot decide.' Her colour was high, but all the inner glow seemed to have gone out of her. 'I am sorry, that was tactless of me, given how you feel.' But despite her distress at his reaction she was watching him with a tenderness in her eyes that he supposed was a reflection of her feelings for the baby. He was constantly wondering about her true feelings, about what was going on behind those wide hazel eyes, even when her face lit up at the sight of him coming into a room or her arms reached for him in bed.

There was noise from outside and he got to his feet, glad to be away from the intensity of his feelings and the searching look in Arabella's eyes as she studied his face. 'Daniel's here,' he told her.

Arabella got to her feet and walked slowly to stand beside him at the window. She curled her hand over his arm and the ache inside subsided a little. She always made him feel good, he realised, wondering at it.

'Perhaps I should find him a nice wife and he can set up his own nursery,' Arabella said.

Elliott watched his cousin as he jumped down from what looked like a smart new Dennet gig. He liked Daniel and his cousin was a good friend to Arabella, who seemed relaxed with him in a way she never was with Elliott. He wondered why he had never felt jealous, but looking down and seeing the pleasure on Arabella's face he felt a jolt of something unpleasantly like it now. 'Matchmaker,' he said.

She laughed at his accusation, and shook her head at him. Elliott kept his arm around Arabella's shoulders when they went down to greet Calne. It was strange, he reflected as Daniel showed him his new gig, how very possessive he felt towards Arabella all of a sudden. Simply territorial instinct and the fact that she was his responsibility, he supposed.

She was stroking the horse, a pretty grey mare, laughing as it blew gustily into her palm in search of titbits. 'She is sweet, Daniel. Have you had her long?'

'A few weeks. Would you like to come for a drive, Bella?'

'I would love to, but—' She looked at Elliott, her face alight at the thought of such a simple treat. He realised that it had never occurred to him to take her out in one of his sporting vehicles. She would be driven to the village or to visit tenants in the gig or the closed carriage and, being Arabella, had not presumed to ask for something more interesting.

'I will take you driving tomorrow in the phaeton,' he promised. 'I would say today, but I promised to meet Henderson to decide on some felling over in Forty Acre Wood.'

'Of course, thank you,' she said with every sign of

pleasure. But he saw her give the mare a last, lingering caress.

'But there is no reason for you not to go with Daniel now.' Why be such a dog in the manger? Calne was a good driver and the mare was prettily behaved and he trusted his cousin. He was rewarded by her smile.

'Thank you, Elliott.' She came and kissed his cheek and he felt ridiculously pleased. 'I will just go and get my bonnet and pelisse, Daniel.'

Elliott waited, chatting to the other man, until she came down with Toby running behind her. He handed her up, watching how the mare reacted, then waved them off and strode away to the stables to have his own hack saddled.

He should have thought to take her out more, spend more time with her alone before the baby came, and then she would not have to turn to his cousin for companionship. It had been easy to enlarge their social circle, but that did not require him to be alone with Arabella, to let her close. Bed was different—he smiled at the thought— but he wished he knew how to make a friend of his wife.

7 December

Sit on the sidelines and be ignored. Doctor Hamilton's words were all too true, Elliott thought, pacing back and forth across the hearth rug in the study. In the grate a fire crackled cheerfully, outside, the first snows of the winter were swirling against the window panes and the short afternoon was drawing in.

Both Arabella and the doctor had been predicting that the baby would arrive the previous week, but now it was the seventh of December and she had been in labour since the small hours when she had woken him, apologising for disturbing his sleep.

Elliott had run for the stables, woken two grooms and sent them for the doctor, then returned, only to be firmly shown the door by Gwen and Mrs Knight. He stood outside staring at the panels and strained his ears. Silence. He began to pace, counting lengths of the corridor. Twenty, thirty. A cry, sharply cut off, and he lost count, ran back and opened the door. He caught a glimpse of Arabella's face, white and serious, but not, thank God, distressed.

'Elliott,' she said, conjuring up a smile from somewhere. 'Do go and lie down and get some sleep, my dear. Nothing will be happening yet.'

Sleep? How the devil did she expect him to sleep? Mrs Knight came and took hold of the door handle, her face managing to be both indulgent and severe at the same time. 'Go away, my lord. This is women's work now. The mistress needs to concentrate and she can't be doing with worrying about not upsetting you.'

He retreated to the study, rang for the fire to be made up and tried to fight the image those words conjured up. Arabella wouldn't want him *upset*. All the things she would be going through that might *upset* him were only too vivid. Like him, Rafe had been a big man—the baby was probably huge...

The sound of the door knocker had him at the entrance before Henlow could reach it. The doctor came in, disgustingly cheerful and completely calm as he brushed the snow from his shoulders. *Anyone would think*, Elliott ranted to himself, *that this was not a crisis.*

Doctor Hamilton looked at him. 'There is nothing you can do, there is no cause for concern, my lord.' He smiled. 'I would have thought you a man of iron nerve. Now, courage—and don't start on the brandy too early.'

Elliott was left at the foot of the stairs, feeling bereft and utterly useless. That had been seven hours ago. The doctor had emerged and taken luncheon, reporting slow but perfectly normal progress. Mary Humble, the girl from the village Arabella had hired as nursery maid, arrived, cheerful and kindly. Mrs Knight came out now and again looking flushed, told him there was nothing to worry about and vanished again. He worried.

When the clock struck four he opened the door and strode across the hall and up the stairs. And heard Arabella's cry. *No*. He was not leaving her any longer. By the sound of it she was past worrying about upsetting him.

The sheet was tented over the bed, Hamilton at the foot, the housekeeper was rubbing Arabella's back and Gwen holding her hand. She was white and sweating and her hair was limp about her face and she looked exhausted, but her eyes opened wide as she saw him. Then another contraction took her and she strained against it, her struggle not to cry out obvious.

'I'm here,' Elliott said, putting Gwen aside and taking Arabella's hand. 'And I am not leaving and you scream as much as you like.' She turned her head on the pillow and looked at him, then closed her fingers around his in a grip like death.

After that he lost touch with time and any reality other than the woman on the bed. As the intensity of the contractions increased, Elliott simply poured all his strength and will into Arabella and prayed for her and for this to be over.

And then the others went still, there was a moment's quiet and the doctor said, 'Now!' bent down and the indignant cry of a child filled the room. Arabella fell back against the pillows and Elliott took her in his arms, kissing her in utter relief.

'Oh, sweetheart, Arabella darling. You brave girl. My brave girl.' She smiled up at him, exhausted yet serene. He had never felt closer to her, never so possessive.

'My lord, do you not want to see the child?' It was Mrs Knight behind him.

'No,' Elliott said baldly. Ludicrously, he had forgotten for a few moments what had brought them to this crisis. He did not want to see the child who had given Arabella so much pain to deliver. Rafe's child. 'I want to see my wife.'

'Who wants her baby in her arms, not you, man,' his housekeeper said as she gave him a sharp jab in the ribs. When he sat back she slipped a small swathed bundle into Arabella's arms. 'There, my lady. A lovely little girl.'

'A girl?' He rounded on Dr Hamilton, who was washing his hands.

'Indeed yes, my lord. A perfectly healthy daughter.' He frowned at Elliott and lowered his voice. 'There's time enough for sons, don't be worrying her ladyship about that now. Let her think you are pleased.'

'I am pleased, damn it,' Elliott retorted. 'I am delighted. I couldn't be happier.'

I have got what I wanted. A daughter. Rafe's daughter.

Not a son. Now my son will be heir. The dark, visceral triumph built inside him until he could have shouted for joy. And then he looked at Arabella, exhausted after hours of pain and effort and risk and the shame washed back. No sooner had she gone through that than he was dreaming of putting her through it all over again. She would show him her daughter and his pleasure would be not for the child, but because it was a girl. *You ungrateful devil*, he thought. *You selfish lout.*

'Elliott?' Bella wanted him, was wondering why he was not at her side. Elliott made himself smile and went to sit, with care, on the edge of the bed. The baby was already at her breast and the sight knocked the breath out of him. 'Isn't she lovely?'

'Lovely,' he agreed, putting out a tentative finger to touch the red, crumpled cheek. 'Like her mother,' he lied valiantly.

'Are you all right?' Arabella asked him. 'You sound—I don't know, upset.'

'Shock,' he said, pushing the hair back from her face with a hand that shook slightly. 'I can see why Dr Hamilton and Mrs Knight wanted to keep me out. Mere men are not strong enough for this.'

Arabella gave a little huff of laughter as though that was all she had the energy for. 'Here,' she said as the baby stopped sucking and began to grizzle. 'Go to your father.'

He found his hands full of the preposterously tiny bundle. The baby frowned at him, all angry red face, blue eyes and a drift of kitten-soft black hair right on top of her head. 'Good afternoon, Miss Calne,' he said, feeling inadequate. She obviously thought him so too, for she closed her eyes and began to cry in earnest. *You are not a boy*, he thought, trying to find some other emotion than one of simple relief that Arabella was all right and the child was a girl.

'Bring her over here, my lord,' said Mrs Knight. 'I'll hold her while Gwen and Mary make her ladyship comfortable.'

'No,' Elliott said, standing up and shifting the baby so she felt safe in his arms. 'I'll take her through to the sitting room for a few minutes.'

'Shh,' he said, rocking her a little. 'Shh. You must learn to do what your papa tells you.' She quietened and opened her eyes. Speech seemed to soothe her. *Papa? I must learn to get used to that. I must learn to love this red-faced little person who has caused such havoc.*

Elliott sat down and talked nonsense softly to her until she went to sleep. When Mrs Knight came back for him the bed had been remade and Arabella was asleep in a fresh nightgown, her hair combed back and held by a simple ribbon. She looked too young to be a mother. His heart contracted and his vision blurred.

'I'll take the little one, shall I, my lord?' It was the new nursery maid, smiling and competent, reaching for the baby.

Elliott handed her over. 'Where is the cradle?'

'In the nursery, my lord.'

'Bring it in here and put it by the bed. Her ladyship will want the child close when she wakes.' They were talking in whispers, but Elliott doubted anything would wake Arabella until the baby cried.

He recalled telling Arabella to use the old nursery

upstairs, being irritated with her when she refused. Now he saw her he understood her need to have the baby close. The cradle, the new white lace-draped one purchased in case of a daughter and not a son and heir, was carried in and the baby settled inside it. Elliott sat down and began to pull off his boots. 'Thank you, everyone. I will stay with my wife until she wakes.'

The new maid seemed startled, but Gwen and Mrs Knight smiled and bustled her out. Doctor Hamilton looked across at him as he closed his bag. 'The next one will be easier,' he said. 'On both of you.' He went out, closing the door softly behind him.

Bella woke feeling weary to the bone, sore and utterly content. For some reason she wanted to cry, so she had a little happy, silent, weep.

'Here,' a deep voice by her ear said when she sniffed and rubbed away the tears. She turned her head on the pillow and there was Elliott, holding a handkerchief.

'Thank you.' She mopped her eyes. 'I'm crying because I'm happy.'

'I know. I am very proud of you.' He leaned in and kissed her gently. 'Clever, brave girl.'

'Where is she?' Bella tried to pull herself up against the pillows.

'Just there beside you. Here, let me help.' Elliott got her settled then lifted the baby from the cradle into her arms.

'You are managing very well with her,' she said, surprise vying with affection.

'Thank you.' His voice was oddly constrained and he did not meet her eyes. 'She is so tiny I am terrified of

doing something wrong.' He reached out a hand to touch
the child's cheek, then drew it back.

'What is it, Elliott?' A cold finger of doubt pierced the
warm glow that was wrapping Bella. 'There is nothing
wrong with her you haven't told me about, is there?'

Chapter Twenty-One

‘**N**o!’ Elliott turned on the bed so she could see his face clearly. ‘She is perfect.’

‘Then what is troubling you?’ Bella twined her fingers into his hand as it spread on the bed, taut to brace him. ‘I can see it in your eyes, Elliott. I know you too well now. Were you very shocked? Mrs Knight was amazed you stayed—I think she expected you to faint or something.’

‘Shocked?’ He grimaced. ‘Stunned is more the word. And utterly in awe of the courage and endurance of women. Men fight and suffer pain in hot blood most of the time and call it courage. Your sex just gets calmly on with producing the next generation without complaint.’

‘I seem to recall complaining. Bitterly,’ Bella said. ‘I think the memory must fade with time. I do not think I would like to do it again for a while, though. But tell me, Elliott. When I knew she was a girl I thought you would be happy.’

He was struggling with himself, like a man trying to

confess his sins. Bella snuggled the baby closer and squeezed his hand tighter. Her family, all together—now she must keep it like that.

'I was so relieved it was a girl,' he said finally, as though admitting to a crime.

'I know.' The way he had felt about the prospect of a boy had made her miserable and apprehensive for months, even though she could understand it and had tried to hide her feelings from him. But why was he not happy now?

'I have been praying it would be a daughter because I did not want Rafe's son to inherit, but ours—yours and mine. You know that. And that is dishonourable of me. I should have been able to put that aside, to be certain I could love and care for his child.'

Male honour! Bella wrestled with what to say that would not make things worse. Elliott looked, and sounded, as though he had been caught cheating at cards or some other masculine enormity. She loved him, but sometimes she simply did not understand him. 'I understand why you felt like that. But it is difficult for me to comprehend why you think it is so wrong,' she said carefully. 'I can see that you do, but it seems perfectly natural to me. Men are territorial and possessive—this is your estate now, your land, your title. Of course you want your son to inherit.'

He seemed taken aback by her lack of condemnation. She wished they had been able to discuss it during her pregnancy. It seemed the shock of the birth had removed his inhibitions. 'I am certain that if Rafe had married you and then died and I had been the child's guardian I would have felt none of this.'

'Because you never expected to inherit,' Bella said. 'Life never turns out as we expect it. We cannot punish ourselves for things that might not have happened.'

'No.' But he did not seem totally convinced.

'Elliott, do you think you can grow to love her?'

'Yes,' he said, reaching to touch the baby's cheek again and this time letting his finger linger, so gentle for such a big man.

'Then, for her sake, can you not forgive yourself for how you felt? You were ashamed of it, you fought against it—must you be perfect?'

'What a cockscomb I would be if I thought that,' he said with a reluctant chuckle. There was silence while she could almost feel him thinking. The baby wrapped its fingers around his index finger and he went very still. 'Yes, for her sake I can forgive myself,' he said. 'And for you, if you ask it.'

Bella reached out and touched his hair, then the baby began to stir and she put it to her breast, shaken all over again by the intensity of her feelings for the child. There was nothing soft there—she would die for this little scrap.

Long, precious minutes passed then she said, 'We must think of names for her.'

'Rafaela?' Elliott suggested, startling her.

'Truly? You would name her after Rafe?'

'Would you mind so very much? I just feel she should have something of her father's, however little he deserved it. Perhaps not as her first name. People knew he and I were not close. But as a second name it would arouse no suspicion. What was your mother's name?'

'Annabelle. My sisters are Margaret and Celina.'

'And my mother was called Margery. M… How about Marguerite? She is a little flower, after all. The Honourable Miss Marguerite Rafaela Calne?'

'Oh, yes! Marguerite, listen to what your papa has called you.' She glanced up and caught Elliott's expression. 'I am sorry, I should not have said *Papa* like that. I was presuming—'

'Correctly. I have already explained to our daughter that she must listen to everything her papa tells her and she stopped crying and stared at me very obediently. A trifle cross-eyed, perhaps, and she was dribbling, but I am sure it was dutiful.'

Bella giggled and Elliott turned until he was lying against the pillows, too, and could put his arm around her. She twisted her head to look up at him, but she could not see his face. Something tense in the line of his jaw made her frown for a moment, then she dismissed it. He was tired.

A family, she thought, sleepily, beginning to nod off again. *We are a family. It is perfect.* And then the recollection came to her that it was not quite perfect, that this man here beside her did not love her. But he was fond of her, she knew that. And protected her and cared about her. He would take pleasure in her body when he returned to her bed. Perhaps that was enough. It would have to be—it was more than many women had.

Elliott tightened his arm around her. He is so tired, she thought. But there was something else to be decided that they had not discussed.

'Who will be her godparents?'

'My great-aunt, I think.'

'And Anne Baynton.'

'Your sisters? You could stand for them in church.'

'Oh, yes. Thank you, Elliott. And men? I think we should ask Daniel.'

'Very well. Daniel and John Baynton and my third cousin the Duke of Avery.'

'Are you close?' A duke, goodness.

'We are good friends. And he is young, rich, influential and everything a young lady needs in a godfather.' He sighed. 'I can see I will have one hell of a time as her father, beating the young men off with sticks. She will have her mother's sweet face—'

'—and your blue eyes.'

'And a duke for a doting godfather. Perhaps I had better dower her with a pittance to keep the mob of young men to a reasonable size.'

'When shall we have the christening?'

'Not until the New Year, I think,' Elliott said. 'People are scattered for Christmas house parties already—the Bayntons have gone up to Yorkshire, Avery will be holding court at Avery Castle in Lincolnshire, Daniel is going to stay with friends in Bristol, he said, and my great-aunt will be setting off to go up to London by easy stages very soon—and coming back just as slowly.

'We will talk to the vicar about a date, write to the godparents and then when you are up and about, we can decide on a guest list and have a house party of our own.'

'And we could invite your aunts from London,' Bella suggested. 'I would like to meet them.' How strange to feel happy and confident about the prospect of a house party when a few months ago she would have been appalled at the thought. If only she could invite her father and Meg and Lina.

'I'll see if Bishop Huntingford will perform the baptism,' Elliott continued, sounding sleepy.

'A duke and a bishop,' Bella marvelled. 'How very grand we have become.' She was answered by snores, a soft little whiffle from the baby and a loud masculine effort from her husband. 'I think I'll join you,' she murmured, closing her eyes and drifting off, more content, despite everything, than she could ever remember being.

6 January 1815

'Your Grace.' Bella sank into the low curtsy that Anne Baynton had spent an hour tutoring her in, only to have both hands seized and be pulled to her feet by one of the best looking young men she had ever seen.

'William,' said the Duke of Avery, kissing her with enthusiasm on both cheeks. 'Elliott, how on earth did you find such a beautiful wife? You don't deserve her, I can tell that just by looking at her.'

'Put her down, Will,' Elliott said with a smile and a look in his eye that said he was prepared to floor anyone, dukes included, if they overstepped the mark.

Bella felt a flutter of absurd excitement. She had been dreading this christening party, but now everything seemed to be perfect.

Elliott had been avoiding her bed, out of consideration and to give her time to recover from the birth, she knew, but since Marguerite's birth he seemed more distant, not closer as she had hoped.

And although he was concerned, and kind, he
showed no signs of doting on the baby as she had hoped
from his first reaction. It had just been relief that she
was a girl, she realised. The child was not his and so
Marguerite would not have his love, only his kindness,
as she did.

But she had much to be happy about, Bella reminded
herself. She had recovered from the birth, Marguerite
was flourishing, the guests for their first house party
were all arriving and seemed delighted with their
welcome and now Elliott was bristling possessively
when another man admired her. It was not love, but it
was certainly gratifying.

She turned and ushered the duke into the hands of a
footman to be shown his room, then rolled her eyes at
Anne Baynton, who was chatting to Elliott's aunts.
Anne smiled back as Henlow opened the door again to
admit the bishop, Mrs Huntingford, his chaplain and
their servants. The ducal curtsy did very well for a
bishop, she decided as greetings were exchanged and
the new arrivals welcomed in.

Yes, she was very lucky, Bella decided after dinner
as the tea tray was brought in. If only Meg and Lina were
here everything would be perfect. Bella looked up and
found Elliott watching her. He strolled over. Oh, yes, and
if her husband loved her. Now that *would* be perfection.

'Magnificent, Lady Hadleigh.'

'You are pleased? I am so glad,' she murmured.
'Everyone seems very comfortable. Just listen to the
level of noise!'

The house party had been swollen by the addition of several of Elliott's friends. The unmarried ones were taking advantage of the presence of several single ladies to flirt outrageously and the two married ones had abandoned their wives to discuss the vital matter of the breeding of foxhounds, a debate in which the bishop was engaging with enthusiasm.

Mrs Huntingford was discussing something earnestly with Lady Abbotsbury and the aunts were fussing over whether the unmarried girls were adequately chaperoned.

'I am more than pleased,' Elliott said. 'I am proud of you, Arabella.'

'Proud?'

'I never dreamed the wet, exhausted, determined little mouse who turned up on my doorstep in May would turn into such a beautiful, confident viscountess.'

'I am not beautiful, you flirt,' Bella protested, laughing to hide the absurd rush of pleasure his words gave her.

'You are when you are happy,' Elliott murmured. 'I must just make sure you are happy all the time, because otherwise you are merely extremely attractive.'

'You do make me happy,' she said, the laughter leaving her to be replaced by something intense, something very serious. 'All the time.'

'I do?' There were times when she thought Elliott's soul was in his eyes, so deep and blue and intense were they. She glimpsed it now, some feeling as real and earnest as the one filling her.

'I… You are so kind to me, Elliott,' she said and the shutters came down.

'Kind.'

'And honourable. And you are a wonderful father.' She had said something wrong, but she did not know what it was. But of course, she was gushing at him and he probably hated that. He never spoke to her of tender feelings, only congratulated her on her competence, on the work she did or how well she looked. She must never forget how he came to marry her or that he might have found a bride whose competence, beauty and fitness for her role as Viscountess of Hadleigh could be taken for granted.

When they had all retired for the night she went into Marguerite's nursery and stood for a while in her night robe, looking down at the sleeping baby.

'Are you coming to bed, Arabella?' Elliott stood in the doorway stark naked, taking her breath with desire, outrage and a shocking desire to giggle.

'Elliott! You've no clothes on!'

'I know. I think Marguerite is too young to notice, don't you?'

'But Mary Humble is most certainly not!' She jerked her head towards the door to the nursery-maid's room.

'Then come and lecture me in private. I've missed you in my bed. Will it be all right?' He scooped her up in his arms and strode through nursery, sitting room and into her bedchamber, Bella reaching out over his shoulder to shut the doors behind them as they went.

'Yes, it will be all right and I do not want to lecture you,' she protested. *I want you to make love to me and tell me that you love me.*

Elliott just grinned and dropped her on to the bed. And he made love to her, very gently. And it was wonderful, as it always was and, as always, he murmured, 'Thank you, Arabella darling,' afterwards as he left her. And Bella wanted to cry because, it seemed, happiness and safety and contentment was not enough. She needed everything: she needed his love.

Chapter Twenty-Two

⁓⁓⁓⁓⁓

The day after the christening it poured with rain, much to Bella's alarm as an inexperienced hostess. What was she going to do with a houseful of guests on a wet Sunday afternoon after Matins and luncheon? She need not have worried. The bishop retired to his room to read sermons, the older ladies gathered round to sew church kneelers and assassinate characters and the younger ones obligingly played with the children and cooed over Marguerite and the Bayntons' new baby, Jonathan.

The men had vanished—some, Bella knew, to play cards or billiards, well away from the bishop's gaze, the others to the stables. She sat and watched the children, rescued the babies from being over-cuddled and thought of very little, lulled by the patter of rain on the windows and the hiss and crackle of the big fire in the grate.

Then John Baynton came in, rain spangling his hair, and bent to whisper something in Anne's ear. She looked up at him and whispered back and Bella read her lips. *I love you too.* The look on their faces as John straight-

ened up and touched his wife's hair before he went out
again took Bella's breath away.

It had been so fleeting, that tender, loving moment, and
yet it showed her exactly what was missing from her own
marriage more vividly than a thousand words could have
done. *I am a coward*, she thought. *I must tell Elliott how
I feel. I will talk to him when the guests have all gone.*

She got up and wandered through the house and at
last found herself beside the window seat in a little-
used wing and sank down to watch the rain running
down the windows. The weather was crying for her—
she did not need to shed a single tear of her own. Inside
she was cold, even though she tried, the sensible,
rational, stoical part of her tried, to say nothing had
changed, that she should still be happy and content with
what she had. Elliott had never pretended to love her;
he was nothing if not honest. It was she who had
changed, she who had fallen in love and now wanted the
impossible, his love too.

Once she had dreamed of a knight on a white charger,
come to rescue her. And the knight was really an evil
goblin and she had deceived herself into love. And now
she could be happy again, if she could only remember
how to be the sensible, patient Bella again, to have no
expectations other than to work hard and do her duty.
But this time she really had fallen for the true knight,
the honourable man who rescued her from the dragon.

He had given her his protection, his rank, his body, his
name for her child, his kindness—and it was not enough.

'Bella? Here you are! Your are freezing—look at
your hands, they are positively blue.' And here Elliott

was, come to rescue her from her own folly once more. 'You'll catch your death of cold—whatever are you doing here?'

'I wanted some peace and quiet before I joined the guests,' she explained, letting her hands lie limp between his big, rough warm ones as he chaffed them. 'I didn't notice how cold it was.'

'Come along and get warm.'

'Yes,' she agreed. She got up and produced a quite successful smile. 'I will come and try to get warm.' But she carefully freed her hand from his and walked alone down the passageway.

'The house to ourselves,' Bella said as she waved at the Duke of Avery's carriage, vanishing into the fog. 'It was a lovely house party.' So much to do to take her mind off her marriage, so many people to talk to. Now they were alone again.

'But three days is quite enough,' Elliott observed. He put his arm round her shoulders and Bella slid out of the embrace as they turned. 'Are you feeling all right this morning?'

'Yes, thank you,' Bella lied. She had hardly slept, tossing and turning, troubled by her thoughts and knowledge that she should tell Elliott how she felt.

'Come into the drawing room,' he said, his hand gentle but inexorable under her elbow. 'I don't think you are well, whatever you say, and there is something I must tell you.'

'I'm all right,' she snapped, cornered.

'Bella, what on earth is the matter?' Elliott shut the

door and came to stand in front of her before the fire. 'This is not like you.'

'No,' she said slowly, feeling all the old restraints and certainties falling away. 'No, it isn't. But you see, I have been thinking and, Elliott, I am sorry, but I find it hurts so much now. I should never have married you.'

'Arabella, darling.' Elliott managed to fold her tight into his arms. 'Listen to me, you really are not well. You are tired. Your nerves are still not calm after the birth. You—'

'Don't *darling* me!' Her face was crushed against his waistcoat and her arms pinned to her sides. His body was hard and strong and her own body stirred in treacherous arousal. Arabella kicked, making no impact at all on his Hessians with her indoor shoes.

Elliott held her away from him a little, his hands tight on her shoulders. 'Arabella, stop this. I don't understand why you bring this up now. Of course we had to marry, it was the right thing, you know that.'

'Yes, of course it was, once you knew. Don't you see—' Bella stared at him, trying to make him understand what she was only just beginning to comprehend herself '—I should have gone the moment I realised Rafe was dead. Now we are trapped. I cannot even run away and leave you—Viscount Hadleigh would not seek a divorce. You are stuck with me and I will be a good wife and breed sons for you. I suppose it will be…convenient.'

'It is not convenient, damn it.' Elliott was losing his temper now too. His eyes were dark sapphires, his mouth a hard line. 'It has never been *convenient*. I did not want to marry you. But I had to and I have had to learn to live with the emotional baggage our marriage brought with it and you will just have to learn to live with it too. I thought I had,' he added bitterly.

Elliott, her tower of strength, her refuge, her honest friend and her lover, was telling her the truth at last. 'Emotional baggage,' she said, all the anger gone, her voice cold and flat to her own ears. 'Of course. You are naturally gallant, naturally kind, but it must be a strain. I thought I was happy. I should be. I am so *sorry* I cannot be happy.' She twisted in his grip and broke free, ran to the door without looking back.

'Arabella, stop,' Elliott called after her. 'Where are you going?'

'To find my sister. I am going to the War Office. Why haven't they written to tell me where she is, where they are paying her widow's pension?' She needed someone to love, someone to love her. Someone who would understand.

There was something in the utter silence that stopped her in her tracks, sent her back to the doorway. 'Elliott? What is it? Have you heard something?'

'Negative news,' he admitted. 'I was going to tell you this morning. There is no trace of Margaret. It seems her marriage to James Halgate was never legal. After the battle of Vittoria where he was killed she seems to have slipped from the records.'

'Meg? But they must know where she is.'

'They do not know. Arabella, listen to me.' He took her by the upper arms as though to restrain her. 'Spain is a vast country, in chaos. This was more than two years ago. Perhaps she has remarried, settled out there, or—you must face it, my dear—she may have died.'

'No! No, I will not believe it. Take me to London, Elliott.'

'It is pouring with rain, you need rest, you have a baby and there is nothing you can do in London, Arabella. I am so sorry. We will think about it, find some contacts in Spain—I can send someone to investigate. But not now, this minute. You must see it is not rational.'

'No, of course not.' Rational? He wanted her to be rational? She was weary of being sensible and stoical. Something cold and hard settled over her, something like the bitter determination that had seized her when Rafe left. Elliott did not love her. Perhaps he could not love, not after an upbringing by remote parents, after a brother who hurt and rejected him. He did not understand how she felt about Meg and Lina, so she must find them herself.

Perhaps if they had a little time apart they could see their feelings for each other more clearly. Perhaps she could learn to do without love. She would come back, of course. It was her duty to be a good wife, to give Elliott an heir, to give Marguerite a proper home. But just now she could not bear to be here.

'No. Of course not.' She turned on her heel and walked away.

What had happened? What had gone wrong? Elliott stared at the half-open door feeling as though his heart had been wrenched out of his chest.

He thought he had made her happy and secure at least, but it seemed it was an illusion that something had shattered and now he did not know how to build it up again.

She would be in her bedchamber, he guessed. Toby sat outside, whining. Elliott tapped on the door, then turned the handle. It was locked. With a muttered oath he strode down the corridor to the sitting-room door. Locked. The nursery door was locked too. He knocked again. 'Arabella?' Silence.

Elliott wheeled round and stalked back to his own room, went through the dressing room and tried the interconnecting door. Locked. 'Arabella, will you please let me in?' He banged on the panels with his closed fist. From close by there was the thin wail of a child abruptly wakened. He felt his temper slipping; Marguerite should be in the nursery with her nursemaid. He banged again, harder with no response.

Locked in the safe were duplicate keys for the whole house. It took him a matter of minutes to return with the ones for the whole suite of rooms. 'Arabella, if you do not open the door I will.'

He waited and at last the door opened. Arabella stood there, pale and dry-eyed. 'Please do not make so much noise, you will frighten Marguerite.'

'Then do not lock the doors,' he said, walking past her into the room.

'I do not want you here. I do not know what to say. I am sorry, I should never have spoken, I just lost my...my will, I suppose.'

'Unfortunately for what you want, Arabella, this

happens to be my house, you are my wife and that is my daughter.' She looked at him sharply. 'Oh, yes, my daughter. Do not attempt to take her away from me— the only person who would suffer from that is her.'

'I was not—' She broke off and turned away to stare out at the chill wet world outside. 'I made vows, Elliott, and I will keep them.'

'Then talk to me, Arabella!' He took her arm, pulled her to him. Even as he spoke Elliott knew he was too rough. He opened his hands a little, but kept her close.

'I do care for you.' Arabella sounded weary. 'I have cared for you almost from the beginning. I admire you and I think you kind and strong. You know I have felt a strong attraction for you or I would not have come to your bed as willingly as I have done. But none of that alters the fact that I should not have married you. Somehow I should have managed. It was wrong and selfish and now we are both hurt and I do not know how to make it better. Please, go away.'

'Arabella, you cannot shut yourself away up here,' Elliott said harshly. 'The servants will be wondering what on earth is going on.'

'Tell them that I am having the vapours or some such female affliction that men think we are prone to.'

Elliott turned on his heel and walked out. He had never heard that brittle tone from Arabella, never seen her so dully angry or refusing to try to please him. Part of him knew she had the right to express her feelings, however much they hurt him. Part of him, the part that was wounded by every word, wanted his compliant, sweet-tempered wife back again.

* * *

Bella watched from her window as Elliott rode out, his gun slung over his shoulder, his shot belt across his chest, the pointers running at the horse's heels. Despite the cold, dank fog he preferred to be away from her. She could not blame him, only herself. Something had snapped, something that, looking back, she supposed she must have kept tightly chained up for years and years.

Years of being the peacemaker, the dutiful daughter. Years of obedience and austerity, of loss and sadness. Then Rafe had betrayed her and she had not even had the words to hit back at him. Now Elliott's words had finally broken the fraying ropes around her restraint and it had spilled out, the confusion and hurt and distress. If she could only have told him she loved him…but that would have been even worse. Would he have lied or would he have told her, kindly and with pity, that he could not return her love?

The urge to go and pick up her child and cuddle her was almost overwhelming—someone, at least, loved her un-conditionally and she could love her back without reserve.

No, there were three: Marguerite and her two sisters. *Where are you, Meg and Lina?* she asked herself as she had, so often. Surely she would know if they were no longer alive? She had to hang on to that thought.

The hurt and the anger stirred again, making her feel sick. She so rarely allowed herself to be angry, let alone give way to it as she had just now.

Bella leaned her forehead against the cold glass. Today she would huddle like a wounded animal in her lair, holding her baby. Tomorrow…tomorrow she would go to London and take Marguerite with her.

Then when she had done all she could to find her sisters she would apologise to Elliott, promise to never speak of her feelings again and, somehow, come to terms with what her marriage was now.

Then Marguerite woke and began to gurgle. 'I'm coming, sweetheart,' she called. 'Mama's here.'

Breakfast was harder than she could have imagined because Elliott behaved so impeccably. He was polite, he smiled and when she sent the servants from the room and tried to speak of the day before he simply shook his head. 'No, it is all right, Arabella. We will forget it and go on. Your nerves were overwrought after the house party.'

She wanted to apologise, to try to explain—not how she felt, but why her self-control had given way. But if he wanted to pretend it had never happened then what could she do but go to London with all that unsaid between them?

There was a tap on the door. 'My lord, excuse me.' It was Henlow and behind him Bella glimpsed some men in working clothes clustered in the hallway. 'Turner has sent to say there is flooding all down the Cat Brook. He's worried the dam at the mill race might give way.'

'I must go.' Elliott stood and went out into the hall. Bella could hear him giving orders as the door closed. 'Send for my horse, Henlow. Jem, all the men off the Home Farm, a wagon, picks and shovels—'

Bella went out into the hallway and tried to appear brisk and cheerful. Her acting abilities were apparently not proof against the butler's knowledge of what went on in the household.

'His lordship will deal with it, my lady. He is the man to have by your side in a crisis. And he will no doubt return in a good mood. I have always observed that hard work balances any inequality of temperament he may be feeling.'

Inequality of temperament, indeed! That was doubtless a butler's code for flaming rows and fists thudding on doors. Was that what he thought of her moods, too? Inequalities of temperament?

'Not that his lordship is much prone to…moods, if I might make so bold, my lady. His late lordship was of a most unpredictable and changeable humour and without his lordship's sweetness of temper and strength of character,' Henlow said, looking as though he was sucking lemons. 'He will come about, my lady.' As though worried that he had said too much, he turned on his heel and hurried off through the green baize door.

Bella went upstairs. Everything was prepared and now she did not even have the worry of evading Elliott. She put the note she had written on the mantelshelf, donned her warmest pelisse, her bonnet and gloves and went to find Mary Humble, who was dressing the baby.

'Come along.' She picked up two of the valises. 'His lordship has had to take most of the footmen off to attend to some emergency with the mill race, we can take these down ourselves.'

The maid followed, baby in one arm, the bag of necessities for the journey in the other hand. She had listened with sympathy to Bella's tale of a family emergency taking her to London urgently. His lordship would follow as soon as he could, Bella had said. But she had to get to her sister.

She repeated the tale in the stable yard and Wilkins, the senior groom left in charge, had no thought of arguing with her ladyship. The coachman came down as the team were harnessed in the travelling chaise, the luggage strapped on behind, all except for the baby's necessities, and one of the undergrooms swung up behind. With a yap Toby leapt in too.

Bella leaned back against the squabs and let the sway of the carriage lull her as she scratched the terrier behind his ear. She would have to come back, she knew that, but just at the moment all she wanted was to be away from Elliott before she blurted out her love for him, drove him even further from her. That, and to do something, anything, to find Meg and Lina.

'We will stay at a hotel, Mary,' she said, producing the London guide she had removed from the library. 'I will see which sounds the most suitable.'

The carriage began to slow as they turned off the main drive on to the lane that ran down to the bridge and then back up before they reached the turnpike road that led towards London. Bella glanced out at the fog and then back to her book. It was not easy to read.

'The Pulteney sounds the finest,' she observed, trying to sound cheerful and positive. 'But it is probably very expensive.' The carriage levelled out, the sound of hooves on wood signalled they had reached the bridge. 'Let's see which—'

There was a rending noise, a creaking and cracking.

The coachman shouted and the groom up behind yelled back, then the carriage tipped and fell sideways and down. Bella grabbed for Marguerite as they crashed to a halt. Cold water rushed in, but her groping hands met nothing but the folds of Mary's gown.

It was almost dark, cold, the baby was screaming. They were in the river.

Chapter Twenty-Three

Elliott splashed out of the river edge, his boots sodden. 'Too late. The dam's gone. Nothing we can do here now, we can't repair it with this much water going down.'

'We'd better take a look at the bridges lower down, my lord,' Murrow, the estate carpenter, said, pushing his hat back on his head and wiping the sweat and mist droplets off his face. 'They're none too strong. I warned his late lordship about them, often a time, but he wouldn't spend the money.'

'We'll go down now. Who's that?' A rider was thundering down the muddy slope. 'Wilkins?'

The groom slid off the horse he had been riding bareback. 'It's her ladyship—the carriage. The bridge collapsed, my lord.' He pointed downstream.

'The carriage? Her ladyship is at home.' But even as he said it the fear was knotting in his stomach. Elliott took the horse's mane and swung up on to its back.

'No, my lord. She said she was going to London.'

Oh God. Arabella. 'Murrow, get all the men down

there. Horses, timbers, ropes.' The carpenter was a good man, he'd know what to do. Elliott turned the horse and gave it its head down the river bank.

When Bella found her footing she was in near darkness and in water. Confusion almost panicked her and then she realised where she was.

'Marguerite! Mary!' The carriage resounded with the baby's screams.

'Here,' the maid gasped and Bella twisted to find the girl holding the baby over her head.

'Give her to me, I am taller than you. Can you find the seat and stand on it?' The carriage was tilted crazily and there was something massive across the only window she could see.

'I think so.' The girl floundered and then rose a little out of the water, her head and shoulders cramped under the roof.

Bella tried for a foothold and managed to get a little higher too. Marguerite's blankets were wet, but not soaked through. 'We can put her into the luggage netting,' she said. 'If we drop her…' The maid scrabbled to hold the net open at one side as Bella pushed the wriggling, screaming bundle into it. The net, attached to the inside of the roof, was at an odd angle, but at least it was clear of the water.

For a moment that was reassuring, then she felt the icy cold in her legs and the weight of her waterlogged clothing beginning to drag. How long could they survive in this? 'Help!' she shouted. 'Help!'

The coachman and groom must be hurt or surely

they would be doing something. 'Are we going to drown?' Mary quavered.

'Of course not,' Bella said. But they could die of cold if someone did not find them soon. 'Just hold on, keep as much of yourself out of the water as possible. Shh, Marguerite, shh, Mama's here.'

The carriage shuddered, slid, and she had the sickening realisation that if it moved any more they would be trapped as it sank. *Oh, Elliott, I am so sorry. I love you. Please come, my love, please come.*

The wreckage of the bridge loomed out of the fog as a bulky figure staggered towards him, a small, frantically barking dog at its heels. Elliott swung off the horse as Toby leapt for his arms. The sound of a baby screaming in fright and discomfort was clear over the rush of water.

'Philips, where's her ladyship?'

'Inside, my lord. And her maid and the baby. Groom's a bit battered, but he's not so bad—he went for help. A big rush of water hit the bridge just as we got on to it.' He ran beside Elliott to the bank. 'It's wedged, but the timbers are giving way, my lord.'

'I can see,' Elliott said, putting the dog down and fighting the urge just to hurl himself into the torrent. 'We need ropes, horses—oh, good man, Murrow.' The carpenter brought a wagon down the hill at a reckless canter, dragged the team to a halt and men began to leap down and unharness the horses.

'Arabella!' he shouted until he thought his lungs would burst and then, faintly, he heard her voice.

'Elliott! Safe…but slipping.'

'We're coming.' He tied a rope around his waist and pulled off his boots, his coat, grabbed another rope and plunged into the water. Behind him he heard Murrow do the same.

It was not deep, but the current was strong and full of wood and branches torn down by the rains. Elliott fought his way to the carriage and made his rope fast, then clambered over the tilted side to cut the traces. The bodies of the horses broke free and were swept downstream, taking some of the strain off the body of the vehicle.

He clambered back as more men joined the carpenter, tying on ropes. 'Arabella?' The window, facing up at the sky, was closed. He dare not break it. There was movement inside and it opened halfway. 'Arabella!'

'Is it safe to take the baby?' she said, her face white; her lips, he saw with horror, were almost blue.

'Yes, give her to me.' He reached in and the squirming, furious bundle was pushed into his hands.

'I'll be back in just a moment. Hold on, Arabella.' Elliott slid and scrambled over the tilting carriage, trying not to rock it, trying to hold tight to the baby. When he reached the water there was a chain of men holding the ropes, breaking the flow for him so he would get to land.

'I'll take her, I've got grandbabies,' said Philips, reaching for Marguerite.

Elliott brushed back the blanket off her face and she stared at him, big blue eyes in a red, indignant face and his heart turned over. 'I love you,' he murmured and pushed her into the gnarled hands. 'Get her dry and warm,' he said as he turned back to the water.

'We've got ropes on it, it won't shift now,' Murrow told him. 'If we can just get that baulk of timber off we can open the door.'

It took three of them, balanced on the carriage, to shift the timber and force open the door. Arabella pushed Mary Humble out, then held up her arms for Elliott.

'I knew you would come. I knew it. I only had to be strong enough to hold on until then.'

'I will always come for you,' he said, pulling her into his arms almost roughly. 'I'll always come for both of you.'

Somehow they reached the bank. Servants from the house were there now with towels and blankets and hot water. 'How do you feel?' He stood there, half-naked, the fog wrapping chill tendrils round him and felt only the touch of her presence. He lifted a hand and stroked his fingers down her cheek and Arabella turned her face into the hollow of his hand and kissed it.

'I am so sorry, Elliott. I just wanted to find Meg, to get away and think.'

'And I should have listened to you. Don't fret, everyone will be all right.' He swept her up in his arms and walked with her to the carriage where Gwen was waiting to envelop her in towels and rugs. Mary Humble was already there, cradling the baby, but she gave her to Arabella as she reached for her.

'Hot baths, Gwen,' he ordered. 'Hurry, now.'

A rapid check that the men were all safe and the groom was being taken care of and Elliott was on horseback again and galloping in the wake of the carriage. He had nearly lost Arabella. Nearly lost both of them. The terror of it clawed at him like a creature, the fear that they might still be in danger from the cold racked him.

Arabella was in the bath when he strode, dripping, into her bedchamber. Gwen tried to shoo him out, but Elliott simply sidestepped her and went round the screen.

'Oh! Oh, Elliott. Marguerite is quite all right. She's warm and none the worse and tucked up.'

He knelt by the tub and reached for the big sponge that she was trying, very ineffectively, to hide behind. Gwen had washed her hair and swathed it in a turban of towelling and she was already turning pink from the effects of the warm water.

'We need you dry and in bed. Look at these washer-woman's fingers.' He held up her water-wrinkled hand to show her. Then, suddenly, the shock of it ambushed him, knocking away his strength and his defences.

'Arabella—' His voice cracked.

'I know. It is all right now,' she soothed, pulling her to him, muddy and sodden as he was. 'It is all right.'

He could feel the hot tears on his cheeks and hoped she would think it was his hair that was dripping on her as she held him, rocking him as best she could, as though he was the one needing looking after, not her.

Arabella, I love you. Darling girl, I love you. The words sounded so loud in his head that for a moment he thought he had spoken them. Elliott turned away abruptly to snatch up a towel and scrub his betraying face with it and heard her gasp. He *had* said it out loud.

'Elliott? You love me?' He swivelled back and met the wide hazel gaze that seemed to reach right down into his soul. 'I love you,' she said, her voice trembling. 'Elliott, I can hardly believe that you can love me too.'

He bent to take her lips as his mind reeled. *She loves me? Arabella loves me.* 'I only just realised. I could have lost you and I didn't know…I didn't understand what I was feeling. Arabella, how could I have been so blind?'

'I was blind, too, you know,' Arabella murmured, reaching out to touch his face. 'I realised when I was in the family chapel that what I felt for you was so different from what I felt for Rafe, so strong, that it had to be love.' She blushed a little, 'And in bed…'

'It did not occur to me that a woman like you only gives herself with that trust and desire, night after night, when she is in love with the man,' Elliott said. He felt as though he was drunk and yet utterly clearheaded. It was wonderful and terrifying. 'I just thought I was fortunate that at least I was able to make you happy in bed.'

A little laugh escaped her. 'Oh, Elliott. Do you realise we have never made love knowing that we love each other?'

Elliott looked at her thoughtfully, his eyes heavy with unspoken desire and Bella's insides became hot and liquid with longing. 'What a very provoking idea, my love. We are going to have to give it so much thought—and probably a great deal of attention—to make certain we express our feelings fully.'

'Now, Elliott. Please.'

'You should rest.' But his eyes burned into her.

'Help me out of the bath and I will go and see Marguerite again and then, if she is well, we will both go and rest…together.'

He let Gwen come back and dry her, dress her in nightgown and robe while he went and washed and changed. He found her again standing by the cradle and put his hand over hers as she stoked the baby's cheek. 'Both my loves, safe and sound.'

When she straightened up from kissing the soft little cheek he took her hand and just walked straight through the intervening rooms and into his bedchamber. He closed the door and leaned against it.

'Elliott, are you sure you are not too tired?'

'I would have to be unconscious to be too tired to make love to you, Arabella.' Elliott's eyes were dark with desire and something else that made her want to laugh with sheer delight.

She laughed, breathless with happiness. 'I love you so much, I want you awake to tell you,' she said as he pulled her to him, his fingers urgent with ribbons and ties.

'I like undressing you from all these fripperies,' he admitted, tossing the négligé into a corner before running his hands gently over her breasts so that the nipples peaked hard against his palms. 'Those nightgowns are like unwrapping a very intriguing parcel.'

Bella tried to sound indignant. 'Parcel? Well, allow me to unwrap you then, my lord.'

'*Arabella.*' It was a groan as she struggled with buttons and shirttails. 'Hurry.'

The fastenings of his breeches gave way to her fingers and she felt the muscles of his stomach contract as she slipped her hand down and circled him. He thrust into her hand, hot and hard and ready for her. They stood, locked together, not moving, his hand cupping her breast, hers encircling the powerful length of him. Bella tightened her hold.

'No. Arabella… Wait.'

'Your boots,' she managed as he swept her up and dropped her on the bed.

'My boots be damned.'

'The covers… Oh! Oh, Elliott. Oh, my love. *Yes.*' Boots, bedding, everything vanished from her consciousness as he came into her with a certainty and a possessive passion that eclipsed everything that had gone before. She was his and he was hers and nothing, it seemed to her through a daze of mounting, aching urgency, would ever be the same again.

He drove her up, beyond breaking point into a sudden, all-consuming climax, then held her, murmuring as he moved gently within her until she was aware again, her fingers tightening on his shoulders as she said against his mouth, 'Love you, I love you. *Elliott.*'

'Arabella. My love.' Elliott kissed her back, claiming her, feeling that this was somehow the first time for them, the first time it had ever mattered so much. He forced control on himself, aware of her body, her breathing, the rising need sweeping through her again, and held on until he felt her begin to break again. 'My love, for ever,' he heard himself say as the passion swept him away. 'Always.'

26 March

'Those beds will be a mass of bloom by summer.' Arabella leaned against Elliott as they looked out of the drawing-room window on to the new flowerbeds Johnson and his men, including young Trubshaw, had cut out of the turf and were just beginning to plant up with the hardier shrubs.

'It is almost the end of March, spring is in the air, Marguerite is flourishing,' she continued. He put his arm around her shoulders and hugged her more tightly. It was still a shock, a joy, to know that she was his and he loved her. 'Is it possible to be happier, do you think?'

'In general, no,' Elliott agreed, loving the way she wriggled with sensual responsiveness as he bent to nibble her earlobe. 'I could think of ways to increase the intensity of the feeling, of course.'

'You always can,' Arabella said. As usual when she remembered that she was supposed to be a respectable viscountess she was trying to sound disapproving and failing completely. 'It so happens that we have absolutely no commitments this afternoon, or this evening. I kept today free because of packing tomorrow for London.'

'Your very first Season, Lady Hadleigh. Are you nervous?' He was glad he had delayed travelling until the weather was better. The time to themselves had been precious. It had taken Arabella a long time to forgive herself for running away from him and to believe that the accident was somehow not her fault. He had tried to find out more about her missing sisters, to no avail, but she had turned to him for comfort and sharing the search and the emotion had brought them closer together.

'Terrified,' she admitted. 'But you will be there so it will not be so bad. I was thinking that perhaps we could go upstairs, and er…*rest* this afternoon.'

'How about resting right now?' Elliott started to turn from the window, his imagination conjuring up an entire menu of unrestful things to do with his wife, then stopped. 'Damnation, there's a carriage coming up the drive. Are we expecting visitors? I don't recognise the team.'

'Or the crest on the door either.' Beside him Arabella craned her neck to try to make it out. The vehicle came to a halt, the door swung open and a tall, broad-shouldered man got out. 'I don't know him, do you?' she said. 'My goodness, what an alarming-looking gentleman. He is positively swarthy, and looks so grim. What a jaw!'

'Army,' Elliott hazarded, studying the upright back and indefinable air of authority as the big man held out his hand to assist a lady to alight.

'What an elegant hat,' Arabella said. 'I wonder if— *Meg*! It is Meg! Elliott—' She ran out of the room without waiting for him, dodged past Henlow who was opening the front door, and flung herself down the steps with Elliott at her heels. 'Meg!'

'Bella!' The modish matron dropped reticule and parasol and launched herself at Arabella. 'It *is* you! We've found you at last. Ross, see, it is Bella! You look so beautiful…'

She burst into tears. Bella burst into tears. Elliott skirted round the two women sobbing in each others' arms and held out his hand to the other man. 'Hadleigh.'

'Brandon.' The men shook and turned back to regard their wives.

Elliott thought vaguely about handkerchiefs and then decided he would wait for the emotion to subside a trifle. 'How did you find us?' he asked.

'My wife was lining drawers and using a pile of newspapers that had mounted up while we were, er…otherwise engaged,' Ross Brandon said. 'She saw her sister's name and there was no stopping her. We went to your Town house first, found the knocker off and Meg insisted on setting out immediately. She was too impatient to write and wait two days for a response.'

Bella turned, wreathed in smiles despite her tear-streaked face. 'Elliott, it *is* Meg and she is Lady Brandon now!'

'I rather gathered that,' he said with a grin, holding out a handkerchief. 'Shall we go in?'

'I'll just get the nurse-maid and the baby,' Brandon said, going back to the carriage and helping a young woman with the baby asleep in her arms to alight.

'Oh, how perfect.' Bella hung over the infant. 'Is it a boy? How old is he?'

'Six weeks,' Meg said. 'Charles Mallory Ross Brandon.'

'And my daughter is twelve weeks old. Come in…come in and see her, her name is Marguerite Rafaela Calne and she is beautiful.' Bella towed her sister towards the door, talking non-stop. 'But, Meg, it is so long, almost seven years. There is so much to tell—where shall we begin?'

* * *

It took almost three hours to learn the basic facts about the years they had spent apart. Bella wept again when she heard that Meg had been deceived into a bigamous marriage with James Halgate and then left destitute in Spain when he was killed in battle. She had encouraged her sister to elope with her childhood sweetheart and he had proved to have feet of clay. But if it were not for that tragedy Meg would never have met the man she was so obviously passionately in love with now.

The tale of how she had met Major Ross Brandon on the quayside in Bordeaux and nursed his wounds in return for her passage back and how they had fallen in love and married, defying scandal, had her flinging her arms around her brother-in-law's neck and kissing him. He might look dour and frightening, but Bella soon realised he adored Meg and doted on his son and she was determined to love him in return.

It was more difficult to tell her own story, for she could not reveal the truth about Marguerite's father to anyone, not even her sister. 'I behaved very imprudently,' she confessed, blushing. 'And Marguerite was born seven months after the wedding.'

'I think it very romantic,' Meg said, beaming at Elliott. 'It was love at first sight, was it not?'

'Do you know,' Elliott said, smiling at Bella, 'it may well have been.' She smiled back. No, she knew it had not been that, but somehow this was better: deeper and truer.

'But what can have happened to Celina?' Meg asked

anxiously. 'I know she ran away in June 1813 because Patrick Jago, my enquiry agent, found out that much.'

'All I know is that she went to an aunt I had never heard of, a sister of Mama's. And, Meg, I am so sorry if this is a shock, but Elliott and I think that Mama did not die, as Papa told us, but ran off with another man.'

Meg *was* shocked, but less surprised by that suggestion than Bella had been. But then, Bella thought, her younger sister had seen a good deal more of the world than she. It was a comfort to talk about it though, to hold her sister as they grieved again for their mother. 'We must advertise for Lina,' she said. 'We cannot give up. One day we will be reunited.'

'Tired?' Elliott asked as they finally went to their room. They had talked themselves to a standstill that evening and Meg and Ross had retired to bed, leaving young Charles tucked up in the nursery next to Marguerite.

'I am too excited to sleep,' Bella admitted. 'I just want to cuddle and enjoy being so happy.'

'Just cuddle?' He raised one dark brow and a warm glow began to spread through her.

'To start with,' Bella said demurely. 'Have I told you, Elliott Calne, just how much I love you?'

'Possibly not for a few hours,' he admitted, as he stood in the middle of the room and shed his dressing gown with his usual total lack of modesty. 'I am open to being reminded.'

'I feel I have a family at last.' Bella removed her négligé and drifted closer, enjoying the heat in his eyes, the tenderness with which he reached out to draw her to him. 'I have a husband who loves me, a beautiful daughter and now a sister again.'

'Come here and cuddle me, then,' Elliott said, his voice husky.

'No,' said Bella, standing on tiptoe to kiss the sensual curve of his lower lip. 'No, I think I need to kiss you all over and tell you between each kiss how much I love you.'

'That sounds an excellent plan,' Elliott murmured, backing away until they fell on to the bed in a tangle of arms and legs. 'Just so long as I can kiss you back. I may not have fallen in love at first sight as your romantical sister believes, but my conscience has never served me a better turn than when it told me to marry you, Arabella Shelley. I could not have found a wife I loved more if I searched the globe.'

And so she began to kiss him and their voices became murmurs and their touching became urgent and finally they lay entwined as the candles guttered and the room became dark and still and full of love.

* * * * *

HISTORICAL

Regency

THE DARK VISCOUNT
by Deborah Simmons

Wilful Miss Sydony Marchant is not one to be afraid, even in the looming shadow of her imposing new home. But if the vast mansion doesn't shock her, the arrival of Viscount Hawthorne will! No longer the boy she once kissed – Bartholomew is now a man with a ruthless glint in his eye...

LORD PORTMAN'S TROUBLESOME WIFE
by Mary Nichols

Normally self-controlled Harry, Lord Portman is unsettled by his attraction to his convenient wife Rosamund, so keeps her at arm's length. When Rosamund falls into danger, Harry must let go of the past and fight for the woman he loves.
The Piccadilly Gentlemen's Club mini-series

THE DUKE'S GOVERNESS BRIDE
by Miranda Jarrett

Dreading the end of her Grand Tour, former governess Jane Wood nervously awaits the arrival of her employer, Richard Farren, Duke of Aston. Widower Richard is stunned by mousey Miss Wood's transformation into the carefree and passionate Jane!

On sale from 1st October 2010
Don't miss out!

HISTORICAL

CONQUERED AND SEDUCED
by Lyn Randal

Two years ago former gladiatrix Severina had no choice
but to flee from her beloved Livius Lucan. Now she needs
his help. And in return Lucan is determined to conquer
this runaway woman – and claim the wedding
night he never had!

THE LAWMAN'S BRIDE
by Cheryl St John

All Sophie wants is to be left alone to build a new life.
Town marshal Clay Connor is upright and honourable; he
deserves more than a woman with a tainted past. But
if Sophie learns to trust again this lawman could
make her new life complete...

THE NOTORIOUS KNIGHT
by Margaret Moore

Sir Bayard may be handsome and secretly make
Lady Gillian rethink her vows never to marry, but she
has no intention of giving in to this presumptuous knight!
Sir Bayard must protect Lady Gillian, but he doesn't
expect to do battle with the lady herself!

On sale from 1st October 2010
Don't miss out!

2 FREE BOOKS
AND A SURPRISE GIFT

We would like to take this opportunity to thank you for reading this Mills & Boon® book by offering you the chance to take TWO more specially selected books from the Historical series absolutely FREE! We're also making this offer to introduce you to the benefits of the Mills & Boon® Book Club™—

- **FREE home delivery**
- **FREE gifts and competitions**
- **FREE monthly Newsletter**
- **Exclusive Mills & Boon Book Club offers**
- **Books available before they're in the shops**

Accepting these FREE books and gift places you under no obligation to buy, you may cancel at any time, even after receiving your free books. Simply complete your details below and return the entire page to the address below. You don't even need a stamp!

YES Please send me 2 free Historical books and a surprise gift. I understand that unless you hear from me, I will receive 4 superb new books every month for just £3.99 each, postage and packing free. I am under no obligation to purchase any books and may cancel my subscription at any time. The free books and gift will be mine to keep in any case.

Ms/Mrs/Miss/Mr ——————————— Initials ———————————

Surname ——————————————————————————

Address ——————————————————————————

————————————————————— Postcode ———————————

E-mail ——————————————————————————

Send this whole page to: Mills & Boon Book Club, Free Book Offer, FREEPOST NAT 10298, Richmond, TW9 1BR